Theft

Theft

A NOVEL

BK LOREN

COUNTERPOINT
BERKELEY

Library of Congress Cataloging-in-Publication Data is available.

ISBN 978-1-58243-819-1

Cover design by Jason Snyder
Interior design by Erin Seaward-Hiatt

Printed in the United States of America

COUNTERPOINT
1919 Fifth Street
Berkeley, CA 94710

www.counterpointpress.com

Distributed by Publishers Group West

10 9 8 7 6 5 4 3 2 1

author's note

The land and wildlife agencies mentioned in *Theft* are fictional. The story of *Theft* intentionally expands the traditional territory of the Mexican grey wolf. Any similarities between existing people, places, and wildlife agencies and the characters, agencies, and places in *Theft* are purely coincidental.

for Lisa Cech
always has been, always will be

". . . although we'd like to believe animals relocate when their habitats are destroyed, most organisms have nowhere to go. They will die rather than move. Worse yet, these losses are usually unseen and writ large all over the world. We are truly thieves, pillaging the future."

—Harry Greene, *Tracks and Shadows: Field Biology as Art*

o n e

Willa, 1980

RIDING THROUGH THE tall-grass sweetness of the Colorado prairie, wheat stalks whipping my legs and the whir of insects—a high-pitched *buzz buzz buzz*—turning me dizzy under that white-yellow heat pouring through the blue sky. My brother Zeb, three years older than me and in high school by now, pedals while I hold tight to his belt loops. It's my bike he's riding, used to be his before he handed it down to me last summer. He takes us through the field and pedals into the neighborhood where the houses are tall and the lawns take up a whole block of land. He slams the brakes on the bike, hops off, lets it fall. "Come on," he says. He stretches his arm out behind him for me to hold his hand. We walk to the side of the house, climb the stairs to the back deck, and he hands me the greasy thick gel, tells me to slather it on. "No gloves, we're pros," he says. We leave no prints, no evidence.

He tells me to slip through the barely open window. I'm small enough, and my body is limber and lithe, even for a kid my age. I slip like a penny into a bank, like a rabbit into a hole, and I drop down into another world, furniture I never did see before—dark, heavy wood bed, chest of drawers, shining oak floors—and the sunlight has all day been fingering its way between the gap in the closed curtains making the wood smell the way only wood smells in the heat, something smoldering. It brims in my nostrils.

On a stand next to a cushioned chair there's a pair of glasses. Black rims, smudged lenses, across the back of the chair a leather belt, the third hole sticking out like a belly button, the notch there worn deep, someone's hands cinching that belt every morning, gut hanging over, white sports shirt tucked in, I can see it all. It's my shortcoming, says Zeb. I see the people who live in a place, not their belongings, and I've got no eye for stealing. But I'm learning.

I stay put, like Zeb says. I watch him move, smooth as a fish in water, see him slinking down the long hallway, his JC Penney jeans too loose and his black T-shirt too tight, Marlboros rolled up in the sleeve, and the muscles in his bony arms tight as rubber bands. "Stay there," he calls again. I shove my greasy hands in my pockets, and the room grows around me huge. I think of Mom. She's the one we're doing all this for, but she doesn't know we're here.

"Hello," I call out, just to hear my own voice echo in the space of this huge place.

"What the hell you hollering at, Willa?" Zeb's voice booms all the way down the long hallway.

I listen. I hear him rummaging through the drawers and closets, careful and fast as he is, a pro. Then I hear something different, a distinct ringing. "You hear that, Zeb?" I stand stock-still, alone in the big room.

"Didn't hear nothing but your goddamned bellowing, Willa."

I know Zeb when he's concentrating. Like I said, he's a fish under water and he can't hear a thing. But I know I heard something, makes my bones feel like rubber melting in hot sun, tickling from the inside out. Doesn't matter. I stand stiff and strong, nothing showing, no fear when you look at me, but there's a bird trapped in my body. I can feel it fluttering in my chest, batting crazy against the walls of my ribcage, caught in too small a space.

I tiptoe over and look out the front window. It's big enough so I can see all the way down the block. No kids playing, like where we live. No bicycles or heaps of tires on front lawns, no tag or jump rope going on in the streets. Eerie place, if you ask me, but I figure Zeb's right. He's usually right. There's nothing to be afraid of, no one coming, and the ringing I heard was just fear buzzing in my head. A thief's got no use for fear.

I take a deep breath. I feel the bird in my chest fold its wings, rest on the branches of my lungs, quiet. Without the cage of my hollowed chest, that bird would fly. But it stays. It rests. I tuck my legs under me and I start to sit down, and just then the phone rings clear as Sunday morning bells, sends me like a pea in a sling-shot back to where Zeb's working. His backpack is stuffed full already, and the room he's in is ransacked. Clothes torn from closets, drawers emptied, anything good selected out, the rest left to the owners.

"What the hell, Willa?"

"They know we're here, Zeb."

"Who?"

"I don't know. But they're calling."

Zeb walks to the phone, puts his hand on the receiver, pretends to pick it up. "Hello," he says. "Willa Robbins? Yes, she's right here."

"Zeb!"

The phone stops ringing. Zeb laughs. "No one knows we're here, Willa. It's just the phone ringing." He bends down, slips his hand into the pocket of my jeans, drops something inside. "For Mom," he says. "Make her feel pretty."

I pull a gold and sapphire necklace from my pocket, and just looking at it socks me in the chest. To see Mom have a reason to wear this, a place to go where she would feel beautiful and graceful and not ugly and twisted up with Parkinson's like she is, the thought of it weakens me. The jewels shimmer like her eyes. Zeb winks at me, then walks out. He moves fast and focused, opens the door of the next room down the hallway, and I'm alone again in this place that's as ransacked as the old farmhouse in the field we crossed to get here. Mom was born and raised in that farmhouse, part of a homestead sometime last century, she says, and she stayed there till my grandparents died and Zeb was born. Couple years after that, Mom and Dad lost it to something they called "eminent domain," so the City could build stores there instead of houses, and that property has been sitting with a FOR SALE billboard on it ever since. Years now and that field has never sold. "As if someone's just going to happen by it and see it for sale out here in the middle of nowhere," Dad says almost every time he's home for dinner, which is not often. He's always on the road, selling things door-to-door.

"Going to pave that road and make it a major thoroughfare, turn our old house into a nice shopping center," Mom says back to him every time. But neither one of them keeps that conversation going. They just keep saying those same two sentences about it, again and again.

There are still signs of Mom's family living in that ramshackle place, the roof all collapsed in on itself now, one of those farm houses you see that sags like a swayback mare, both of them good for nothing, people say. The windowpanes are all broken out, and there are no doors, and the walls are only half-standing, so you can just walk on in and see the cobwebbed containers still sitting there on the rotted-out remnants of the kitchen counter. There's a rocking chair that creaks and rocks on its own, too, no one rocking it, and strands of tattered curtains blow in the breeze.

All the kids in our neighborhood play in that old house, and me and Zeb have sworn not to tell it was where Mom lived when she was growing up, because it's shameful, she says, to lose a place like that to eminent domain, just a fancy way of saying the place was condemned. But everyone knows anyway, even if we don't say it out loud. We take turns walking through the empty house, see who can stay inside the longest without getting spooked by a ghost, which is usually just some crow flying through, or a field mouse scurrying past. All the same, there's some kind of presence there, and we feel it.

It's like me and Zeb in this house now. Whoever lives here will feel the ghost of us when they come back, find their home torn open like a wound, their belongings no longer private. I ball my right hand into a fist, feel the weight of the sapphire necklace there. "Mom doesn't need jewelry, Zeb. She needs to get healed," I call down the hallway.

"What the hell you think I'm working on, Willa?"

"Johnny's Pharmacy's right up the hill from us."

He comes down the hallway now, leans in close to my face, and whispers, "You think I don't know that, Willa? You think breaking into a business like that is easy? Hell, I get enough money and we can buy her the help she needs, right? We can *buy* it." He huffs a little, stands up straight again. "Nothing wrong with having her feel pretty while she's waiting to get better."

He heads back down the hall, and I open my palm, look at the necklace. He's right. It would look beautiful on Mom. The decision's tough to make, but I make it. I tuck that piece of jewelry into the gap between the mattress and headboard of the bed. It could have fallen there. That's what the mother who lives here will think when she finds it. *It must have fallen that night I was getting ready to go out.* I don't want Mom wearing it anyway, not after this other lady's had it around her perfumed neck for so many years.

After I hide the necklace, I hear the ringing again, fainter this time. But there's no sense telling Zeb about it. I walk back out to the living room and wait. I stand there shivering in the smoldering heat.

A few minutes later, Zeb walks down the hall, stands next to me. He opens his canvas knapsack, shows me the stack of green bills there—scattered tens and twenties. All that cash sitting on top of the fishing bait, the cheese balls, salmon eggs, and night crawlers. There's a stench to the thing, let me tell you, and the house too hot and stuffy inside to begin with. The smell gets caught in the place where my nose meets my throat, sticks in that soft spot where I can't swallow it down or make it come up.

Zeb reaches deeper into his knapsack, pulls back the top layer of money and jewelry. He shows me a gun so small the whole thing could fit in my hand. Its snub-nosed silver barrel is engraved all the way to the place where the bullet comes out, ivory white handle engraved too.

"You can't take that," I tell him.

"Thirty-eight special, Smith and Wesson. Custom collector's item. You bet I'm taking it. It's what I came for." He covers the gun back up, then hands me a ten-dollar bill and rests his hand on my shoulder. "Buy yourself something good with that, Willa."

"How'd you know that thing was here?"

"I always know what I'm looking for."

"Yeah, but how'd you *know*?"

"I knew. That's all. Let's go."

We walk out the front door, back door makes us look suspicious, Zeb says. He walks proud, like he owns this house. He hops on his bike, and I take my seat behind him, holding his waist as he pedals. I hear the sirens starting up. "Goddamnit, Zeb, they're coming, just like I said."

He laughs.

"Pedal fast," I tell him, looking over my shoulder, waiting for the red lights to bear down on us.

He pedals, and I feel the weight of our take in his knapsack, hear the gun clinking against the fishing bait and tackle, and I try but cannot recall a day in my life when I was not already guilty of stealing, Zeb taking me with him from day one of my thoughts.

Pretty soon, we're a good long way from the far side of the field, almost back to our neighborhood and the sirens are still whining, but it's okay because now we're not there and if they're coming for us, we're home safe, just two kids playing in their own neighborhood. I can hear Zeb's friends, Billy and Levon, laughing by the fishing pond, and in the distance I see a small red dot of a cop's light pulsing—can see it cruising between the houses across the field—and just then, Zeb swings his bike around and pedals back toward the place we just left.

"What're you doing, Zeb?" I think of hopping off, but Zeb pedals fast, sits halfway down on my legs, pinning me.

"You see that cop?" he asks.

"Yeah, I saw him."

"I want to see what's going on."

"You *know* what's going on."

He hikes his knapsack up tighter on his shoulders and pedals harder. "You don't know what you're talking about. I want to see what the cops are doing. I gotta learn about these things." He rips across the field, and pretty soon we're back in the big-house neighborhood. Zeb flies off the bike, his lanky legs clearing the center bar, and I have no choice but to jump off with him, let the bike fall. He flops onto the lawn across the street from the house, bends his legs over the curb, elbows on knees, chin resting in his palms, and his eyes fixed on the scene of our crime. He's out of breath, says, "Yeah, they're in there, all right."

The door of the house we just robbed is open. Cops meander in the front yard, walk into the house with their hands on their holsters, on guard.

"Think they'll come over here?" Zeb says.

I clench my jaw to keep my teeth from chattering.

Zeb laughs a little. "What's wrong, Willa? This is the best part." He nudges my shoulder, and I push him away. "You want me to do the pharmacy, but you don't want to help me learn." His voice is a hiss.

"All right," I tell him. "I'm fine."

The tallest cop walks across the street, swinging his flashlight in one hand, though it's broad daylight. "Look. He's coming over here!" Zeb whispers.

"Seen anything strange going on in that house?" the cop asks.

Zeb's canvas pack spews the scent of cheese balls and fish. He sits there with his neatly combed hair and his tidy T-shirt, no Marlboros wrapped in his sleeve now.

"Seen any strangers driving around this neighborhood?"

"No, sir."

"You live nearby?"

"Not too far, sir. Just across the field. My mom's family used to own most of that field, you know. There's a pond there, too. Fishing." He points.

The officer smiles and pats Zeb right on the backpack with his huge, bare palm. Zeb smiles, keeps his eyes wide open, looking at the house with the curiosity and wonder of someone who is innocent.

"Catch any fish there, son?"

"Lots. Yeah. Not today but most days I catch largemouth bass."

"Is that right?"

"Yes, sir."

"Your dad ever take you up fishing in the mountains?"

Zeb shakes his head. "My Dad works too much for fishing."

"Doesn't know what he's missing, does he?"

Zeb quits his *yes sirs* and *no sirs* now. He just eyes the cop and shrugs. "My dad's always working. My mom's sick and so he's always working. You got just the one job?"

"What's that, son?"

"My Dad works more than one job."

"Is that right?" the cops says. When the cop turns to me, Zeb stares at him hard. "How about you? You seen anything unusual around here?" the cop asks me. He doesn't mean it, doesn't think a girl like me could know anything. I can tell by the way he smiles down on me and half-chuckles his question. There's no need to answer.

"All right then. You two better run along. This is no place for a couple of kids right now."

When the cop turns around, I scuff my tennies, hole in the toe, along the concrete gutter. I feel the blood oozing up to the surface, and it feels good. It feels certain.

Zeb moans and straddles the bike, pats the seat for me to hop on behind him, and we ride back through the field, tall grass whipping my bare ankles, high altitude sun prickling the back of my neck.

When we get close to our side of the field again, I hear the other kids playing. I don't want to be with them. No one knows what me and Zeb do, and I feel their not-knowing like a fire in me. "Let me off here," I call out, and Zeb lets the bike fall, and we both take off running different directions.

I run toward our house, fling the door open, and stand in the threshold panting like a chased dog. I can feel fear shaking my body, so I hold myself upright, arms crossed over my chest tight, breathing smooth and quiet, and all the same, Mom, standing over her walker in her threadbare floral apron, turns from chopping vegetables in the kitchen and says, "Well, you're all out of breath. What've you been up to?" She smiles. She always smiles when I walk in the room, and it's something I can't stand, the way her love wraps around me when I've been out all day stealing with Zeb. Her shaky hands offer me a knife, and I grab a bag of carrots from the fridge, start chopping right alongside her.

"Been out with your brother today?"

"Little bit, yeah." I notice her perfect hands, her long, tapered fingernails, when mine are just stubby nubs. As long as her hands are doing something, they're not as twisted up as they are when she's doing nothing, and it makes me want her to keep moving forever. She chops vegetables like a regular mom, and once I give into it, it feels good being with her, cooking, listening to James Taylor singing on the record player. The house is stuffy inside; the air thick, clinging tight to me, feels good against my skin, the comfort of it all.

From the window, me and Mom watch Zeb out in the field, the skinny, angled silhouette of him. He's walking with my best friend, Brenda, and the little gun he just stole is still in the front pocket of his baggy jeans. I can see it hammocked there, swinging every time he takes a step. He's carrying his hunting shotgun over his shoulder, too. He stops walking, sets the butt of the shotgun on the ground, and leans it so Brenda can balance it for him while she stands next to him. He lights a cigarette, and the smoke curls from his nostrils. Mom shakes her head, and I can't tell if it's the old house making her sad or Zeb. "How many times I've asked your brother not to carry that gun outside. And with Brenda right there with him." She stops chopping, and it's like an electric current runs all the way down her left arm, coming out through her trembling hand.

"Shooting birds," I tell her. "He promised he wouldn't shoot birds anymore." Zeb knows me and Mom both love birds.

"He'd better not be shooting birds, or anything else for that matter." She's angry, and firm, but there's nothing she can do to stop him. Not in her condition. "He shouldn't be smoking, either," she says. "I hope he doesn't smoke when you're with him."

"He does." I regret saying it soon as I hear it out loud.

She shakes her head. "Where's Brenda's father, anyway?" she asks. "Letting her run around all day like he does. That man had no business adopting a daughter, taking her off an Indian reservation, to boot." She whispers the adoption part shamefully, like she always does.

Zeb and Brenda walk through the old house, the east wall fallen down so me and Mom can see inside it like a huge, square skeleton outlining the place where Mom grew up. Zeb and Brenda duck out of sight when they sit behind the crumbling wall. At first I can see the smoke from Zeb's cigarette trailing above the crumbled wall. But pretty soon, it disappears too.

I lift my hand from the cutting board, rest it on Mom's shaky hand, and she starts peeling potatoes, as if I hadn't touched her at all. "That's grandma's rocking chair in that house, isn't it? The chair where you first felt Zeb kicking in your tummy."

She looks out at the old house, says nothing. I stay close to her, our fingers brushing occasionally as we work.

"You must've moved out of that place fast, leaving all that stuff inside it." She keeps peeling and I keep talking, and I can see her wanting me to shut up, but I don't. "Wish we could go visit that house together someday, you and me."

Finally she stops busying herself. She sets the peeler aside and rests her palms in mine. I feel the shudder of her disease surfacing on her skin, and I brace myself against it, let her trembling enter my own body so maybe I can take it away from her. The morning I spent stealing with Zeb washes away, and the world slows down to something smaller, something better.

She shuffles with her Parkinson's feet over to the chest of drawers under the TV and pulls out the old photo albums. Most of the time when I ask about the house, she finds something else to talk about. Today, she pulls out these old photos. I sit next to her and she shows me. The house in the pictures looks small but sturdy, like something from my *Little House on the Prairie* books. I trace the outline of it and let my fingers pass over the tidy barbed-wire fence my grandfather built. It looks new, but it's sagging and straggly in the field now. I see the horses grazing in the background. "Nuisance," Mom says, almost smiling. That was the name of her family's horse.

I see the old mare, but I can't stop looking at a grove of apple trees and some pines landscaping her yard, because they're the same trees I see every day, still standing in the field now. I turn the page and look at a faded black-and-white photo of Mom when she was younger than I am now. She's standing under the shade of my favorite climbing tree, with her own brother on one side of her, and another kid, a tall, lanky boy, on the other side. All three kids have on overalls with frayed hems that hang about six inches too short, and their bare, boney legs are splashed with mud. They wear leather shoes, not tennies, and they hold a line between them with six fish dangling from it like huge clothespins. They're smiling like they're about to burst.

"We had lots of fun when we were kids," Mom says.

"We could have fun there now. You and me. Go fishing there someday."

"There's some good fish in that pond. Used to be."

"Still is. I catch good fish there all the time."

She nods, and her hand stills long enough for her to turn the page, but it goes back to trembling soon as she rests it in her lap. I watch her, and I know what they say is wrong. I know this disease will not keep getting worse in her. I know she'll fight it off, strong as she is. We sit there, me and Mom, and I look from the black-and-white photos out into the field, where the blue sky aches above the wheat-colored grasses and the trees still stand like they used to a hundred years back.

Just then Brenda and Zeb stand up. Zeb lights another cigarette, and Mom's trembling comes back. "Damn Zeb," I whisper, and Mom turns her head enough so that I know she heard me. But she doesn't say a word. Brenda shoulders the shotgun for Zeb now, and they walk together out toward the pond, hitting each other as they walk until Brenda finally breaks off from him and heads back toward home. Couple minutes later, when Zeb's alone in the field,

I hear the pop of his gun, and I feel Mom jerk against it. I close my eyes, quit looking out the window. I don't want to see what he's shooting.

.   .   .

BY NOW, THE DAY has worn Mom out. So I help her to her bedroom, and she naps. I lay next to her reading one of my library books till I can't stand the indoors air anymore. There's no trembling when she sleeps, so I bend over and kiss her on her cheek. I can't kiss her when she's awake because her trembling scares me so much. But when she's sleeping, it's like she's almost normal. I leave her sleeping, and I head out to the field. I walk out to my favorite spot by the pond and lay down, my arms crossed under my head, thinking. The coolness of the earth seeps through my thin T-shirt, chills my back.

The day is working its way toward evening now, so I start to get up, and I see Zeb walking toward me, alone, no guns this time, far as I can tell. I want him to leave. I want this field all to myself, I want this sky. If Mom can't be here with me on account of her Parkinson's, I want to be alone. I don't want my brother walking the same ground as me. But he keeps heading toward me in a straight line, and I see his hands clasped in front of him. He's holding something close to his chest. "I don't need whatever you got for me, Zeb. Don't want one of your damn presents," I call out to him.

He doesn't answer, just keeps walking till he stands right in front of me, opens his clasped hands, and sunlight streams out of them, the bright yellow feathers on the breast of a meadowlark, a bird he shot and killed earlier today. At first, I want to walk away from him and never see him again. But then I see his sadness, and something gives way in me. The world feels shrouded now, like me and Zeb are the only people in it. I move closer to him, open my palms under his, and he empties the bird in. It hits with more weight than I'd expected, its head spilling over the side of my palms like water from a fountain, limp. "You did this," I tell him.

He flinches at my words, and I feel the bird's body. It is warm in the way only living things are warm. I can feel its heart beating too, the pressure of its breathing.

"I think it's living, Zeb," I whisper. Against his toughness, his eyes widen with hope. I hold that bird in the hollow of my palms, like my hands are praying around it. "It's the color of daffodils." I pet the meadowlark's throat. "Does it get colored that way when it sings?"

"A bird can't get colored from singing," Zeb says. But I know he's wrong. The yellow of this bird is bright and saturated with the sound of the meadow in springtime. There's this bubble around me and Zeb now, a world within a world made of me and my brother, but somehow Brenda's voice pierces it. She calls from across the field, and me and Zeb both start walking away from her without thinking about it, our shoulders pressed close together, forming a barricade against her

Pretty soon, though, we hear Brenda's voice right behind us. "What're you two doing? Whatchya got?" We keep walking till she hovers long enough, asking us over and over, and finally I stop and turn around, open my hands to her, and watch her fall silent. She bends closer, then looks at Zeb. She eyes him mean, then she pulls her long, black hair into a ponytail and looks at me, questioning.

"You were here, Brenda, you know how this bird got shot."

"We were just walking with the guns," she says. "Not shooting them. There's no damn reason for killing a bird like this."

Zeb just looks at her. He has nothing to say, just takes Brenda's anger like it was due him. The world changes then, and what felt like a shroud around me and Zeb shifts and becomes a quiet that engulfs me and Brenda. Zeb steps back. "What're you planning to do with that bird, Willa?" Brenda asks.

"Gonna doctor it."

She whispers but at the same time keeps her anger going. "Can't doctor it, Willa. Far as I can tell from looking at it, Zeb shot it full on." She's five inches taller and two years older than I am, held back in school the same year I jumped ahead, not on account of her being stupid, but on account of her father taking her out of school to nurse his hangovers too many days, when he isn't even her real dad. So me and Brenda are in the same grade now, but she still thinks she knows more than I do.

"You can't even see where this bird's been shot," I tell her. "I could make a splint if the wing's broken, could feed it with an eye dropper till it gets stronger. I've seen people do it on TV."

She reaches into my hands and lifts one wing of the bird with her forefinger and thumb. The meadowlark's flight feathers spread out like a deck of playing cards. She points to the holes peppering the body under the wing, the distinct scatter of birdshot. It weakens me. "Looks like rain gone hard on the skin," I tell her. "That must have been what the bird thought when it hit. Rain gone hard on the skin."

"It didn't think anything, Willa. It's a *bird*." She glares at Zeb standing behind me now, and I expect him to come at her hard, the way these two fight most days. But he just reaches in and touches the bird one last time, no arguing or temper, and then he walks away, leaves us both standing there without him. It's what I wanted all along, for him not to be near me, but when he walks away, I feel an ache, something that only fades when I fight against it.

The only thing that matters now is the meadowlark. "Look," I say to Brenda, whispering again. "Nothing got in its eyes. They look like tiny black seeds, don't they?" She comes in closer to me, and we huddle around the bird. I close the bird's eyes with one finger. Its lids are wrinkled and scaly, like a reptile's. I glance up, see Zeb on the edge of the field, his back hunched as he walks away, his arms crossed over his stomach, like he might be feeling sick.

Brenda sees me looking at him, shakes her head. "He's an asshole," she says. Then she goes back to whispering. "This bird is suffering," she says.

"Yeah. It is."

She tosses her arm around my shoulder, and together we walk toward the pond. The evening sky has turned swollen and quiet.

"This bird is suffering," Brenda says, again, and she's not talking to me, she's just repeating things into the air. When we reach the water, she squats down, opens her palms, and asks me to hand the bird over, which is something I cannot do.

"It's my bird, Brenda."

"You can't own a bird, Willa."

"I know. But I know what you're planning to do with it."

"Because it's best."

I can't stand what she's saying, and I want to come at her like Zeb does sometimes, with fists. She's tall and big boned, and when she's not with me, people tell me she's grumpy and hateable. But I know it's just her being scared and pissed off at things other people don't understand. I also know, deep down, that what she's saying is true. The bird is suffering, and there's nothing to change that or turn back time. "Well, let me do it then," I tell her.

"*Will* you?" she says.

It's hard to do, but I nod, yes. She agrees, and we both kneel down side by side on the banks of the pond. I could not do this without her being there with me. I could not do it alone. I know this in the pores of my bones.

I look out across the field, sun on the down side of the day and the jagged mountains turning pink along the ridges, dark blue underneath. I think, *This will be the last sky this bird will ever see*, and I know there's no way to make it any different.

I feel the cool water of the pond wrap around the backs of my hands. It trickles through the gaps between my fingers, pooling around the bird, which struggles as soon as I dip it in. I didn't think it had any fight left in its body, but it does.

I've been told it's a caring thing to do, no matter how hard it is. You've got to help a suffering thing die. So I keep my hands clasped tight, close my fingers around its narrow neck, and I twist the head. I feel a *crack*, and the bird goes dead. Tears well up in my eyes.

"Is it done?" Brenda says.

"It's done." The meadowlark buoys to the surface of the pond, looks half the size it was when it was living, its slack skin and fragile bones visible beneath its sulfur yellow feathers. "Goddamn Zeb," Brenda whispers. She reaches into the water, scoops the bird up in her palms.

"What're you doing?" I ask. She starts walking, and I follow. "Where're you taking that bird?"

"Going to bury it." It feels right, so we walk together to a place by the edge of the field where we know the claylike dirt of this land turns softer, having been farmed for so many years by my own family. There, we both start digging with our hands. "Think we should put it in a box?" I ask.

"No box."

"Like a person. So it can go on from here."

"No box. Just earth. It's all it needs," Brenda says.

When the little pocket we hollow out is about the size of a big avocado, we stop. She takes a moment, then asks me if I'm ready. "Go ahead. Put it in," I tell her. Together, we place the bird in the grave, let our fingers slip out from underneath it. We cover it back up with soil.

"Better get back home now," she says. She stands up and walks away fast.

I stay. I pick up two stalks of dried wheat, one long, one shorter. I wrap the shorter stalk around the longer stalk about three quarters of the way up, make a cross for the grave.

"Let it be, Willa." Brenda's voice stretches back across the field, the way sounds echo on a summer evening. I press my finger into the earth, poke a dependable hole there, set the bottom end of the cross into the ground. Then I run to catch up with my friend.

A few steps from where we both split off to go to our own houses, I look back. The cross has fallen. The grave is an empty mound.

Willa

I HADN'T THOUGHT ABOUT Zeb for a long time. Or maybe I thought about him all the time, his presence like a dull hum circling my brain, the way birds of prey circle without being noticed by animals busy on the ground. The peregrine falcon flies fifteen thousand feet above the earth and has been clocked in a dive at over two hundred miles an hour. A songbird has little chance of maneuvering out of a peregrine's line of sight. The falcon hits its mark midair.

The phone call came like that: a quick hit, a surprise, but not a surprise. It was just a matter of time.

"He's gone into the woods," the voice said.

From my house on the Chuparosas Mesa, I could see the late summer weather moving in from the north, beyond the Sangre de Cristos, low clouds drifting across the New Mexico border from Colorado, the home I'd left behind, a place I could never squeeze out of my bones—the field where Zeb and I played when we were kids, the mountains that surrounded the place. That land felt like blood relation, to me, like the heart-and-soul substance of a family that had long since been undone. The voice on the phone kept on, and all those memories I thought had vanished came rushing through me, vivid and clear as the present day. They shook me. What the voice was saying shook me, too. So much time had passed, twenty-five years or so. How could they revive this incident now?

"There's no time statute in killing someone," the voice said. "You understand that, Miss Robbins, don't you?" He addressed me formally, not out of respect, but condescension.

"I understand a lot of things."

"Precisely. That's why we're calling you. We figure you might be the only one who could track him through the San Juans effectively. Pretty rugged territory there, you know."

"Track him?"

"Bring him out of the woods."

My gut was in a knot, but this last bit made me smile a little. Zeb had finally found a way to live in the place he loved, the backwoods of the San Juan range in southern Colorado, his favorite place when we were growing up. "Look, he was a *kid*," I said, finally. "We were both kids."

There was a grunt on the other end of the line, followed by a rehearsed litany of recent offenses they couldn't pin on Zeb, but which this guy said he "just knew" Zeb had committed. His voice had started out all cool and calm in the beginning, but as he talked about Zeb, I could hear him getting more and more agitated, even excited. "Yeah, your brother, he does all these petty little thefts, you know, minor pot deals, punk pranks: defacing property, breaking into stores and changing the damn prices on things, shit like that."

"He changes prices?"

"Yeah, lowers them to his liking. Maybe he thinks it's funny. Hell, I don't know. But he doesn't do it in his own little hippie town. No. He makes a trip down the mountain to the chain stores to do it, one after the other, doesn't leave a damn trace, except for writing numbers all over everything. Shit like that, you know, and so me and my guys, we drive up the mountain and we haul his ass in, question him, and—" He stalled to catch his breath and his voice came out almost whiny. "We question him and the sonofabitch looks squeaky clean."

I almost laugh a little, but what the guy says next takes away any chance of that. His voice goes from being frustrated and excited to mean and deadly serious. "We have him on *this*, though," the man said. "Homicide. Killing a man." His cocky laughter came like a machine gun now. "Killing a man is no petty theft, you know. Zeb's done. We have him now."

My gut sunk. I knew exactly what he was talking about. There was no way to pretend. "I don't understand. There's no new evidence." Any proof they'd gathered since Zeb had killed Chet had to be over twenty-five years old.

"We don't need much evidence, Miss Robbins," he said. "We have a confession, *written*, along with his description of what happened that day, right down to the last detail. Things only the killer would know. You know what he did? He emailed it to us. Sent it to a few state offices too, just to make sure, you know. *Emailed it*, like a damn party invitation."

I could feel my throat tightening, my mind reeling back to the time it all happened. I felt the person I was now shrinking away underneath the kid I was back then, stealing right alongside Zeb. "It doesn't make sense. If my brother turned himself in, why would he run?"

"You tell me how your brother's mind works, and we'll both know." He had a point there. Zeb's thoughts had always been a jungle. "Probably some stupid impulse decision, and we got email to thank for that, right? Can you be here Monday?" he said.

I gulped for air, felt my lungs fill with the New Mexico evening. I loved this place now, and I couldn't imagine leaving it. From the living room where I stood, I could see Magda standing in my kitchen, making fresh chorizo that smelled of smoke and chilies. I looked out the window and saw her husband, Cario, walking across the open desert, a blue-jeaned, blue-shirted dot on the purple horizon. Every evening and every morning, Cario and Magda made the trek from their little adobe home, about a quarter mile away, to my place. We shared breakfast, dinner, conversation. Some nights, Christina stopped by on her way home from work, too, and the four of us had good food, a rich and vibrant love between us, though love was a word I was careful with around Christina. Still, this was the life I had made for myself, my makeshift, mongrel family. I'd lived here most of my adult life, had built my home from the ground up, had found peace, a way to live comfortably—things I never thought possible when I was growing up with Zeb.

I carried the phone with me as I walked outside, leaned against my truck, the wheel wells as rusty as the earth I stood on, same red color that soaked the marrow of my bones. When I thought of going back to Colorado, I longed for it, yet it frightened me. I worried that this call, so out of the blue, was a set up for what I'd done. I wondered if they had somehow figured out that I was as guilty of taking a life as Zeb. I'd worked hard to bury what I knew, to redefine it to myself, to tell the story a different way. But there were the bony, hard facts of it. I was responsible for my own mother's death. Did they know that? Was that the unspoken reason for the call?

"There's a good chance I won't have any more luck find-ing Zeb than you," I said. "If you already spent a day and a half tracking him, with dogs, I can't sniff things out any better than a canine."

"I'm told you're one of the best trackers around."

"Overstatement."

"So you know damn well that tracking is 90 percent getting inside the head of whatever or whoever you're tracking. And you *know* Zeb." He was right on all counts. "And he's your brother, for chrissake. You find him, he comes out alive. *We* find him, and—" He left it to me to fill in the blank. There was silence on his end of the line. He knew he had me.

"Okay," I said. "I'll come." My words felt hollow.

"Good."

I had lowered the receiver away from my ear, ready to hang up, when his voice came at me again, sounding like a Dragnet man. "Without you, Willa, our choices are limited. If you don't show, I'll have to give my men the right to shoot."

My jaw tightened. I watched Cario, his bow-legged Mexican cowboy gait. He opened the screen door, walked into my house. I couldn't stand the thought of leaving him and Magda. "I'll be there. I'm glad to do it," I said into the phone. I hung up.

It wasn't a complete lie. To have a reason and a way to see Zeb again—I'd been waiting for that since we went our separate ways so long ago, the tug between us still visceral across place and time. The man was right. I knew everything about Zeb. And Zeb knew almost everything about me. I'd had what felt like a bird batting around in my chest since I was a kid, something caged and trying to get out. This was it: my chance to release it, once and for all. I needed to see Zeb again.

I skirted a conversation with Cario and Magda by walking around to the back door. I walked into my room, started packing, the phone call echoing through my head as resonant and haunting as the wolf howls I'd heard yesterday in the canyon.

* * *

I HAD SPENT THE day and night before working outside the borders of Días de Ojos National Forest, tracking Hector (called AM108 by the Wilderness and Water Agency reintroduction project) and Ciela (AF138), two Mexican grey wolves who had removal orders on their heads for allegedly feeding their young with meat from slow, dumb cattle, rather than wild deer, javelina, or elk.

Even after working in the field for so long, I'd never learned not to fall in love with the animals I tracked. Hector and Ciela were two of the first wolves in Días de Ojos to mate and reproduce in the wild, the offspring of Sky (AF118) and Kody (AM97) who had been released into the forest five years earlier.

Mexican wolves aren't the same as the Yellowstone wolves getting all the press. They're the most endangered sub-species of wolf in the world, and the most endangered mammal in North America. Because they don't have a national park like Yellowstone protecting them, they're more fragile. In National Parks, no ranching is allowed. National forests, however, depend on ranching. But reintroducing wolves to forest mixed with cattle ranchland was like putting sharks in a tank with guppies and then killing the sharks if the guppies didn't survive. Pretty soon, the tank is empty. Though the Wilderness and Water Agency had tried to buy the ranchers out of their easements, none were selling. The only way the WWA had convinced the ranchers to agree to the mandatory reintroduction of the endangered wolf was to have the animals declared "nonessential experimental species." They were still "endangered," but this special designation allowed for more "management flexibility" with Mexican wolves, which meant they could be shot and killed, "if necessary." The double bind was inescapable: The WWA was responsible for releasing 100 percent of the wolves in the southwest states. It was also responsible for killing—either by shooting or botched relocations—most of the same wolves they'd released.

Hector and Ciela, though, had been born in the wild, had never been touched by human hands, never been collared with a transmitter. They were truly wild wolves. The Wilderness and Water Agency had agreed to monitor them by foot-tracking and helicopter only, and I worked for two large nonprofit wildlife defense organizations as an independent overseer. Just this year, the WWA had finally stopped shooting Mexican wolves for crossing out of the Días de Ojos boundaries. Hector and Ciela were the first wolves allowed to successfully migrate off the protected area, and they had made their way far from the ranchers' properties. Because of this, they had a chance of surviving. They were the embodiment of hope.

But Halvorson, a rancher from near the Navajo Nation border, said he'd witnessed Ciela and Hector and their pack (called the West Canyon pack) killing his cattle. Though Halvorson admitted he thought wolves should be extirpated and had made false claims about wolves before, the WWA said the ID was certain. Hector and Ciela's offense had gone on too long. They'd killed his livestock three times now, and Halvorson claimed he had run them out of the territory with ATVs and rifle blanks. But each time, the wolves had found their way back to their home again.

I'd tracked these wolves and found little evidence of these claims. The wolves scavenged dead, mismanaged cattle now and again, but had never killed. They were excellent hunters, and they had successfully raised their first litter. Three pups had survived to adolescence. But unless I could prove Hector and Ciela innocent once and for all, that would be their last litter. I was their final appeal.

"Hell, Halvorson's being nice about it, Willa. He could've shot them and been done with it," Andy my contact at WWA had told me.

"Yeah," I said. "Tell him thanks."

So I'd spent a few days and nights with my belly pressed close to the earth, enveloped in the musty scent of leaves and dirt, watching Ciela and Hector. Over the past year, I'd gained their trust. Not the kind of trust that made them immune to humans. I'd seen them run from the slightest suggestion of human movement. But they were used to my scent, in particular. I stayed under constant cover, but I no longer needed to look through the narrow tunnel of binoculars or a scope. Now I was able to get close enough to observe individual details: the rich black outline around Hector's grey eyes, shaped in a narrow almond; the slight glitch in Ciela's gait that told the story of a battle she'd had that we, in all our "close observation," had missed, something that had left her permanently wounded, but thriving all the same. The will to survive inhabited her bones.

That day, I'd been ecstatic when I watched her and Hector and two other West Canyon wolves chase and kill an adult mule deer. It was one of two successful wild hunts I'd witnessed in the past few months. It might have been enough to save Hector and Ciela, if I argued my point well. But I was the only person who had witnessed their kills. Now I could not be there to talk to WWA in person. I'd written a report, told every last detail of Ciela and Hector's success. Still, as I packed for Colorado, the fate of the wolves worried the margins of my heart.

*   *   *

I STOOD IN MY bedroom, tossing clothes and gear into my duffle, trying to explain all this to Cario and Magda who stood, now, in my doorway, questioning me.

"I don't like it," Cario said. He took me by the hand and led me into the living room, so he could keep watching TV while he talked. "You don't know your brother anymore, Willa. He could be dangerous, even to you."

"Could be," I said. I set my duffle bag down and watched a few minutes of *Anatomía de Grey*. On the screen, two patients in the ER had a large pole running through the middle of their bodies.

At a commercial break, Magda patted my thigh. "This is not good." She pointed to the TV screen, stood up, and imitated my voice in a perfect American accent. "Why is this entertainment?

These bleeding people in pain? Take my TV why don't you? Take it to your own damn house." She quit imitating me now and sat back down on the sofa. The soft, fleshy wrinkles on her cheeks, usually smile lines, turned to crevices of worry. "You're watching *Grey's Anatomy*, Willa, and for the love of Mary and Joseph and sweet baby Jesus, you are not complaining about it." She shook her head. "You're not yourself. You're not right in the head." She knocked her knuckles against my skull, took a break of silence, then reloaded. "And what about your *friend*, Christina?" She emphasized the word, reminding me that Christina meant more to me than a friend should, in her opinion. "Have you told her your hair-brained idea? Call her. She'll tell you no. She's got good sense."

I was absorbed in the TV.

"Have you called Raymond? He'll tell you: 'Loco.' He'll tell you: 'Stay.'" She lost her train of thought for a moment, and I was relieved. "You know, Raymond owes me twenty dollars. Last poker game we had here on the mesa. Remember?" She nudged Cario. "I took Raymond for twenty dollars and he did not pay up."

"Sí, Sí. Out of the hundreds he usually wins from you, that you've never paid him," Cario said.

"Ver la televisión," Magda said, to Cario. Then to me, "Going to Colorado, Willa. It's not good."

My whole life was happening in double exposures now. One film played Magda and Cario sitting in my living room, joking about good times we'd had out here on this mesa. And behind that image, the film of my childhood played. "I'll be back before Raymond owes you another twenty," I said. I tried for a smile. Magda didn't. "I have to stop by and see him anyway. Got some wolves he needs to look after for me."

"Tell him to look after my twenty dollars." She gestured to my small duffle bag. "That's all you're taking?"

"Won't be there long."

"Mierda santo," a whisper meant for Cario's ears only. "Nuestra niña es una locura."

"Sí, está loca," Cario said, though his eyes never left the TV.

"You bet I'm crazy. I live out on this godforsaken mesa with you two," I said.

This time, Magda found a smile, but it faded fast. "Your brother, Mija. Let him be." She stood up, took my hand, and led me to my bedroom. "Sleep on it."

"Eres mi familia, you know," I said.

"Por supuesto. Somos familia." She hugged me, closed the door, then walked back to my living room, my TV, and her husband.

＊　＊　＊

NEXT MORNING, SOON AS the sun oozed red over the horizon, I woke up and headed out. I heard the warped screen door slam behind me, then swing back to its halfway open position, as it always did. I walked out into the sounds of morning, the ravens starting up already, songbirds beginning, coyotes fading, and there, across the mesa, I saw Magda, standing on her porch, waving goodbye. If there had been a tug when I said goodbye to Zeb or to Mom long ago, that same tug went out to Magda now. I felt pulled back to Colorado, the place I'd grown up, and at the same time, tied here, to New Mexico, this land, these people, this love.

I took the long way through town so I could drive by Chris's little adobe house. I had every intention of knocking on the door, saying goodbye, letting her know what was going on. But the house was dark, and I told myself it would be best not to wake her. The engine of my truck rumbled, the sparse lights of my little town becoming a distant constellation that faded to darkness in the rearview mirror.

Zeb

THE ROAD DIMINISHED IN both directions, around the bend before him, behind him in a thin whip that trailed for some

time before it disappeared in his rearview mirror. Late summer wheat lay flattened by wind and heat, strapped across the
hillsides like the greying hair of a blonde woman, strawlike and
dull by now.

There are some things you cannot change, you just cannot change.

The engine brake hissed and sputtered, the only sound in
the predawn night. Hand over hand, his whole body working,
he steered the Peterbilt up the exit ramp, to the stoplight. With
the driver side window rolled down, the morning cool brushed
across his bare arms, lean and more muscular than they should
have been for his forty-some years. The chill felt good to him.
He sat for a few seconds in the quiet, then felt the engine rumble in his chest as he pressed the pedal. He pulled the rig into
the bay.

He logged his hours by the splash of moonlight through the
cab window, didn't want the dome light on, hated the goddamn
interrogation lights of cities that dimmed the stars above, hated
anything that took away from the darkness, made something as
abundant as stars struggle to do their job. Most things he loved
had dimmed.

He pulled the leather ties from his ponytail, let his dark hair
fall around his shoulders now, then closed the log book, walked
across the lot, turned in his time sheet without so much as a good
goddamn to the other drivers milling around and shooting the
shit after their shifts. He made his way to the bare tables where
three computers sat, drivers checking email and writing to their
families. Zeb sat down, pulled up the same pages he always looked
at, the ones that told of the work his sister was doing in New
Mexico, though they never said exactly where in New Mexico.
Some secluded place kept top secret from the general public, for
good reason, but still. How to find her, wherever she was now.
It worried him. He would give up most of what he had now to
see her again. He hovered too long over his email, then made a
decision he'd keep to himself. After he hit "send," he stared at
the computer a while longer. Then he signed off and walked back
outside, across the lot.

An hour's drive lay head of him, and about two miles from home, he killed the lights of his '68 Chevy truck, drove in darkness, sensed his way around the curves of familiar blacktop and intersections that lay as open and forgiving as a young woman's body. His wife was no longer young, no longer the girl he'd grown up with in the field. Brenda was at home in bed now, fat, snoring, her black hair streaked with wires of grey. The glowing embers of his cigarette outlined her form every time he inhaled, the bearlike heap of her beneath woolen blankets, the smell of her sharp, whiskeyed breath as she exhaled in her sleep. He could see her silhouette even as he drove.

In the long gravel driveway, he released the clutch, let the engine die before turning the key. He still missed his old Australian shepherd, Hitch, who had greeted him along this road for nearly five years, his ghosted outline still visible to Zeb along this path. He tried to shake the memory of the mountain lion that had taken Hitch, but the spirit of that cat was embedded in him to the bone. The first time he'd seen the lion, he'd been walking through the meadow near his cabin. It was a fall day, no snow yet, and he had just settled into his cabin, his first real home as an adult (something he'd never imagined would be possible for him).

At first, she was completely shadowed by the trees. But light changed fast in the highlands, and the shadows shifted, and where once there was nothing, now there were three lions, a female with two kits that were almost full grown. Female cougars keep their offspring with them for up to three years before sending them into their own territories, and these kits, Zeb figured, were a season or two away from being pushed out. The family was sharing a recent kill, a doe, as far as he could tell.

Zeb watched from his distance as the cougars pulled at the fresh meat, their muzzles thick with blood in a way photos in souvenir shops never showed, uncomfortable as people are with an animal that is both beautiful *and* deadly. He watched silently until the female lion dragged the remains of the doe deeper into the woods and covered the carcass with leaves and debris.

The following winter, he was walking home alone after a day of unsuccessful bow hunting. Twilight had turned to dusk and dusk to dark, the seam of the day now folded over into night. He inhaled the menthol air, let it flood his lungs. It felt good to him, and his constant vigilance lagged. In that vulnerable moment, without so much as the snap of a twig as a warning, a mountain lion was on him. It knocked him to the ground, and he felt his skin pop as the knifelike claws sunk into his fleshy shoulder muscles. He felt his own warm blood covering his skin, and then he went numb and strong with adrenalin. With the butt of his bow he hammered the animal between the eyes, and the cougar fell back enough to let him reach for his handgun, aim, and pull the trigger. The animal went down instantly, no struggle, no suffering.

He stood there, shaken. It was a young cat, just pushed out of his mother's care, in search of his own territory now. But with houses and subdivisions crawling up the mountainside like they were, new territory for mountain lions was meager. Zeb knew this young male was the offspring of the female he'd seen with her two kits at the edge of the meadow. It had been a while since he'd broken the law, and now a dead mountain lion, out of season, lay in front of him. As he looked down at the blood and earth, he knew this lion would go to waste in the woods. Scavengers would pick at it till it rotted. With the bears already asleep for the winter, there was no predator large enough to consume this much meat. So he bled the animal from the neck, then took out his hunting knife and split the lion from ribcage to anus. He field dressed it like a deer, and he hauled the remains home. It was the first time he had tasted the meat of another hunter.

He blinked as he drove now, trying to shake the memory. He leaned into the steering wheel and coasted home.

His bad leg caught on some sharp spur he could feel on his hip bone as he stepped out of the truck, and he limped without hiding it now, no one watching at this time in the morning anyway.

At the corral, he bent at the waist and slipped between the wood slats of the fence. "Lita, Chey." He clicked his tongue between his back teeth and jaw. "C'mon girl, c'mon, boy." Cheyenne, the bay, trotted over, his dusky mane swaying. "Yeah, boy, yeah." The horse bowed to meet him, and Zeb rested his own forehead against the blaze on Chey's nose, stroked the sides of the horse's muscled neck, saying, "Yeah, boy. Hungry? Yeah, let's get you fed." He pulled armfuls of hay from the feed shed, walked back out to the troughs, kicked at Bonnie and Clyde, the two old mules who had lumbered out of the stable, shooing them away from Chey's bin, "Git, now, git," then he spread enough hay on the ground to feed them, too. "Lita, Rosalita," he called again, louder. He clicked his tongue.

In the lightening dusk, he saw the silhouette of her neck. It rose from the earth like a sapling tree. "Well, come on, girl. Gonna let Bonnie and Clyde steal your breakfast?" He kicked again at the mules. "Y'old robbers."

Rosalita, the small paint pony Zeb favored, struggled to stand, her front hooves flailing. Then the reaching arc of her neck gave up and folded. Her head hit the earth with a thud.

For a split second Zeb's eyes widened like a boy's. He felt like a boy again, the veins in his neck thick with fear, his heart a wild and bloodied thing snared in a steel trap. From his distance he watched the muscles in Rosalita's whole body go limp in the certain way of death. He set his jaw, willed himself numb. He slapped the flanks of the bay stallion, let Bonnie press her stubbly, soft muzzle into his hip, felt the heat of her body in the cool morning, and gave her an extra good scrub behind the ears. He took out a cigarette, made motion to light it, then tucked it back into the front pocket of the flannel shirt he'd ripped the sleeves off of while driving through the Mojave, the damned heat that had scorched him all across the lowlands. He folded his arms over his chest, shivered, then walked toward Rosalita.

"Lita. My Rosalita," his voice cracking now. The horse's flanks were torn clean, a row of knives dragged along them, the red striations of muscle pulsing visibly, the hieroglyphics of a wild cat engraved in her flesh. It had always bothered him that there was so little blood in dying. The white and brown hair of her hide was bloodied, yes, but very little blood had touched the ground, and what did just darkened the already red Colorado dirt, soaked in too fast to notice. Shaking, he placed a gentle finger on one of the deep puncture wounds in her neck.

He rested his open palm on her heart, felt her breathing. Zeb never wore a watch, just went by rhythms. About thirty-five breaths a minute, he figured, more than twice her average breathing rate. "Rosalita," a whisper now. The scimitar calls of killdeers divided the morning from the night. His own breath was fast and shallow in his chest. "Jesus." His knees gave way and he crumpled to the ground next to the horse, his body leaning into the soft part of her chest, the wide *V* just below her ribcage.

Sunrise came like an afterthought to the mountains where Zeb lived. Fourteen-thousand foot peaks stood like gods guarding the Arkansas river, the granite tree line on each mountain marking the place where oxygen thinned and most forms of life quit trying. By the time the sun brimmed over those giants, it had been warming the lowlands for hours, no ceremony left in the dawn. As the sun rose that morning, Zeb felt Rosalita's heart stop. "It's all right, Lita," he whispered. "I'm here. I'm here." He rested his head on her chest, listened to life slip out of her.

A few minutes later he stood and walked into the house.

"Well, you're dragging your withered ass in late this morning," Brenda said. She tossed her meaty arms around his neck, so sun tanned from the road that it matched the dark brown of her own skin. She kissed him flat on the lips, a kiss he did not return.

"Got home at the regular time," he said.

"Not that I seen of you."

He sat down at the scarred wood table.

Brenda gave up, waved her hand toward the electric range. "There's cold eggs used to be hot waiting for you in the oven."

Zeb helped himself, scraped the dried eggs, bacon, and hash browns onto his plate. He stared out the small kitchen window, saw nothing, then saw something. He dropped the plate, let the yellowed eggs bounce off onto the counter. "Sonofabitch, it's her."

"You're on your own for the joe, too," Brenda said. "I drank myself a pot already." She poured vodka into her morning OJ, swished it around in the glass.

"Yeah, all right," Zeb said, not to Brenda.

"Fire ants gnawing your panties this morning?" She shook her head. "Obsessed with that damn mountain lion again?"

He walked into the living room, grabbed a rifle, felt the satisfying click when he cocked it, and headed outside, walking fast, numb to whatever it was that had made him limp earlier.

The cougar slinked through ribbons of sunlight that fell through Doug firs and aspen. That cat could have been a shadow itself if it hadn't moved with such intention, if it had moved mindlessly, like wind. But a predator's moves always have purpose, have power. Especially a cat.

Zeb raised his rifle, and the scope brought the lion so close he could see her breathing, mouth open slightly, pink tongue, muzzle outlined by whiskers quivering with each inhalation, the wary pant of a cat: cautious, and at the same time fearless. He could see, too, the barrel of his rifle jerking, the throb of his heart made visible in his aim. He was an excellent marksman, but this time he tried to steady the gun, and couldn't.

"Goddamn." He lowered the rifle. It was a rule he lived by: Never point a gun unless you plan to shoot it, and never take that shot unless you're sure it will hit dead on.

The big cat skulked from the wooded hillside out into the meadow, her graceful body moving low to the ground, a predator with a hunted look in its eyes. Away from the shelter of trees, the animal turned almost small under the wide, mountain sky. He watched the cat cross, and then— And then what? The world had split in two, far as Zeb could tell. Along the horizon, a seam had opened up, as if the sky had always been only loosely stitched to the land anyway, and the cat had disappeared into the space in-between. Though it was walking, sauntering, really, and though Zeb had his eyes right on it, the cat vanished into the woods.

The sun was high in the sky now, but it didn't warm anything, just turned it brighter and more crisp in the autumn air.

Zeb stood still, watching. Then listening, then sniffing the wind like an animal.

After a while, he went back to Rosalita. There was his life inside the cabin, waiting for him. His love for Brenda had never been a passion. It was love, yes, the kind of love that has tendrils rooted in childhood, something beautiful, but something lost, a nostalgia even before it had a chance to become real in the present.

Then there was the life he had here, outdoors. The times he felt most like himself were the times he'd spent out in the woods, alone, or riding Rosalita. The longer he spent outdoors, the more the truck stops and highways faded away and his memory skipped a few decades and settled back on his life growing up, the house he was born in but could not remember, save for the rotted bones of it that stood in the field where his mother was born. He'd spent the best part of his earliest days in that neighborhood, growing up with his sister. He didn't want any of it back. That wasn't it. His future gnawed at him more deeply than any memory he could conjure, the vagueness of it, like smoke with no source of fire, just a dreary haze rising from something dowsed. He'd outlived most of what he loved, and what remained was shrinking away fast. Like the field; like his mother and the cruel and persistent illness that had crippled her; like wilderness.

There were some things you could not change. He knew that. But when he'd sent that email, he'd made one decision. And with his hand there on Rosalita's dying body, he made another: to change his future, his life.

∘　∘　∘

A FEW DAYS AFTER that he woke a little later than usual and saw the trail of police cars winding their way on the skinny road that switch-backed its way up the mountainside below him. They were silent from this distance, their diminished red lights flashing through the morning fog. Four of them, and no one else living near his place on this mountain. Just Zeb and Brenda.

The cars approached closer now, and he felt something ping in his chest, as if his lungs were strung with musical wire and a sharp sound played in him, something as comforting and familiar as an old song: seductive and certain and alive. His confession had been the right thing to do. He had finally made the right choice.

He walked outside to get a better look at their arrival. He saw his own breath in the late autumn chill, and he stuffed his hands in the pockets of his Lee jeans. He could hear Brenda calling him from inside, as usual, telling him his breakfast was made and she was not going to hold it for him, and she would let it get cold, and the coffee, too, and when was the last time they'd sat down together for breakfast anyway. And then she quit talking.

With his head cocked a little sideways, he almost smiled. He walked back into the house, tossed the rubbery eggs Brenda had made into the trash, stood at the stove, and started cooking his own breakfast.

Through the narrow doorway of the cabin, he could see Brenda crashed out in a heap on the musty, plaid, living room sofa. She would be surprised to hear a knock at the door, to see anyone other than him in her house. In a dozen years they had not invited anyone to their home, did all their visiting at the feed store or Gnarly's Saloon instead, Zeb preferring, as he did, to choose the times when he was feeling talkative, even gregarious, and protect the times when he was not. Over the years, his gregarious times had come down to a few dozen long nights at Gnarly's spent joking about some of his best pranks, but mostly telling stories of his childhood with his sister, stories the townies took as tall tales and bragging, but Zeb took as a chance to try and figure it all out. Brenda avoided joining him on these occasions, her version of each of his stories differing from his, and both of them being right. Still, he knew she would wake with a start at the strange sound of a knock on the door, her sodden consciousness trying for the sharpness it had had in her youth.

He flipped the eggs in the pan, liked over-easy better than scrambled anyway, and waited for the bacon to sizzle white around the edges, the meaty parts crispy and charred, and he lifted the frying pan and the breakfast slid onto his plate. He sat down at the table and ate. A cool sensation like rivers rushed through his muscles. Any minute, the cabin door would open. Brenda would wake and not understand what was happening. The salty eggs tasted good on his tongue, the home-cooked meal a comfort to him now.

He stood at the window sink, washing his plate, and sponged the egg grease into the sink. He wiped his hands on his jeans, watched the red lights flicker through the trees that striped the horizon, then he walked to the living room, took a handgun from the mantle, a box of ammo from a drawer in the coffee table he'd made of beetle-kill pine that he'd harvested himself, walked to the back door, and hurled the gun and ammo into the air. They landed past the tree-lined edge of his property.

"Brenda," he said, standing above her as she slept on the couch. "Brenda." He shook her shoulder, and she roused. He was surprised at the feeling that swelled in his chest when her eyes opened and connected with his. He wanted to say something, but instead, he just looked at her, almost kissed her, but didn't. She squinted at him, shook her head in annoyance, and slept again.

"Tell them you don't know anything," he said, finally. He walked down the short hallway to the kitchen.

"Tell who?"

"Anyone. When they come asking for me." He added, "Please."

He heard her gruff laugh coming from the living room now. "Is that what you're thinking? Someone's coming for you?" she said. "They could care less about your petty stealing, your little pranks. Delusions of grandeur, sweetheart, delusions of grandeur."

He leaned on the small windowsill in the kitchen, watched the police cars finally emerge from the narrow, tree-shrouded drive that led to his place, something settling down inside him as he watched. He saw them, their sedan wheels bobbing, barely able to hold the muddied road, a black and white SUV behind two cars, an impressive parade. It frightened him. And it felt good.

The chair legs stumbled across the knotty wood floor of the kitchen as he pulled out a chair and sat back down at the table.

Brenda was already snoring again, the sound like a wind through the cavern of the living room.

The knock came just after he took his seat, and he pressed his face into his palms, inhaled deeply, felt the ache of a held-back smile in his jaws. They were polite enough to knock. He considered pulling the door open for them, reaching out his hand in greeting, but it was just a consideration. His heart jackhammered in his chest, alive and slamming through the years of cement and pavement time had packed around it.

From there on out, the cops did what he knew they'd do. They called his full name. Zebulon Pike Robbins. They threatened him. They announced their warrant for his arrest. Brenda slept. Then the toughest among them jiggled the door handle, hoping the door was locked so he could bust it down—Zeb knew this, knew too much about them and how their thoughts twisted around in their brains. He knew the constant anger inside that gave the cops a reason for living, knew it like it was his own blood, but darker.

The toughest cop opened the door first. It pushed open easily, and then the rest of the blue uniforms spilled in. But by that time, Zeb had already slipped through the floor-door in the work shed and made his way through the narrow cave of the bomb shelter that had been built by Clean Dan, the crazy recluse who had lived in the cabin before Zeb. As Zeb made his way up the hillside, he imagined Brenda fully awake now, standing in the kitchen half drunk and trying to make sense of it all. That swell of emotion came to his chest again, and it puzzled him and he quelled it, and he kept on walking up the mountainside.

·　·　·

HE KNEW WHAT WOULD happen next. He knew they'd call in other forces, bring the dogs out. With the powerful scent glands they had balled up inside their noses, dogs could see without laying eyes on things. A canine sniffs the air and has all the information anyone needs about a place: the mood, the danger, the food sources. Zeb understood the cops and the dogs, the ferocity and drive both shared.

He also knew this: The most dangerous part of any weapon is the end of it. The blade of a knife is half as damaging as the point. The middle of a chain is soft when it wraps around you, though the end of it can shred the skin. It was against all instinct and human intuition, but Zeb had learned over the years that when someone attacked you, moving *in*, not backing away, was always the best defense.

So as the men hunting him dispersed into the field, he methodically circled back to the center. It wasn't haphazard or even overconfident. It was analytical. He watched their steps and made his decisions. He needed them to want him, and he needed them not to find him. He was driven by this crazy hope he had about maybe seeing his sister one more time. She was a tracker, after all. She knew him, and she knew these woods.

He knew he had advantages over the cops. He understood this land better than anyone, the crevices and open spaces, the places any well-trained hunting party would look, and the ones they would likely overlook. For every step they took into the woods, Zeb took two back toward home. He watched them expand around him. He stayed at the center. By the time the back-up police wagon came with the canines, he'd already circled back onto his own property, the starting point. On the way, he'd picked up the handgun and ammo he'd tossed, just in case, and he tucked them into his pockets. A few cops guarded the periphery of the home, but none were near good old Clean Dan's shelter, an easy way in and out.

Now, he sat in the workroom of his cabin wrapped in a deer-skin clothing he'd tanned and sewn recently. Its musky scent might confound the dogs, at least momentarily. He looked out the narrow window, saw the cops walking back and forth to their cars, doors hanging open like heavy wings, cherry tops circling like Christmas lights among evergreens, radios squawking in almost-victory. In the midst of it all, his eyes rested on Rosalita. Even in death, that beautiful horse comforted him. He'd seen her born on this land and had stayed with her till she died, and in all that time, nothing had restrained her or made her anything other than *horse*. Even her death was a part of this landscape, violence being a part of how everything lived out here.

Keeping one eye on the window, he sat down, pulled a bag of Drum tobacco from a leather pouch. When he opened it, the smell of fresh tobacco mingled with the scent of the leather. The dogs were off leash now. It thrilled him and humbled him to be hunted by dogs. He took a pinch from the tobacco pouch, placed it in the white paper, then rolled the smoke tightly, licked its seam, and smoothed it over. He heard voices in the kitchen, and the sound startled him. One officer had stayed back, with Brenda. It was something he hadn't planned on, and it made his neck throb and his throat tighten. He'd wanted to talk to Brenda before he left. He'd wanted to tell her what was on his mind. He listened hard, trying to drown out the pounding of his own heart in his ears.

Brenda was sober, even lucid now. He heard her ask the man if he cared for coffee, and Zeb's heart thrummed.

"No, Ma'am," came the voice.

"You saying what you got on him?" Brenda asked.

"What we got on him's a confession. Written and detailed down to the last iota."

"What's he confessing to that's causing this kind of hullabaloo?"

"He your husband, Ma'am?"

"We never had a ceremony. But we're pretty damn sick of each other by now and here we are living in this damn house together anyway, so I think that qualifies."

This was the part of Brenda Zeb had grown to love. She was raw, open, even beautiful in her thick strength and abiding anger.

"No ceremony, no information," the man said.

"Sonsabitches," Brenda said.

"He got any real family you know of?" the man asked.

Brenda laughed. "Yeah. He's got a father. Good luck talking to him because he hasn't talked to anyone in over ten years. And he's got a sister who's a damn good friend of mine who I haven't seen since the Dead Sea was just sick. She tracks wolves in some remote corner of the planet that even Zeb can't find, so good luck there, too."

Zeb half smiled. He could hear Brenda cleaning up the kitchen, something she did on the rare occasions when she could not find words to express the intensity of her emotions. She banged pots and pans loudly, made the silverware sing like out of tune wind chimes. "He means something to me, you know," she said after a while. Said it calmly and with measure.

"Yes, Ma'am." There was a silence. No cleaning. No one walking on the creaky wood floor. Then the sudden sound of a chair scraping the wood and the man's hard-soled heels walking out the door.

Zeb's breathing slowed now. He knew why he and Brenda had stayed together all these years, in spite of everything. They could read each other like rivers, the fluidity, the steadiness, the soft rage of water shaping something as solid as rock, softening its ragged edges. He didn't light the smoke he'd rolled. Instead, he tucked it into his front pocket. When the voices in the kitchen went silent and the men in the field were no longer visible, he knew his chance for talking to Brenda had passed. He knew he would put her at risk if he told her anything. He slept that night in his home for the last time, listening to Brenda's footsteps on the wood floor, her occasional swearing at nothing. In the middle of the night, he heard her slamming doors and swearing louder. Then she left the house, got into her truck, and took off. He knew she would be okay then. He knew she understood his position.

In the morning, he made his way down the mountain, away from the commotion, into town.

Willa, 1980

WE HAVE TO DRAW blood. A finger prick won't do. We've gone more than half the summer and have not renewed our blood-sister

pact. Brenda says it's because she's too grown up for it now. She
has moved on to other things, boys and makeup and stuff like that.

"Besides that, your brother's bad news," she says, to me.

"You want to do this or not?"

"He had that gun yesterday, Willa. Not his regular bird gun.
He had that little gun, too."

"You were out there with him before I got there, Brenda. You
oughta know."

"I wasn't *with* him."

"We saw you from the window. Me and Mom watched you
and Zeb."

"Yeah, so."

"Yeah, so you're lying and you'd rather be with Zeb than me
these days."

She laughs. "Where'd he get a gun like that anyway?" she
says. "That little job is not a hunting gun, you know."

"A gun's a gun. You ready to do this or not, Brenda?"

"I'm just saying, he's bad news."

"You like him."

"He scares me."

"Your dad scares me."

She laughs. "He's not such an ass when he's not drunk."

"Well, he's never not drunk. And you think Zeb's cute, you
say it all the time. Can't say that much for your dad." I point
toward Chet and Dolly Thatcher's front yard. It's the only
house with a green lawn and a paved sidewalk like the houses
across the field. It looks out of place side-by-side with all the
other identical houses sitting like Monopoly pieces on our side
of the field. I tell Brenda that too. "That damn green lawn
makes the Thatchers think they're better than everyone else in
the neighborhood."

She shrugs. "Least our houses are better than that damned
condemned shack like the one in the field," Brenda tells me.

"It wasn't condemned. It was eminent domained."

"Same thing. That's what my dad says."

"Screw your dad. You doing this thing with me or not?"

She hems and haws. "That's *the Thatchers'* sidewalk, Willa."

"I know it's the Thatchers'. Only sidewalk in our neighborhood, far as I can see."

"Yeah, and if we get caught—"

"We won't get caught."

Brenda studies the white pavement.

I point to the sidewalk.

Brenda flips her long black hair over one shoulder, a habit she has when she's nervous. "All right. The concrete's better than gravel, like you said."

The sidewalk is just on the other side of Chet and Dolly's cherished rose bushes. Other yards have bicycles, trikes, kites, stacks of tires, sometimes an old stove or fridge in them. We use all those things for hide-and-seek, or for bases in softball. But no one uses the Thatchers' yard for anything. If you cross it, I mean if your toe touches it when you're running from third base to home, or weaving your way out of a tackle in football, Chet'll come outside, shaking his fists, yelling *goddamn, shit, fuck*—words that would make us laugh if it wasn't Chet Thatcher saying them at us.

Every evening Chet waters his precious lawn and Dolly prunes her rose bushes, and the kids in the neighborhood all stare because we know too much about them. What we hear going on sometimes behind their closed blinds is a story no one will ever tell. We talk about other things that go on, like when Billy's mom paddles him right out on the front lawn, or when Brenda's daddy sits in his lawn chair, asleep, liquored-up and drooling. We laugh at shit like that. But when we hear Dolly's voice crying out, when we hear Chet yelling at her, all of us—Brenda, me, all the kids, even Zeb—we stop playing whatever game we're playing. "Gotta go now," we say. "Gotta go home." In ten minutes, our neighborhood turns completely quiet. No one laughing. No one calling out new rules to a game, no one crying because they didn't win the last game. There's probably the sound of Dolly's voice still, but there's no one left to hear it. Everyone is home, safe.

Me and Brenda stare at the Thatcher yard. We know what Chet is capable of. All the same, I take a deep breath and call out, "Let's do it!" and we grip each other's hands, and Brenda hollers, "Go!"

We run a streak across my yard and enter Thatcher territory, and then things slow down. I see my white tennies churning, see Chet's green lawn beneath them, see my own legs sprinting right next to Brenda's, and when we get to the edge of Chet's concrete strip, I call out, "Now!" We flatten out our bodies in midair and land with our knee bones hard on the pavement. After that, things speed up again. We stand up fast and sprint to get to the other side of the street, knees throbbing, a held-back laugh pinching our throats.

Bright red blood streams from bright red circles on our knees, flesh torn open good. We run to the field, find a quiet place with no one else around. Already I can feel the blood tightening on my skinned knee. Brenda sits on the ground, her knees pulled into her chest. I sit across from her and we both suck in wind from the corners of our mouths, hissing against the sting. The patches on our knees are a bloody red sheen, and we press the dark circles of our wounds together, my skin so white next to Brenda's, white as her sisters' and her father's skin. We lean in closer, and I feel our blood crossing over.

"Your mama doing all right?" Brenda says.

"Yeah, she's all right."

The summer breeze touches our split-open skin, makes the wound feel like a thousand tiny needles.

"She ever go to a doctor about her condition?"

"Can't afford it much, Brenda."

"Yeah. It'd be good if you could, though."

"It'd be real good, yeah. Hey, I saw your daddy sitting outside in his lawn chair the other day."

"He wave to you?"

"He stood up and hugged me and we had a nice walk around the block."

"Really?"

"Shit no, Brenda. What do you think?" I press my knee tighter into hers. "Ever wonder what your real daddy's like, Bren? Your Indian father?"

She shakes her head no.

"If he looks like you, or anything?"

She snorts a little. "My real daddy? I'll tell you what my real daddy's doing. He's drunk and useless and living on the poorest land in the union, Willa. He's out there on that Indian reservation, and he can't even buy dinner for his own damn self, let alone for a kid like me."

"Think so?"

"Yeah."

"That what your dad tells you?"

She shrugs. "He's the only one who would know, right?"

I think about it. "I guess so, yeah."

We sit quiet, pressing our knees together a little longer, till the sting finally fades. "Our blood's crossed over by now. I can feel it," I tell her.

Brenda nods. "It's crossed."

We separate our knees and strings of blood stretch like sticky red strands of a spider web between us. The pulling apart makes us bleed fresh again.

"Can't clean it," I remind her.

"I know. I won't."

* * *

SOME GIRLS HAVE A kind of chant or contract to seal their pact. Me and Brenda seal it with one pure red rose petal. This means going to Chet and Dolly Thatcher's yard again. They're the only ones with flowers, and right close to the flowers is their dog, sitting sad and sorry in a little chain-link pen.

"Don't get that dog barking," Brenda says.

"We won't."

We walk along the rose hedge with our hands in our pockets, bring them out only to snatch a rose. The dog sits with one shoulder pressed up against the fence, looking at us, wagging its tail in the dirt. Its mouth hangs open, smiling that dog smile.

I cup my hand around a rose bud. It pops like a knuckle when I pluck it from the stem. The dog stands up. "Good pup. Yeah." I hold the flower in the flat of my palm, sort through petal after petal, looking for one that is solid red.

We go through several rose bushes, thorns shaped like little peaks of stiffened egg whites in the meringue pies Mom makes. If the petals have white on their tips, we let the whole rose drop to the ground. The blooms burst like silent fireworks when they hit.

"Think they're home?"

I look at Chet and Dolly's grey-in-summer windows. "Looks to me like they're never home." Zeb has a sense about these things, but I don't. He can tell at a glance when someone is home, sizes any situation up fast. I don't have those kind of smarts.

Brenda tiptoes alongside the hedge. The dog paws under the chain link fence at our discarded petals. Brenda pulls another flower from the stem, drops it, and the dog noses for it, then starts in barking, butt in the air, wagging his tail like he wants to play.

"Good boy, hush, boy, hush." Me and Brenda talk to the dog at the same time, but he just keeps barking, and then I hear the Thatchers' door pull open.

"Holy shit," I whisper, and together me and Brenda take off running. We huddle behind a corner of my house. I can hear Chet's hard-soled shoes clicking on the concrete. "Don't look," I tell Brenda, "Don't look!"

Doesn't matter if we look or not. We can hear the beating going on. The dog yelps and cries, and I hear the sound of Chet's strap coming down on it, over and over. We sit and listen, eyes straight ahead, and I see the tears coming to Brenda, and I wish to God I could cry, too. It's something else that starts up in me, though, something sharp and violent, and I can't help it—I turn and look over my shoulder.

Chet's back is to me. His arm pumps up and down, belt catching on the fence sometimes, other times hitting with a solid thump. The dog does everything it can to get away. But it ends up quiet in the corner, laying limp.

Chet goes back into the house, wrapping his belt around his fisted knuckles like a boxer's taped hands, and I'll be damned if that dog doesn't get up on all fours and walk toward Chet. It doesn't growl or bear its teeth like I want it to. It doesn't take a bite out of Chet's fat ass. It wags its tail, its whole butt going back and forth, its head down, looking up all sheepish like it's saying it's sorry. It wants Chet to pet it.

"Fucking Chet," I whisper.

"Come on," Brenda says.

It's so hard to turn away from that pup, the way he keeps believing and hoping. But Brenda tugs my shoulder, and I turn away and we walk down the street. When we reach her doorstep, she opens her fisted hand, a perfect red rose petal there, no white at the tip. "Blood sisters," she says.

"Blood sisters. Yeah." But it's weakened now. My knee hurts, and I can't remember why Brenda and I pretended to be blood sisters anyway. That feeling's gone and I stand there blankly, wondering how someone as worthless as Chet could take something so valuable away.

* * *

BEFORE BEDTIME THAT NIGHT, I scour my hands with Lava, the soap Zeb uses after he works on lawn mower engines, cars, guns. It feels like sandpaper on my skin. Brenda has told me about her aunt who died from not washing her hands before supper. Zeb says it's bullshit, but I scrub my hands till they turn bright pink, anyway.

Mom comes and tucks me in. She used to read to me, but she can't do that anymore, her own will slipping away from her day

by day. "You look all balled up," she says, and I notice her voice is
falling away, too, becoming a soft whisper even when she means
to be strong and gentle. I pull the covers up close around my neck.
"That can't be comfortable," she says, "You're all tight. Don't you
want to stretch out?"

I shake my head no, and she bends over and kisses each eyelid.
"Sleep sweet," she says, and she tells me she loves me and I want
to say the same thing back to her but I feel her fading away. I keep
my hands hidden under the sheets. That day, they made a dog
get a beating; they stole. I dream of them sometimes, my wrists
bloody stumps, my fingers shriveled like burned branches, black
with disease. They have done evil things, I know, but I want to
wake with them in the morning. I do not want my hands taken
from me in the night.

•   •   •

IT'S STILL THE MIDDLE of the night, but before he comes around
the corner, I can feel the door opening. Zeb steps close to me,
kneels down by my bed. "Don't you ever sleep?"

"I *was* sleeping till you opened that door," I tell him.

"You can't hear that door opening."

"Well, I did."

"Okay, c'mon," he says.

"What?"

"Got something I need you for."

"Johnny's pharmacy?"

"I told you a million times I'm not good enough for that job
yet, Willa."

I cross my arms and turn over, facing the wall. "Then I'm not
going with you, Zeb. I am *not* stealing anything."

"Yeah, you are."

"No I'm not."

"Willa. You are. Just quit."

I keep facing the wall. I tuck my hands into my armpits.

He sighs. "Look, you know the Thatcher dog?"

My stomach tightens soon as he says it. "I know the Thatcher dog, yeah."

"Gonna save it."

I turn and look at him.

"You *in* or *out?*"

"What're you going do?"

"Save the dog."

"How?"

"You in or out?"

Even in the dusky light I can see his smile. He looks like a scruffy young Elvis, kind of pretty, a little bit tough. I search his pockets with my eyes to see if he's still carrying that gun. There's nothing. So I release my hands from under the sheets, swing my legs over the side of the bed.

"I'm not swiping anything with you, Zeb."

"Get your shoes on."

I grab a jacket and zip it up over my pajamas. Me and Zeb walk out of my room and down the hallway. Half of me wants Mom to wake up and find us and tell us both we're in big trouble and send us straight back to bed. But I know she can't hear us, and even if she could, there's nothing she could do, not in her condition. So we tiptoe through the living room and step out.

There's a different color to things in the night. Night-green lawns, night-silver cottonwoods by the pond in the field. The dog is almost complete shadow now, shrunk away in his night-sleeping corner.

"That poor pup's canine teeth haunt him," Zeb says. "He was meant to be wild, like a wolf." When we come up on the dog, he flips to all fours. "Look at that: *Instinct*," Zeb says. "Beautiful."

"Don't get that dog barking, Zeb."

"The Thatchers are gone up to their cabin. Chet's got two homes, you know, says he's fixing this one up to sell it so he can 'get the hell outa dodge.' That's what the fucker actually said to Dad one day when he was out there watering his lawn every night like he does. Anyway, this old dog can howl at the moon if he wants, can't you boy, yeah. No one's coming for him."

The dog stretches his whole body into an arc, butt in the air, muzzle pointed toward the sky. He makes a moaning sound. "Hey boy," says Zeb, and the dog comes wagging over, jowls loose, slobbering. I squeeze my whole hand through the diamond shaped wire of the chain-link fence. Zeb can only fit a few fingers through. But the pup leans in, and we both scrub him good behind the ears, the way he likes.

"I've never heard jackass Thatcher call him by a name," Zeb says. "Hey boy, good pup." The dog pushes his nose through the fence, tongue working me and Zeb, chin to forehead. "Good dog, yeah, good boy."

The dog starts off running, runs to the other end of the short pen then back to where we're standing, then back again to the other end, all of five strides, over and over, the pen too tight around him.

"He's running crazy like that damn fox. Remember that fox I told you about?"

"Yeah, Zeb, about a million times I remember your damn fox story. You were camping in the San Juans with your Boy Scout troop when you saw him."

"Yeah, I was. Wish I could set this dog loose in the wild, like I should have done with that fox. I could go with him," Zeb whispers. "He'd be better off fending for his own instead of being fed by Chet and beaten by Chet with the same regularity. They fucking beat you down, don't they? Yeah boy, yeah."

Zeb looks up. "All right, we've got to hurry, Willa."

"Thought you said they were out of town?"

"Yeah. But I made a deal with myself that if I go a week without stealing, Mom'll get healed. Starting midnight tonight, no more stealing. It'll all go away if I can just do that one thing."

"Well, I made a deal with myself that I'm not stealing anything with you, Zeb. Like I said."

"We're not stealing. We're saving the dog."

"Dog's right here."

The dog wags his tail, stands on his hind legs, and rests his feet on the chain-link. He starts licking toward me, his tongue lapping up nothing but air. Zeb points to the Thatcher's open window, exactly the same slim crack people always leave in their windows and I can never figure out why. It's just a matter of closing the window an inch to keep their houses safe and tight.

Zeb slathers the Vaseline on his hands, and I feel my body start to shake. "I told you I wasn't swiping anything."

"My hands won't fit through that opening," he says. He jabs the Vaseline my direction. "I just need you to push it open a little bit for me. That's all. Then you can go."

He's talking all matter-of-fact, like he can't hear a single word I say about not stealing, and then a light comes on in the Thatcher bathroom and I hit the green lawn and lay flat on my stomach, my heart beating hard enough to make my whole body throb. Zeb leans back against the windowsill, looks down at me. "What the hell, Willa?" He laughs.

I grab his ankle and try to pull him down with me. "Light!" I whisper and point, "Light!"

"I see the light."

"I'm not getting caught, Zeb. I am *not* getting caught and you're a liar, you told me we weren't stealing anything, damn it, Zeb."

He cranes his neck backward, eyes to the stars, shaking his head. Then he looks down at me. "You think I'd do anything to get you in trouble? I wouldn't get you caught, no way." He offers me a hand up. "I'd take the blame completely, Willa, you know I would. I would never do anything to hurt you." I offer him my hand. He pulls me up. "I told you I was saving the dog, and I keep my word, don't I? I keep my word to you." He brushes off the front of my clothes, combs the hair back from my face with his fingertips. "I wouldn't hurt you."

I stand there, shaking, confused.

"Okay," he says after a while. "All right." He pats my bottom, something he knows I hate, and he points me toward home. "Go. I'll figure a way on my own."

I walk a few steps away from him, then stop and look over my shoulder. He takes out some kind of tool from his pocket, walks toward the back door, bends down to the doorknob, begins working on it.

"Zeb," I whisper, just loud enough so he can hear. "How do you know they're not home?"

He's absorbed, doesn't answer, and then there's a *click*, and the back door swings open. The light turns off in the bathroom, and I watch the shadow of a man pass by.

"Shit, Zeb, no!" I run to him and grab his hand, pulling him my direction. "I saw someone Zeb! I saw someone in the bathroom!"

"You didn't see anyone."

"I was standing right there and *I saw someone*. Come on."

He yanks his hand from my grip, tells me to go home. He takes a step into the house, and I tug with all my weight against him.

"Damnit, Willa, let go. There's no one here."

I hear a creaking sound like wood underfoot. My eyes go wide.

"That was me." He points down to his feet, makes the creaking sound again.

"But I saw someone."

Zeb walks into the house with me hanging from his arm, backpedaling against him. Inside, we both stop. The place is quiet No lights anywhere.

"What if Chet has a gun?" I ask.

"He can't have a gun because *he* is not *here*." Zeb shakes his head. "Jesus, Willa, you're acting like a regular kid. Just— *git*."

A regular kid is about the worst thing Zeb could ever call me. So I take a deep breath and steel myself against my own will. "Okay. I'm *in*," I tell him.

He looks at me for too long a time, then smiles. "What if someone's home?"

"There's no one home here, Zeb. You can see, there's no one home." I let go of his hand and lead the way into the house, still shaking inside.

We stand in the middle of Chet and Dolly's living room now, *inside* the forbidden house with its forbidden yard. There's something smothering here, like the air in the place is yellow and damp. The wood paneling turns the living room dark as a cave, but there's a little scalloped wooden shelf above their curtains. It's just a foot or so below the ceiling, and it's jammed with stuffed animals and elves and ceramic figurines, a circus of sad, big-eyed animals glaring down from Thatcher heaven. I think they're supposed to look playful or cute. But they look like little monsters, evil things.

"Freaky, huh? Like little goblins," Zeb says. He never says anything like that, and it sends a goose bump chill tickling my neck. He laughs. Just then, the automatic light timer clicks loudly, and a light comes on in the bedroom. "Oh, look, someone's home," he says.

I jerk my head that direction, and he laughs again. "Come on, Zeb, cut it out!"

He leads me down the hallway. The light is still on in the bedroom, and Zeb waits at the door. The light in the living room dims and Zeb jolts with fear, which sends my heart like a fist into my throat. He laughs so loud the dog starts barking again.

"Shit, Zeb, I said I'm in. Quit teasing me."

He puts his hand on the doorknob of the bedroom, turns it slowly so it clicks real soft. He looks at me, raises his eyebrows. He still believes I think Chet and Dolly are in that room. He's halfway right. He slaps the door open. It bangs against the wall, swings back toward us, and I gasp. He stops the door with his palm. The bed is empty, all made up and tucked in tight at the corners.

"Like I said. They're at the cabin."

It feels like cold water splashing my face on a hot day, that feeling of fear turned to relief, the exhilarating part of stealing. I can't help laughing with Zeb now. I trust him. I should've trusted him all along.

There's a smell in the Thatcher's bedroom, something mustier than in most places we've been, even though the place looks clean. I breathe in quick little sniffs, trying to keep the stink out of my nostrils. The room is cramped but orderly, no clothes on the floor, no laundry. But the furniture is crammed into the place, making it harder for Zeb to move around. He squeezes through the tight space between the bed and chest of drawers and heads straight for the clothes closet. I stand there, still basking in that sweet exhilaration. In a minute, Zeb comes out of the closet with a hanger that holds nothing but belts. The bent part of the hanger twists through the opening in the buckles, and they're stacked buckle-on-buckle, about half a dozen of them. One by one, he takes the belts from the hook, shoves them in his knapsack. Then he heads back into the closet, finds another hanger with two more belts on it, takes them, too.

"Fucker," he says. "Let his pants fall down off his fat ass. Moon the neighborhood with his fat white butt."

I smile, proud to be Zeb's sister.

He looks through the closet one more time, carefully. "Looks like I got them all." He taps my shoulder. "We're done," he says. He points with his head toward the door, and I lead the way out, my whole body feeling light and good.

While I walk out to pet the dog, Zeb takes care to lock up the Thatcher's house, just as it had been before we came. He wipes the door handle with his T-shirt, even though we know the Vaseline keeps the prints from taking hold. He doesn't like leaving even a thin sheen of Vaseline behind, so he wipes things clean. When he's done, he joins me by the fence, reaches through the gate as best he can, and pats the dog. "Yeah, good boy, good boy." He points to a pile of dry food in the corner and a basin of water big enough for a horse. "They leave him that way for a week. Like food and water's all he needs. You'd like to be up there in that cabin with them, wouldn't you. Yeah boy, I know."

Zeb

LATE MORNING, AFTER THE men had been searching the back-woods for a day and a half, Zeb made his way down the side of the mountain. He passed a few neighbors' cabins nestled into the thick evergreen woods, saw the windows glowing, and felt some-thing like a connection to the folks living there, a bond that had happened without him noticing over time. It wasn't deep or even intimate, but it was a bond all the same, something he felt tied to.

He crossed the open field where he'd spent long summer days riding Rosalita. As connected as he felt with the families living in those cabins, it was nothing compared to what he felt with Rosalita. The joy he'd shared with that animal was something he'd never been able to achieve with humans, what with all the talk and double talk humans did. Rosalita was languageless, and his bond with her was all the stronger because of it. He didn't so much *remember* riding her across this field as he *felt* it still happen-ing, as if the land had absorbed and retained every memory he had of the place. Just walking across the meadow brought those days back to life again. Some things can't be taken away.

It was late afternoon by the time he made his way to Gnarly's. When he arrived, the doors were unlocked, but the place was not officially open. Inside, helping himself to an early shot or two of whiskey, sat Ody, the town blacksmith and farrier, the one who had fashioned Chey and Rosalita's shoes over the years. When Zeb entered, Ody stood up and slapped him on the back. "Impressive show yesterday, my friend." He laughed. "It was a goddamn parade of lights winding up to your place, right." He walked to the top-shelf whiskey, selected the Buffalo Trace, and poured two shots. "On me," he said. Zeb took a seat at the bar and Ody joined him. "Zeb Robbins. Always good for a little home entertainment."

"Those guys had a right yesterday," Zeb said. Ody shook his head and laughed.

There was a red and white target hand-painted on a thick piece of plywood that made up the side of one wall of the bar. Without words, with just a glance of friendly competi-tion, the two men stood up. Hanging from Ody's belt was his weapon of choice, a hatchet, the one he used for hunting rabbits and other small game. He took it from his sheath, and Zeb walked to the target and unwedged one of four hatchets already lodged in the wood of the target. "You couldn't hit the side of a barn," Ody laughed.

"Yeah. Luckily, we're not aiming for the side of a barn." Zeb laughed too. For the next half hour or so, the two men stood at an imaginary line and tossed the hatchets into the bull's-eye, shredding the wood there. It surprised Ody, who thought he had the corner on hatchet hunting, was known for being able to make a clean hit on something as small and quick as a rabbit running through heavy brush. "Shit, Zeb, you gotta come into town more often," Ody said, after a while.

"Yeah, it's crossed my mind," said Zeb.

Out of breath, Ody sat down at the bar again. "So what's the deal this time around? Did you break into that new health food store and reprice everything on the shelves?"

Zeb shook his head. "I never reprice everything. Just, you know, the cheese for twenty-two dollars a pound. Shit like that." Ody laughed and Zeb smiled along with him.

Closer to opening time, Frank, the owner and bar tender, came in, saw Zeb sitting there, and smiled wide. He slapped Zeb on the back with pride. "Fuckin Zeb Robbins," Frank said. "On the run again, my friend?"

"Something like that, yeah," Zeb said.

"Well, we gotchya covered," Frank said. "Everyone around here, we look after our own. Couldn't pry a speck of information out of anyone I'd allow in Gnarly's. You know that."

"I know," Zeb said.

Ody handed Frank some cash for the whiskey they'd drunk, and Frank walked behind the bar and started getting ready for the evening. Ginger, Nick, Thad, and Bobby came in carrying their guitars and fiddles, and Zeb and Ody helped them set up on the small stage.

"Special requests tonight?" Bobby asked.

"Something good," Zeb said.

"Like Gram Parsons," Ody said, and the lead singer, Ginger, barely in her twenties, shook her head at the two old men and their weary tastes. It wasn't long after that when Gnarly's started filling up with locals, most gathering earlier than usual tonight to hear the news about what was happening up at Zeb's place. They wanted to get the true story straight from the man himself.

But Zeb had nothing to say about it. As far as he was concerned, there was no news he could tell any of the folks at Gnarly's. They'd seen the red lights streaming up the mountainside and had been telling their own stories about it all day long, none of which were true in the beginning. But they'd become true now as far as the people telling them were concerned, and there was nothing Zeb could have said that would have made their stories wrong and the story he knew right. "He was running three hundred kilos of pot in his truck," Cullum said, and his wife, Sonya, tapped him on the arm and corrected it to two hundred fifty pounds, not kilos," and Zeb listened and laughed.

"Your boss, Mike, tell you to run it?" someone else asked, and Zeb didn't shake his head yes and he didn't say no, but the story kept on without him. Some said the pot was stuffed inside Mexican mangoes that had come all the way from Oaxaca, and Zeb had somehow gotten past the border patrol going south and coming back into the States, who knows how. When they looked to Zeb, he just shrugged and said, "Yeah, mangoes," and everyone laughed and said it was just like Zeb to do something like that. Whatever stories they were telling didn't matter to Zeb because all their words added up to understanding one thing: Zeb was now officially on the run, and they were all about protecting him. That was all that mattered. It was something Zeb appreciated, but did not fully understand: the way his mountain friends loved a fugitive, as if running away and not fitting in was the only way to fit in in these hills—or anywhere else for that matter, and they all played that same role together.

As the night unfolded, he listened to the music and the gossip and watched the lie that would follow him unfold into a story more appealing than the truth, woven, as it was, with the threads of people who had known him and grown to love him over the years. The delicate weight of seeing things for the last time came to him as he studied the knotty wood paneling, the names of people he knew carved into it like some lovers carved their names into living trees, and the smell of old beer and cigarettes saturating his nostrils in the best way. He knew it would be the last time he saw this place, and he knew now that the last time he'd seen Brenda would be the last time he saw her, too, and he tried to etch her face into his memory, the turn of her head when they had met the second time, as strangers, long after their childhood days were gone, the touch of her hand when he came home before dawn and slept next to her till morning broke. He tried to remember the last time he'd seen his mother and father and sister, too, but their faces had vanished. Whoever had said "Time heals" must have been stoned out bad, he thought. Time heals nothing, except maybe a goddamn sore throat, and sometimes not even that.

If anything was going to hook him and make him turn back on the decision he'd made, remembering Brenda and hanging out here with his friends at Gnarly's should have done it. But though they hovered near him, it always felt like people were at an unreachable distance. He ached to close that gap—an ache that had been with him since he could recall, since childhood— but the anvil wedged between him and his own life sunk deeper into his gut with every sunrise and sunset.

This decision was a liberation. Frank, the quiet man who turned into a chatty bartender as the night went on, kept Zeb's beer glass filled with the best on tap and dropped shots of whiskey his way when needed. The stories of what had made the police cars wind up to Zeb's house that morning blossomed and grew more fantastic with every shot or brew ordered. "You crazy fuck!" Frank hollered out, eventually. "Hey everyone, we got crazy Zeb Robbins sitting right here in our bar!" He slapped Zeb on the back, and a few of the people cheered, and most drank up in honor of Zeb. "How'd you do it?" Frank asked. "How'd you get your crazy ass down the mountain when they were trailing you. *With dogs?*"

Zeb shrugged. "I just walked away."

"Crazy ass, Zeb man. You're a fuckin ninja, dude."

Zeb smiled. *Crazy ass Frank*, he thought to himself.

Frank went about his business, serving others their whiskey
and beer.

Frank's wife, Shawna, sat across the bar from Zeb, wearing
her tight white jeans and her bright blue ruffly cowboy shirt. Her
blonde hair fell around her fragile shoulders, and she was so different from Brenda that for years everything about her had repulsed
him. Her son, Tommy, was a friend to Zeb, and so was Frank, but
whenever Zeb had to talk to Shawna, it was like he was talking to
someone who didn't speak his own language. But tonight, something about her fascinated him. What made her dress up every
damn day, what made her curl her hair just so and spray it till it
shone like hard candy? What made that woman care?

A little drunker than he'd intended to be, he stood up and
walked to the other side of the bar, and he took Shawna's hand. Her
eyes went wide when he approached, and she made that coy little
whimper that had always annoyed Zeb, but which tonight made
him smile, even laugh with affection. She would never have considered touching Zeb's weathered and scraped hands in the past,
but now they danced together on the well-worn wooden floor,
two-stepping and line dancing. When a slow song started up, Zeb
hesitated, and she ignored his awkwardness and pulled him close
to her. He felt her slender body close to his as the band slipped from
some new fangled tune into a soulful, gut-shredding Gram and
Emmylou song. Zeb knew he had to let Shawna go after that, and
he did, and he walked back to the bar where Frank had another
shot waiting for him, and Ginger kept on singing another tune.

Zeb drank his beer, his back hunched low over the bar and
friends from town lining up to congratulate him on his getaway
that, right about then, felt nothing like a getaway at all, but a trap. He
realized that he was hooked in strong to this place and these people,
and even so, he could not bridge the distance he felt, the distance and
the love constantly working against each other inside him. Someone
called out a request for the band to play another Gram Parsons tune,
and Zeb seconded that with a simple nod and a raise of his glass.
"That guy got himself burned," Zeb said to whoever was listening.

"What're you talking about?" Frank said.

"Gram Parsons. Had his roadie take his body out to Joshua Tree and burn it after he died."

Someone in the crowd said that sort of thing was illegal, and someone else laughed because who among them had ever been stopped by something illegal when a friend was in need? Zeb continued on with the story, telling how Gram Parsons had asked his roadie to steal his body when he died and to make a huge conflagration of his flesh out in the California desert. "Not long after that, Parsons died and his roadie did exactly that," Zeb said.

"No shit," someone said, and the crowd kept on talking about it.

By that time, the night had worked itself around to early morning again, two o'clock, and the place was still hopping. But Zeb felt done. He asked Frank if he had a place for him to sleep. It had been a long day, and he needed someplace safe where he could hide out just for a day or two. "I'll leave without telling you when or where I'm going. You won't have any information about me that might get you involved."

Frank turned quiet now and quit bragging about Zeb being in their presence. He said nothing, just opened a back door to a small bedroom where he let people sleep off their drink. In the small room, Zeb lay on the cot-like bed listening to the sounds of the people he'd known and loved and had shot the shit with and danced with and often avoided, even though he loved them. As the crowd thinned out and the music stopped, he finally slept. With the drink and the week's events heavy on him, he slept through most of the next day, too. He knew his mind was too muddled to make any move now, so he waited another day in Frank's small room.

But the next morning, Frank knocked on the door.

"They come asking you questions?" Zeb asked.

Frank waved him away. "Like talking to a steel trap," Frank said. "I got nothing for them." Zeb sat on the bed, and Frank leaned against the wall and spoke not with excitement, but with an odd sense of wonder, even confusion. "Lot of people in town following this thing," Frank said. "You know how they are. They got their radio scanners, that sort of thing."

Zeb nodded. Frank shifted his weight, nervous about what he was saying. "I don't know what you did. I don't know what they think they got you on this time, Zeb. But they're pretty serious about it, and—" Frank almost smiled. "And the thing is, they're bringing in a girl."

Zeb looked up.

"To track you down. Some girl from New Mexico. That's what the scanners are picking up."

Zeb listened to Frank talk, and his heart sunk deeper into his chest, a good sinking, something that made him feel more like himself than he could remember, more peaceful than he had felt in years, maybe ever. *Goddamn*, he thought. They had done it. They had brought Willa to him. He listened intently now. Frank shrugged, but grew more serious again. "I don't know what bringing in a girl will do, but they're not letting up this time, Zeb. They're keeping at it."

Zeb nodded again. "Good to know," he said. He could see Frank looking around at the walls, getting more and more nervous about Zeb taking refuge in his place of business, but not wanting to say anything. "Don't worry," Zeb said. "I'll be on my way."

"I'm not saying you have to leave," Frank said.

"No. I am," Zeb said. "It's time."

Frank looked at him to make certain. Zeb didn't look back at Frank. He new that even a glance could implicate him and make him think he knew more than he did about Zeb's plans. "Thanks, Frank." Zeb said. He could smell the smoky walls of the bar in the next room, could remember vividly the nights he'd spent drinking and dancing with Brenda in Gnarly's. "Next time you come here, I'll be gone."

It took Frank a few awkward seconds to turn and leave.

·   ·   ·

THE FIRST SNOWFALL OF the season came on the night Zeb set out from Gnarly's. Not the spitting kind of snow that usually comes between fall and winter, but the kind when huge, wet flakes looked like stars taking their last breath before hissing and dissolving into the earth. Already it was blanketing the land, making it impossible for him to walk without leaving imprints significant enough to be tracked even by the least skilled of his trackers. And so he walked in a large irregular circle that cut through the meadow, over the rockier part of the land, through a dense copse, traveling a mile or more before he began circling inward, methodically, making erratic offshoots that eventually led back to the same chaotic trail. He walked fast and warily. The new team, including Willa, would pick up his trail soon enough, and, as long as he completed this pattern before they caught their first sign of him, he could buy some time. He didn't worry about Willa's safety or whether she would be the one to find him first. She was the same kid he'd grown up with; she was smarter than the other trackers. He wondered what tricks they had used to get her to agree to turning him in, but he hoped he would have time alone with her to share a word before the others reached him. That's all he wanted: time.

He completed the last circle; then he walked through the trees. From that moment on, he forgot about his trackers. Now it was the end of *them* tracking *him*. It was the beginning of him tracking the lion that had killed Rosalita. If he acted like prey, his followers would treat him like prey. And so he turned himself from the hunted to the hunter, a subtle shift of psychology that could make all the difference. Because it was more than the weight of the footfall that left an imprint to be followed. It was the state of mind too, each thought leaving an afterimage that set the track down and informed whoever was trailing you. It was evident in the space between each imprint (speed), the weight of the imprint (determination), the solidity or shakiness of the impression (confidence in the direction you're traveling).

Bottom line was, his mind was off his trackers and fixed on the cougar now. He remembered that when he'd killed the young male, he'd offered some meat to Brenda, and she had shunned it. "The meat doesn't matter. It's the spirit," she told him. He ignored her American Indian bullshit, except that he kept hearing her words in his head like a chant after that. Any lion meat he didn't eat, he placed in prominent places on rocks around his home, an offering to the ravens, foxes, and rodents. He split the skull and offered the brains to the scavengers, too. He did not want to keep anything that looked like a trophy of this cat.

But as he placed the meat there, he saw the green-lit eyes of the female mountain lion lurking in the trees. By morning, when he rose at dawn to feed the animals before he headed in to work, that lion was still there. She sat in the open, not hidden. She didn't move as he tossed hay to the mules and horses. She watched him.

He thought of speaking to her then. The words came to him, an apology, and then the words felt useless, even silly. Her offspring was sitting inside his gut, the male lion, her son, becoming Zeb's own muscle and bone. It became clear to him that the mountain lion was consciously prowling the edges of his land, not hunting deer, but hunting him.

"So she lives up there in the woods," Brenda said. "Mountain lions live here. Doesn't mean she's got eyes for you."

But not long after that, Zeb found the remains of a stray dog he'd been feeding every evening for the past few weeks. It had been mutilated, its body eaten. After that, his beloved Aussie, Hitch, went missing, too, and his obsession with the cougar took over. When he was on the road, driving for Mike, he would sometimes see the cougar crossing the highway, ghostlike, but vivid. In the aftermath, he would realize it had been a deer, or sometimes nothing. But his mind stayed with her all the same. Zeb and the cat were in constant conversation.

It was the cougar that had tunneled into his brain and led him to the decisions he'd made recently. It was the cougar that made his confession real. It was the cougar that made him long for his blood relations. He felt half cat, half human, and always on the outside of everything. When he found Rosalita that morning, he knew it was time.

＊　＊　＊

HE WALKED BACK FURTHER into the woods now. He built a debris hut, nothing more than a tunnel of branches and leaves to warm him so he could rest until evening fell. He needed to sort through some things in his mind. He needed to unclench some things from his heart. It wasn't lack of love that was driving him. It never had been. If anything, it was too much love and his inability to embrace it. He felt the heaviness of Brenda's body, a solace to him. He remembered the ugliness of his mother's twisted limbs, how they hid the beauty that was the core of her. He longed for the strength of his sister's spirit, her innocence. He needed to take some time to let it all go. With layers of sticks and mulch protecting him like a sleeping bag made of earth, the trackers, if they came this way, would likely walk right past him. The scent of this kind of shelter could even waylay police dogs, his own scent buried beneath the strength of musk and urine that soaked the forest floor. It was a good place once he built it. This was home to him. This rotted forest, decomposing and regrowing, constantly. He would wait.

Willa, 1980

THE DAY CHET COMES back from the cabin starts out like any other Sunday. Before daylight, I turn over in my bed and see Zeb sitting cross-legged on my floor. "C'mon," he says. "The fish are waiting." He stands up, two fishing poles and tackle boxes in his hands, and walks out. I toss off the covers, trade my pajamas for overalls, and I meet him out back. He hands me my pole and tackle box. Together, we peek in on Mom, who is still sleeping, alone, while Dad's already up delivering milk, one of his part-time jobs.

"Think she'll be okay while we're out?" I ask.

Zeb stands at her doorway and pushes the door open a crack. The covers twist around her legs but don't cover her back or arms.

Her skin droops from her skeleton like wet clothes on a hanger. It scares me. I can see Zeb's jaw tightening, too. "Dad'll be home in half an hour," he says. "I think she's okay."

Zeb stands there longer, like he's looking for something.

"Let's go," I tell him. He stands still. I hear Mom breathing, and I'm glad for it, but the heaviness of the sound, like a wheelbarrow running over wet gravel, frightens me. "Zeb!" I whisper. I nudge him.

After a while, he turns and knocks my shoulder, hard. "C'mon, let's go," he says.

We walk out under the half-night, half-dawn sky. I can feel the morning in my nostrils, the smell of wet hay and earth, the air not yet thick with the noise and the dust of the day. We walk through the field, past the house where Zeb was born, our tennies and the legs of our pants soaked with dew. Bullfrogs hum.

Zeb sits beside me on the shore of the pond while I set up my rod and reel, then he walks to his favorite place among the rushes. It feels sometimes like me and Zeb have a fishing line and hook inside us. When he walks away from me, I feel a tug in the center of my chest. I'm still shaken from seeing Mom like that, and that hook between me and Zeb feels like it's deeper because of it, like it's bleeding and sinking into me even more.

I sit quiet for a while, long enough that the sadness about Mom fades and being away from Zeb finally feels good, and the surface of the pond turns from silvery-black to blue with pink edges. The sound of bullfrogs gives way to insects buzzing. Fish jump now and again, but my pole and Zeb's stay as still as the herons we see hunting here. The sun warms my skin through my overalls, and I feel like I never want to move from this quiet place. When my pole bends toward the pond once, I know it's nothing to jump up about. A few seconds later, though, the arc in that pole bends to a half a circle, painting a picture of the size of the fish I'm about to catch.

I jump to my feet, let the fish run the line out a little, then I jerk the pole back to set the hook. My reel goes *tick-tick-tick*, and I drag the fish in, watching it flop out of the water, its silver sides glinting in the sun. I have it almost to shore, and there's no telling if that fish is coming out of the water, or if I'm going in.

Zeb watches from across the pond. When he sees me struggling, he understands the size of my catch. He digs the handle of his pole into the ground, sets it with a rock, and comes running to my side of the pond.

He has his arms around my shoulders in seconds, helping me turn my reel and pull. "Steady, steady," he says, but he's no steadier than I am, and that fish is fighting like a bucking bronco.

"Sonofabitch!"

"He's a beaut, Zeb!"

"He's a sonofabitch!"

We pull. The fish is suspended above the pond now, thrashing on the end of the line, no letting up.

"Jesus, Zeb, he's a monster!"

"Just pull him in, Willa, *pull him in!*"

"I'm trying!" And right about then I give the pole over to Zeb, duck underneath his arms, and wade quickly out into the pond. With the water nearly up to my chest, I reach up and grab the flopping fish with my hands.

"Good job, Willa! Yeah! Steady him. Steady him."

We work together to get this monster to shore. I try my best to tame the thing, and the reel ticks faster, and then *snap*, the line breaks, and my huge fish slithers down the front of my overalls, hits the pond, and slips back under the smooth surface.

Zeb walks toward me, lifting his knees high and splashing into the pond. Then he stops. He shades his brow with one hand, looks out across the bright water. "I'll be damned. That fish is gone." His voice is high and confused.

"We let it get lose, Zeb." The smooth surface of the pond sparkles, no sign that fish ever existed. "I guess it's getting time for church, anyway." But my escaped fish has Zeb's full attention now. "Hey, *I'm going*," I tell him, but he just keeps looking out across the pond. I walk back home alone, thinking about how close I came to that beautiful catch.

*   *   *

WHEN ZEB TURNED SIXTEEN, Mom and Dad gave him a choice
about going to church, and he pretty much chooses *no* all the time.
He says praying is like talking into one of those fake walkie-talkies
made of two tin cans connected by a string, says you just hear
the echo of your own voice coming back at you, magnified by
the Campbell's soup can, and you call it God. Me and Mom
and Dad ignore him, and we drive to the Advent Lutheran together. They used to drop me off at Sunday school and then
go on to the big church themselves. I couldn't stand Sunday
school, though, sitting there and listening to Miss Spraddle and
her spring-tulip voice, telling us all about Jesus and his lambs,
singing, "Jesus loves me, this I know," as if there was nothing
to the guilt of it all. So some time back, I asked Mom and Dad
if I could skip Sunday school and go to the place where I could
get the forgiveness I need. "I'm proud of you being able to listen
and sit still through the whole church service," Mom says while
we're driving.

Dad's still sleepy and cranky from his early morning job and
pissed off about the job at the factory he has to go to later. "Nothing wrong with a kid going to Sunday school, Maggie," he says.
"Church is too adult for Willa."

"I'm not a kid, Dad. I'm twelve."

"Then you're ready for catechism. You can't sit still in church."

Truth is, I sit still more than Dad does, and Mom can't sit
still at all. "We can use your help, too," Mom says, to me, going
against Dad. "It's too hard on your father, getting me in and out
of the car."

Dad looks at her mean when she says it, but there's no argument in him. Mom's body has quit moving as much as it used to,
and it's board-stiff and painful all the time, she says. Dad has to
lift her in and out of the wheel chair because her legs don't move at
all anymore, and her joints are so stiff that Dad has to bend them
into place after he gets her in the chair. But nothing stays in place.

Mom's body has its own mind, and it has nothing to do with sitting in one place. Dad keeps his grumpy, tired face on for a long time, but after a while, he says, "Don't be stupid, Maggie. Willa's not strong enough to help me."

It stings when he says it, and then Mom says, "Well then you don't know Willa," and keeps it simple like that, and her belief in me stings twice as much as Dad's disapproval. I'm proud that Mom thinks I'm strong enough to help her, but I know Dad is right. I sit quiet. Mom notices and reaches her hand to the back seat, rests it on my knee, and when she touches me like that, there's no shaking or stiffness I can see in her. I *know* this disease will not get the better of her.

When we get there, the bells chime and people walk in their Sunday best, the headachy smell of women's perfume everywhere. The church has ceilings as high as the houses on the other side of the field. I take my seat and choose my hymnbook. I sing when Mom and Dad sing, stand when they stand, and sit when they sit. I want to go up to the altar when the pastor says, *take, eat, this is the body of Christ he gave for you*, but I stay in my seat and watch Dad wheel Mom up to the front where everyone kneels, except my mom, and she has a hard time getting the little cup of wine to her lips without spilling it. I have to turn away from watching. So I study the stained glass window that shows Jesus opening his robed arms to the little lambs surrounding Him. The colors look like Lifesaver candies to me, the sun streaming through in rays of cherry, lemon, grape, and lime. I think of it: Jesus the Lifesaver.

When everyone comes back from drinking the wine with the cracker, we all press the palms of our hands together in prayer, and I notice that all these praying hands are shaped just like fish jumping out of a pond. I imagine this is what Jesus sees when he looks down from heaven—the church like a well-stocked pond—and I finally understand what Miss Spraddle meant when she said *Jesus is a fisher of men*. He has his hooks out for us, and He'll snag our hands when we're praying and pull us straight up to heaven. Right then, I look over at Mom and press her

praying hands down into her lap. She gives me the eye, then raises her hands back up into prayer, and I slap them down this time,
wrestling with her to keep her fish-hands in her lap so Jesus will
not snag them. Dad opens his praying eyes now and sees my bad
behavior. He shakes his head and gives me the stern look, but
I keep wrestling with Mom until Dad takes both of my hands
and pins them to my lap. It feels horrible, like my whole body
is trapped, and I want to scream, but I'm helpless, and so I turn
my prayer away from whatever the pastor's saying. I squeeze my
eyes and pray harder than I've ever prayed. I pray when the time
comes for Jesus to reel Mom in, she will be like the fish I hooked
this morning. She'll struggle out of His grip and slip down the
front of Jesus's robe and right back into the pond of the living. I
realize this is why her limbs flop around sometimes, because He
has her suspended on His line above the water, and she is writhing to get free. I pray Mom's line will snap soon.

Dad keeps pressing hard on my hands, and I keep stiffening
against it. I pray right then and there that I'll be like that fish, too.
When my time comes, I hope I'll struggle in the bright sun and
Jesus the Fisherman will be exhausted when I swim away, back to
my life here on earth. I pray this for Zeb and Dad, too.

After the prayer, the pastor takes up the collection. By now
Dad has let go of my hands. He's still cranky, and he whispers to
Mom, "Always a price tag," then takes a one-dollar bill and tucks
it in the collection envelope and signs his name on the back.

This is the part I've been waiting for. I see the collection plate
in the row ahead of me, the velvet-lined bowl passing from one
person to the next, and I can smell the sweaty cash when it's right
next to me. I take the plate in my own hands, place my ten-dollar
bill in there naked, no envelope. "She gave almost a whole year's
allowance," Mom whispers to Dad, trying to get his anger at me
to disappear. He looks at the ten-dollar bill Zeb gave me and raises
his eyebrows in surprise. "She should put that in savings," he
whispers to Mom, even angrier at me now, and the pastor calls
out "Jesus saves," and the collection ends. The organ player is joy-
ous about the whole affair. She hits the keys, and everyone in the

church jumps to their feet and bursts into song. *Holy holy holy, Lord God Almighty. All thy works shall praise thy Name in Earth and Sky and Sea. Holy Holy Holy.*

In the midst of all this joy, Dad forgets about being angry, and I am glad about that. I can feel the forgiveness wrapping around me like water now. *Holy holy holy.*

On the way out of church, Dad holds my hand tighter than usual. He looks hard at Mom. "Ten dollars, up in smoke," he says.

I can't understand what Dad's so mad about. Letting go of that ten felt like heaven, to me.

By the time I get home, I feel light and happy. I change my clothes real fast, and I run to find Zeb out in the field. "Hey Willa," he says. "Done talking in your walkie-talkie?"

I got nothing to say back to him. And somehow that makes him quit acting so tough. He puts his hand on my shoulder. "C'mon. I'll buy you a pop."

We walk together up the hill to Johnny's filling station and pharmacy. "Hey Johnny," Zeb calls out, when we cross his tiny, paved lot.

Johnny's there in his blue and white pinstriped overalls, red oval patch encircling his name in cursive above his left chest pocket. *Johnny.* He pumps gas and talks to a pretty girl driving a white convertible Mustang.

"Man! Look at that cherry ragtop 'stang," Zeb says. He ogles the car, cranes his neck backward as we walk into the store. Inside, Zeb finally quits staring at the car and heads straight for the Fanta machine. It's one of those vendors with all the bottle caps of sodas showing through a skinny glass door to the right. Slip in a quarter, and the clamps release so you can pull out the soda of your choice: Grape Fanta; Orange Fanta; A&W Root beer. Zeb drops in fifty cents, pulls out the orange-capped bottle and hands it to me, then pulls out a grape one for himself. Right next to it is the cage where Mr. Alarcon, the pharmacist, works. It's closed today, but Zeb eyes the pills shelved there.

"Easy take," he says. "Once you're in the main part of the store, it's an easy take." He's half talking to himself. Behind the cash register sits a big metal case holding columns of cigarettes: Winston; Lucky Strike; Kool; Pall Mall. Zeb taps his quarters on the glass countertop, waiting. "Think you could fit through that tiny window there?" he asks me.

I glance up, see the window, and shiver. "I could do it," I tell him, and just then Johnny walks into the store for a split second, grabs a key from behind the counter, and ignores me and Zeb.

Zeb stops tapping his quarters and stares at Johnny.

I see his anger growing, and I point inside the glass case. "Hey Zeb, I like those rabbit's foot key chains. You like those key chains at all?"

Zeb quits staring now. "Which one you like, Willa?"

"I don't know. The green one."

Zeb reaches over the counter to the backside, slides the door of the case open, and picks out the green rabbit's foot. He sets it on the counter. "You like it, we'll buy it for you."

Johnny checks the oil in the Mustang. The girl rests her forearm on the rolled down window, and Johnny cranes his neck around the raised hood so he can smile at her like a monkey.

Zeb watches them, then steps behind the counter and selects his own Pall Mall reds. He walks over to the pharmacy cage, lifts me up, sizing my body against the entrance to the cage. "You could do it, Willa." He sets me back down. "One take is all Mom needs. I'd clean the whole damn pharmacy out." He says it like he knows.

I start shivering. "I'm in," I tell him, and it's almost like I can't control the words coming out of me. I want Mom to be healed.

The pretty girl has paid Johnny, and he's already tucked the dollar bills into the pocket of his overalls. But he still stands there smiling and talking. Zeb looks out the window, then rubs his ankles together like he has an itch he just can't scratch. He hooks the sole of one shoe on the hem of his jeans, pushes the pant leg up, shows me the pearl handle, the snub nose barrel of that gun he stole half-tucked inside his sock, held tight with a handmade holster—Zeb's own craftsmanship. "Fucking Johnny," he says. "Look at him out there. Younger than Dad and he owns this place." He stares, and Johnny leans against the Mustang, flirting.

Finally, Zeb laughs, taps the counter one more time with his quarters, then stabs his hands into his pockets, rabbit's foot and Pall Malls right along with them. He reaches over the counter, slams the cash button on the register. The drawer slides open, and he grabs a couple twenties. On the way out the door, he snags the red licorice that is placed exactly where it ought to be if people intend to buy it on whim, and where it ought not to be if they don't intend to pay for it at all.

"Hey Zeb. Get what you need okay?" says Johnny.

Zeb takes a swig of his soda, holds it high. "Got it, Johnny. Thanks!"

I walk fast behind him, barely able to keep up. "You shouldn't have done that, Zeb."

He keeps walking fast.

"You made that promise. You made that deal about not stealing and Mom getting better."

"It was a stupid promise, Willa. I know what Mom needs, and it's right there." He swings one arm back toward Johnny's pharmacy. "It's not some stupid ass promise."

We walk home without saying a word. When we round the corner, we see Dolly and Chet standing in their front yard, just back from their mountain trip. It's edging toward evening by now, and Chet has the hose in his hand, watering the lawn, just like he does every day at this time. I can't even look at him, knowing what me and Zeb have done. But Zeb suddenly turns all chirpy. He waves like a real pal to both of them.

Dolly waves and walks toward us, looking sideways at Chet. She's overly kind and happy like she always seems when they're out in public. "Good to see you, kids. How's your mother doing?"

"Not good," Zeb says.

"Your mother's a strong lady. You know that." Dolly has on a purple robe with a white collar that looks like a party doily. She scooches up close to us. Chet keeps watering the lawn, does not

even turn his eyes when Dolly bats her eyelashes at Zeb and whispers, "Oh *he's* gone off the deep end now." She looks toward Chet
and rolls her eyes, then leans into Zeb. She pets his upper arm and
whispers. "Funniest thing. Oh, I shouldn't be telling you."

"What?"

She shakes her head.

"No, really, what?"

She leans her whole body into Zeb, and right then, Chet
glances over. "He's gone bonkers," Dolly says.

"Well, I don't know, Mr. Thatcher's okay if—"

"No, I mean it, Zeb. He lost all his belts, every dadburned one
of them." She's nearly giddy by now. She rests both palms on Zeb's
chest so he has to back away to keep her face from touching his.
"And he's claiming someone came in and took them." Tears fill
her eyes to help her hold back from bursting into a laugh.

Zeb looks down at me, keeping his cool, but a smile curls the
corner of his lips, something only I can see because I know him
like my own self. I start thinking of horrible things then—cancer,
the world without birds in it, Mom's Parkinson's—*horrible* things
just to keep from bursting out laughing, myself. I hold it back so
much my jaw aches.

"He honestly believes someone broke into the house and stole
nothing but his belts." She glances back at Chet to make sure she's
safe whispering to Zeb like this. "'Well, tell the insurance man,' I
said to him." Her fingernails dig into Zeb's chest, and she laughs
that wheezing kind of whisper-laugh that sounds like she's choking.

Zeb puts on his best performance, commiserating about the
missing belts.

"Chet swears the latch on the back door was fiddled with, too.
Proof, he says. Says 'I'm going to have to fix that thing now.'" She
imitates Chet's gruff voice, and I can see the anger in Zeb's eyes
light up. He hates leaving behind any kind of sign. Dolly goes on
about the latch, and I see Zeb doubling up his fists.

Right about then, Chet turns the water off and drops the
hose. He looks square at Dolly cuddling up to Zeb, then drills
those beady blue eyes of his into my brother.

Dolly notices, too. She stops clinging to Zeb. She takes a step back, collects herself by rubbing her hands over her robe as if she is pressing out the wrinkles, then she talks in a too-high voice, changes the subject. "And Chet's put in a new lawn, Zeb, and we hope the kids'll stay off'n it, so it could get a good healthy chance at growing." She looks sweetly at Chet, but I can see the muscles in his jawbone flexing, and he starts taking these real slow, deliberate steps toward Dolly, me, and Zeb. Dolly keeps up the fakey voice. "Me and Chet don't want to be the neighborhood ogres, Zeb, but you know how it is."

"I understand, Mrs. Thatcher. I'll keep an eye out, yes." Zeb follows Dolly's lead, his voice all out of pitch, too. He nods hello to Chet. "Good evening, Mr. Thatcher."

"Think so, huh?" Chet says. He walks closer, and his waist is just below my eye level. I see the belt he is wearing, and at just about that time I see Zeb's eyes catch on that belt, too, and he goes from doubling his fists to shoving them into his pockets because we did not think of the belt Chet was wearing.

Chet stands right in front of Dolly now.

"The fuck," Zeb says, underneath his breath, and he pats his chest pocket for the cigarettes he knows aren't there.

"What'd you say, boy?" Chet is not whispering.

The dog sits quiet in his little fenced-in area behind Chet and Dolly, and I pray he doesn't start barking again, not with Chet already this pissed off. Dolly's eyes turn little and wrinkly. She backs away from Chet, squinting and blinking. Zeb watches her. He stares at Chet's belt. Then he looks up, riveting his eyes on Chet, and just when I think he's going to lose his temper, his shoulders relax. He shakes his head, gives Chet this look of outright disgust, then turns his back on him. He takes my hand, and we walk one step away, and I think everything is going to be all right. Dolly has backed off, and Chet has not said *shit* or *fuck* or *bitch*, and everything's fine. But that asshole Chet cannot leave well enough alone. He calls out, "I asked what you said to me, boy!"

Zeb's fingers tighten around my hand.

"Goddamnit, boy!"

Thank God Zeb keeps walking. I close my eyes tight for a second and will him to keep walking, which he does, and so Chet finally shuts up. I can't see Chet, but I can hear his footsteps on the paved sidewalk, the sound fading away, and I feel a relief—until I hear a scream, and my knees buckle. The sound comes from Dolly. Zeb stops and turns. Chet tells Dolly to get in the house, and when she doesn't move fast enough, he grabs a fistful of her short hair, whips her head around with a *crack*. She stumbles forward and falls, skinning her hands and knees on the sidewalk. Right then, the dog starts barking, too, and Chet hollers at it to shut the hell up.

I wish I could say what happens next, but I can't. All I know is that one minute Zeb is standing next to me, and then, all of a sudden, he's like a bug on Chet's big, barrel back, pounding with his fists. There's nothing that makes any sense about it. How Zeb got there, what he thought he was going to do next, or how he thinks he's going to get out alive. I think of running, but my legs won't go. I cannot leave my brother in this bad situation, but no one's around to help us, and then, suddenly, I can't believe what I am seeing. There's no need for anyone to help us because Zeb has somehow made his way from Chet's back around to the front of Chet's face, and skinny Zeb has knocked fat Chet to the ground. Zeb straddles Chet like he straddles me when we're play-wrestling, but this time, Zeb is fighting hard, and I do not mean sucker punching.

Things happen like a home movie when the film breaks and we have to splice it back together. The picture jumps ahead. One second there's no one in the whole neighborhood but me, Zeb, Chet, and Dolly Thatcher, and the next second, kids are everywhere, standing in a circle around Zeb and Chet, streaming in from the field, pouring out of their houses, yelling, "Get him, Zeb, go! Yeah!" They're cheering Zeb on, and Chet is laying on his back swinging up at Zeb. I hear the sound of Chet's fleshy body being hit, see the skin of his face split like a too-ripe plum, and there is blood on Zeb's arms now, splattering all the way up to the hemline of his short-sleeved shirt. He has this wild look in his eyes, like he can't see anything in the world but Chet, Zeb a fish underwater when he is concentrating, and there is no pulling him out of his bloody pond.

"You sorry, sad fuck," I hear Zeb saying, "You good for nothing son of a fucking bitch." It comes out of him in this voice that he can barely squeeze from his lungs. He keeps saying it over and over, "You fuck, you fucker," and the dog starts barking and Zeb hits harder and harder until Dolly comes at Zeb from behind, wraps her arms around him in a bear hug, and tries to pull him off.

She doesn't. She can't. But Zeb feels her arms, and it makes him come to the surface of his pond just before he drowns. He gasps. He stands up. His heart is beating so fast I can see it throbbing in the earthworm-like vein on the side of his neck. He's breathing like he's running, but he's stock still and silent. He looks down at Chet, wipes the corner of his lip, shoves his hands in his pockets, and smiles. It's a pissed-off kind of smile, but it's a smile all the same. Then, real deliberately, he reaches down to his ankle, takes out the gun, crouches low, and presses the snubbed barrel against Chet's temple. I hear him whisper, "I can tell your future, old man." And I hear myself telling my brother "no," but nothing comes out of my mouth.

He holds that gun there a long time, ten seconds maybe, a whole lifetime ticking inside each one of those seconds. The field and sky disappear, and it feels like just me and Zeb and Chet in the world right now. The tug between me and my brother aches. I whisper to him, my lips moving without me controlling them, and I think he feels me telling him to stop, but just then, he leans in closer to Chet, and I see his forearm muscles swell, and his bony hand squeezes tight, and the hammer of the gun slams down. The *click* echoes through my head.

And then, nothing. No gunshot. No bullets.

He sits up, still pinning Chet, and looks at me, smiling again. Just then, Chet rolls out of Zeb's pin. Everything's a blur again, and next thing I know, Chet's standing up and pointing Zeb's own gun at Zeb. He's pointing it loosely, dangling it from his skinned hand. "I can tell your future, too, boy," he says. "You got none." Then he laughs softly, tucks Zeb's gun in his pocket, and walks away.

Zeb stands up, wipes the blood from his hands onto his blue jeans. It looks like an oil smear there, like after he's been working on a car.

Willa

I CROSSED OVER THE New Mexico-Navajo border about noon, when the sun had shrunk to a white hot dime at the top of the scorching, October sky. Red spires of rock stood sunburned and shadowless on the roadside, the black tar beneath my tires half melted and soft, even in autumn. "You can see this red rock as holy, or you can see it as bloodied." That's what Brenda's biological father, Raymond Kabotie, said the first time we met. I was in high school by then. Zeb was gone already, and Brenda had run away from home, too. I hadn't seen either one of them in over a year. But Raymond had driven to Colorado from the reservation, looking for Brenda, because once she found him, she ran away from him, too.

I'd always figured Brenda would runaway from her adopted home because she'd never talk about her real family, and if you brought it up to her, anger spilled out of her like lava. It seemed pretty clear that she was going to have to find her family roots if she was ever going to be at peace. So sure enough, when Brenda turned sixteen she ran away from our neighborhood, seeking out her own flesh and blood.

What I didn't predict was that once she found Raymond, she'd run away from him, too. I'll never forget the first time I met him, when I opened our front door that day and he said, "You're Willa Robbins?"

I nodded.

"She talked about you all the time. You're her best friend. Have you seen her? My Brenda?" He had this expression on his face, a smile so hopeful and full of pain at the same time that my chest almost cracked open just talking to him. I invited him in, and he met Mom. Dad was on the road.

He stuck out his hand to shake Mom's in greeting, but when she couldn't respond, he said, "Parkinson's?" No shyness about it, no turning his head away from Mom's crippledness. It was something no one but a doctor had ever said to Mom before.

For a second I worried it might make her feel bad, but her eyes lit up, and she said, "Yes," as if it was a relief just to have someone call it what it was.

"Evil disease," he said. "My own mama had it."

Mom's voice had shrunk to a mere whisper by then, and it was hard for her to hold her head up. She looked like a baby bird sometimes, her head too big for her bony body. But her spirit was still intact. You could see it leaking out of her, all that life that had no way to express itself in her weakened body. Raymond kept on talking to her about his mother, the days he'd spent helping her. "I learned a lot about it, watching my own mom trying to fight that beast off," he said. Raymond stood up then and went to Mom's side. "You mind?" he said, taking her hand.

Mom nodded to let him know it was okay. He explained to her that the Parkinson's made her think she was falling forward. "Yes," Mom whispered, "That's the way it feels," and Raymond said, "But you're not falling. It's a trick your brain's playing on you. If you can trick it back, pitch your body backward a little, get yourself a pair of old boots like mine," he looked at the worn down heels that made him walk with his weight pitched back and his body low to the ground, "it might help you walk." He prompted her to stand up, and she did, and he wrapped his strong arms around her, her face pressed into his leather vest. He looked at me. "And you," he said, "You can help your mom walk by tapping the top of her toe with your own foot." He lowered his cowboy boot gently onto Mom's toe, and sure enough, she picked up her feet and began shuffling forward more easily than she had in months.

Raymond smiled. "Sometimes you just gotta remind your brain that your body is bigger and stronger than it is." He and Mom walked across the room like that, and then pretty soon it seemed like they were dancing. He wrapped one arm around her shoulder, and they moved almost gracefully together. I fell in love with Raymond right then and there. He led Mom back to her seat in her chair. "Evil disease," he said, "Downright evil," and I could see Mom feeling grateful for his blunt understanding.

When he quit paying all the attention to Mom, he turned to me. "So—" He stalled a little. "You haven't seen hide nor hair of Brenda, huh?"

I'd been hoping that he had news for me about her when he first introduced himself, and the emptiness it caused when he told me she'd left his place agitated me to the bone. "She give you a reason for leaving?" I asked.

He looked around the house, cast his eyes upward in that way that tough men do when they're trying to keep their eyes from watering. "She had her reasons," he said. "I just— I tried to keep her there, with me. But she just turned eighteen. She's got a right." He stopped again and stared hard at the ceiling, blinking with his huge chest stuttering a little. "She's got a right, but she doesn't have anything else. No skills. No money. No way to make a life for herself. And she doesn't like it when I say it, but she's innocent, so innocent. She doesn't understand that sometimes a man has to do something he doesn't believe in just to make his way in the world."

I could see Raymond looking out the window toward the field, searching for some way to get himself out of a conversation he'd never planned on having. "That house out there, that's where Mom was born," I told him.

It gave him a chance to gather himself back up. He looked at me with knowing thanks. "That right?" he said.

"Eminent domain," Mom said to him.

He laughed a little. "Took it right out from under you, huh?" It was the first time I saw Mom light up when she was talking about the land, another relief because Raymond understood things right along with her.

"We could go walking out there if you want," I told him.

"I'd like that," he said.

That afternoon, Raymond and I walked the field, and he showed me how alive the place still was, even though we thought it had been ruined when the house was condemned. "No," he said, "Look at all these stories, all this sign!" We spent till dusk studying the afterimages of all the animals that had passed through there, animals I'd never seen, even though I spent almost every summer day there: field mice, voles, rabbits, quail, pheasants, foxes, coyotes. He showed me how to find owl pellets with the bones and fur of prey clumped into a tight little ball, and he showed me the remains of the nests of meadowlarks on the ground, when I thought all birds lived in trees. We walked farther than I'd ever walked in the field, and we saw prairie dogs, burrowing owls, and the first rattlesnake I'd ever laid eyes on. Raymond pointed out how its scales tiled themselves along its body like a bird's feathers. It was like seeing a whole new world in a place I thought I knew well already.

Right then I was hooked. I knew I'd someday learn to track animals, and I dreamed of being as good as Raymond.

Before he left that afternoon we made a pact to keep in touch, to tell each other if we heard anything from Brenda. It was twenty-some years later now, and Raymond's hair had greyed, and I'd grown up, but I still got the kid-jitters before seeing him. He was a man I admired, a mentor, a friend.

*　*　*

UP AHEAD, BLURRED BY a wave of midday desert heat, sat the *Snack-n-Pump*, the familiar convenience store where Raymond worked, the word GAS painted in bright turquoise on the stucco, and ghosted behind it: CAFÉ, then CIGARETTES, then SOUVENIRS, each word still visible in a sketchy outline. No one had bothered to cross out one word before painting over it with another, and so this timeline of American vices greeted tourists to Indian land. I turned my blinker on by habit, no one else driving this desolate highway, and pulled into the dusty lot where I was surprised to see a white and gold Lexus SUV.

From my truck, looking in through the smudged, plate glass windows, I saw Raymond and his skinny friend, Simon, standing side by side behind the counter. A well-coifed, middle-aged blonde woman made her purchase: gasoline, gum, an arrowhead souvenir or Kachina keychain, something from the kitsch bin. I walked into the store, waved huge, and Raymond smiled and jutted his chin toward me to say hello. He kept his attention on his customer.

I grabbed a bag of red licorice from the shelf, a bottle of water—five bucks—from the cooler. By the time I got to the counter, Simon was bent at the waist, his wiry arms wrapped around his belly, laughing without making a sound. Raymond gave him a big, friendly slap on the back. "And my friend here, Grandfather Simon, he's the most spiritual one of all, completely in touch with nature and everything. He never wastes any buffalo he kills." Raymond all but lifted Simon by his thin black T-shirt and turned him around to face the woman. "Do you, Grandfather Simon?"

Simon wiggled out of Raymond's grip now, stood up stiffly and looked straight at the woman. I tossed my purchases on the counter. The customer nodded, sad-faced. "It's a shame what we've done to your people," she said. "I'm sorry."

"Excuse me?" Simon said.

"And thank you so much," she said. She held up her gum and arrowhead.

Raymond dipped his head in one nod.

"Oh, and how far is it into Sedona?" she asked.

"Sedona?" He looked at me and chuckled. "Why are people always going to Sedona?" The woman sized me up, and Raymond raised his thick arm, pointed north. "Up the highway, about two hours, longer on the scenic route, either way you take the exit just after Oak Creek and then Bob's your uncle."

"Bob's my uncle?"

"Yup. Bob's your uncle. You'll be in Sedona."

She forced a smile, and I was glad Raymond hadn't undone her mercilessly, his usual habit with tourists. But then, as she opened the door, he called out, "Ma'am, you'll see lots of my namesake along that highway. Might interest you." He pointed to the name tag on his blue shirt, his initials.

The woman placed her hand over her heart in thanks and looked closer at his tag. "RK?"

"Road Kill, Raymond to some, but my Indian name's Road Kill." He offered a handshake.

I could see her pulling back instinctively, but there her hand was, sitting limp inside his grip. He squeezed tighter now, and she smiled harder. "Road Kill." She practiced his name, and he kept up his wide smile.

"This here is Simon Goes-Extinct. We try to keep up with the times, you know."

I leaned on the counter, shook my head. The man would never change. His deep chuckle echoed over the click of the woman's shoes as she hurried across the floor, out the door.

"So how the hell are you?"

"You're such an ass, Raymond." I smiled.

"Raymond Road Kill."

"Raymond Pain-in-the-Ass."

Simon got a howl out of that one, and Raymond opened his arms and wrapped me in one of his smothering hugs. "What's news? Got some wolves ready for freedom today?"

"Not this time. I'm heading home."

"Lucky chica. Give Cario and Magda my love, will you? Damn, I gotta get down to their place. I owe Magda twenty bucks, and a lesson at poker," Raymond said.

"The other home. Colorado."

His smile went hollow. He waited to see if I had something else to say. I didn't. So he started sorting the buffalo jerky on the end cap.

"So, how long you gonna be there?" Simon asked, trying to fill the silence. His arms fluttered from cash register to counter to the cigarette rack. If he'd been born in more traditional times, he'd have been named for some kind of small flitting animal, a hummingbird or bee. "In Colorado, I mean, back where you were from a long time ago. You're just visiting there, right? Not staying. She's just visiting Colorado, Raymond. She's not moving there, or anything."

Raymond hissed.

"You know, Raymond," I said, carefully, "She'll make her way back someday. Brenda will come back around to you."

"Well, she's doing it on granny time. Going on how long now?"

"So maybe she takes after her father? Slow and easy." I tried to nudge his arm, but he dodged me, then started sorting the candy.

"You know, I never chose to give her up for adoption."

"I know. It was a government decision. She was taken from you. It's fucked up, Raymond."

"They had no right. No reason. It would never have happened that way outside the reservation." He talked through his teeth, stayed focused on this task. "I have no idea where my own daughter is."

"I miss her, too," I said. "And I *know* she misses you."

"Not bad enough, eh?" He forced a new topic. "So, anyway, same road going into Colorado is the same road coming out. We'll catch you on the flip-flop, right?"

"Well, yeah. I'm hoping there is a flip-flop." His look questioned me. "I'm tracking some rugged terrain."

"You always track rugged terrain."

"Not usually tracking my own brother, though."

He stopped stocking the buffalo jerky. "What crazy shit are you into now?" He sat on the counter and leaned in close to me. "*Tell*," he said.

I told him about the phone call, said Zeb had turned himself in, a confession. But, crazy as he is, after he'd confessed, Zeb took off into the woods. "They searched for him for a couple of days. Nothing. Now they say I'm the only one who knows him well enough to track him."

"They got a point there." He tapped his own head with one finger. "Tracking's all up here, so you're a good choice. They're smart," he said. "So the cops had your brother right there, confession and all, and he ran?"

"Seems so."

"Hell, if they fucked up and let him get loose, it's on them. Right? They got nothing on you, Willa. You don't owe them spit in a rain puddle."

"You don't have to fuck up for Zeb to slip out from under you."

"Your brother's pretty wily?"

I nodded. "If he doesn't want them to, they won't find him."

"Sounds like your brother's a coyote."

I half-smiled.

"You ain't catching no coyote, you know that, don't you?"

"I'm a decent tracker. I had a good teacher."

"Yeah, I'm a good teacher. And a good tracker. And *I* ain't catching no coyote. What the hell, Willa? I don't get it. Why you chasing down your own blood, putting yourself at risk?"

"Fifty-percent of Zeb is me. If he doesn't want to come out, there's no way they'll get him. At least, not living." I hoped it sounded like an answer.

Raymond went quiet again, studying me. "Here's the thing, Willa. Whatever's going on, whatever *real* reason you got for going back, it is not good enough. You're in over your head. You got no reason to go there. You've told me a few stories about your brother. Tracking him is stupider than sleeping alone outside with those wolves like you do."

"Speaking of which," I said.

"Speaking of which, you are changing the subject, my friend."

"Ciela and Hector."

"*My* wolves? What about them?"

There was little that meant more to Raymond than keeping these wolves alive and thriving on this land. Contrary to the WWA's findings, Raymond said Mexican grey wolves had been on Navajo, Zuni, and Hopi land since before the Mayflower, and they'd stayed the whole time, no interruption, no extirpation. "Sure, there were animals we Indians might've overhunted at times. I'm not claiming tribal sainthood here. But those wolves have been here all along. Thinned out as they got from being shot elsewhere, they never left this ground."

The WWA had their statistics, and the Indians had their lives, their day-by-day observations across centuries, something that no study or pile of statistics could even touch.

But even though they knew Raymond had more knowledge about native wildlife than most of their biologists, Raymond's credibility with WWA had been dented. He had an unlicensed rehab center, of sorts, in his own backyard—abandoned grey-hound dogs, sometimes coyotes or birds of prey that he nursed back to health—and he was part of a small group of folks who volunteered with a handful of big shot biologists from universities who believed in "Pleistocene rewilding," which meant restoring devastated ecosystems in America with wildlife from thirteen thousand years ago. He'd helped reintroduce the Bolson tortoise, which was fine, according to the law. But when he and two "rogue" professors started trying to make their own connections, hell-bent on restoring jaguars from south of the border back to New Mexico and Arizona—no matter what any law said—Raymond became a "person of interest" to every wildlife agency in the Southwest. So when the WWA found a pack of Mexican grey wolves on Navajo land, they accused Raymond of "importing" them, and they immediately deported the wolves to the established rehab territory. But soon enough, those wolves—followed by Ciela and Hector—were back on Navajo land again, and again the blame went to Raymond.

"I never touched those wolves," he told WWA, and he reiterated to them that they'd been on this land all along, unobserved by their wildlife officials. It was a constant argument between Raymond and the WWA.

When I told him Ciela and Hector had a bullet with their names engraved on it waiting for them, and that just a couple days back, I'd witnessed them hunt a deer successfully—something that *might* save their lives, if documented—he forgot all about probing deeper into my reasons for going to Colorado.

"Fuckers!" he said. He slammed the rack of buffalo jerky and Slim Jims. "Those wolves are officially off limits to them."

"They're not off limits to anyone. They're classified as a special, non-essential species. Anyone can kill them if they can prove a need."

He smacked the rack of jerky harder this time, and Simon ducked and covered. "I could help," Simon offered. "I could witness it with you, Raymond."

"Two Indians witnessing wolves killing a deer. That ought to change their minds, yeah." Raymond paced the store, going nowhere, trying to calm himself. He took a deep breath and came back to me. "This is jackass-stupid, Willa. The WWA is jackass-stupid on a normal day, but you're competing with them now, going away to chase your coyote brother when all this shit is going down."

"I'll be back in a week or two."

"You have no idea when you'll be back."

"I just— I need you to watch Ciela and Hector, for me. Track them. Witness them hunting, not killing cattle. Get some evidence of it, if you can. Andy—he's the *one* guy at Wilderness and Water who knows you're the best. He'll listen to you."

"Andy got me arrested."

"He didn't have a choice."

"They always have a choice."

"Please, Raymond, just tell him you saw Ciela and Hector, he'll call off the shooting, at least till I get back. He's the top guy there, Raymond. He's not a bullshitter. And he knows you're good."

"He sure didn't help me when they dragged my ass to jail."

I shrugged. "Were you bringing in jaguars?"

"Jaguars, other large predators, shit, they've been on this land since who knows when? Getting them back here's the only thing that'll restore this land to the way it was, the way it needs to be."

"You might be right. But were you bringing in jaguars?"

"They keep people humble, too. Large predators, they remind us we're part of the food chain. Arrogant shits that we are."

"So you *were* bringing them in."

"Never brought one single big cat onto this land."

"But you tried. You set it up. And you *paid* for it. Paid an undercover cop, if I recall right."

He turned his head away. No answer.

I sighed. "Look. You're Ciela and Hector's only hope while I'm gone, Raymond."

He inhaled, and his huge chest nearly split the buttons on his shirt. "All right. Done," he said, on the exhale. "I'll do everything I can. I'll witness the wolves. I'll talk to Andy." He shook his head, resisting my request, but I had his word. I knew that's all I needed.

· · ·

I STAYED THAT NIGHT at Raymond's house. His pack of greyhounds—he had at least a dozen of them that he'd "confiscated" from men who used the hounds to hunt coyotes—wandered in and out of the open doors, the sheer size of them weaving through Raymond's small hut like schools of fish winding around rocks in a river. Raymond and I drank beer, told stories, talked wolves, petted the hounds, and sat silently, the silence charged with everything that had bound us together over the years, our families both fragmented in their own ways, then healed a bit by our mutual love for Cario and Magda. We also shared a passion for wilderness, and we were part of witnessing the constant fragmentation of that, too. Either one of us would have done just about anything to keep at least some corner of that wilderness whole. The land itself had become our extended family, the anchor we would always return to.

"You know," Raymond said, as the night wore on, "I don't know what reason you got for going to Colorado, Willa. But it ain't Zeb."

I sat quiet.

He tapped his beer can with his pointer finger, then took the last swig and crumpled the can in his fist. "Better be a damn good reason," he said. "Better be worth the lives of those wolves." He stood up, tossed the can in a bin, then kissed my head, like a father. He stood above me and held my head to his stomach, stroking my hair. I smelled the sweat of him, and it smelled good. I could have stayed there in that huge hug longer, but he let me go, then said, "Last chance. You can sleep in the big, comfy bed, and I'll gladly take the couch."

I stared at him, wanted to remember every last detail of what he looked like before I went to sleep. "Thanks. But I like the couch. And I'll be up and out early. I don't want to wake you," I said.

"Seriously. Last chance," he repeated.

I smiled and waved him away.

"Sweet dreams, Willa," he said. I heard the heels of his boots thump down the short hallway. I slept that night on the same musty, sagging couch where I always slept, the one that had been his bed during the short time Brenda lived with him and he let her have the private room.

*   *   *

I LEFT AT ABOUT five in the morning, tiptoeing past the dogs before Raymond woke, already one day late according to the cops' schedule, and several days early according to mine. I drove along the mud-solid road that led back to the highway, and in that darkness, a group of teenagers had a game of hoops going. The basket was made of a restaurant-sized Crisco can they'd roped around one of the sandstone spires, the ball a red rubber playground ball like the one I used for four-square in elementary school. They played skins versus shirts, one girl among them, and they were playing hard enough that the sweat on their chests caught light from the sinking full moon, their skinny legs cutting fast around cactus and pinon pine. They dribbled surprisingly easily on uneven ground.

I'd played this kind of basketball with Raymond and his friends during a few of my visits—two-against-one, me and Simon against Raymond. We used a bike rim Raymond had nailed to a telephone pole near the convenience store as our hoop. When Cario and Magda were there, they'd cheer for Simon and me, and boo Raymond, who always ended up at twenty-one before we broke ten.

"You can't even dribble on this damn dirt!" I'd holler to Raymond, and he'd whoosh right by Simon and me and dunk the ball in the bike rim.

"Helps your ball handling," he'd say. "Anyone can dribble on them smooth courts they make in the city. Shit. This is real playing!" And Raymond would laugh and pass by us while we stood there gawking, and Magda and Cario sat there booing, all of us laughing and drinking beer as we played.

Even by reservation standards, though, it didn't make sense for these kids to be playing here, on the side of the long, empty road in the middle of nowhere. But then I saw the powder blue Chevy pickup in a sand bank rolled upside down like a flipped tortoise. Fresh gas and oil leaked from its seams. Its cab had folded flat when it hit the ground, and one wheel had broken off from the axle, the tire and rim now halfway down the highway, in the middle of the road. The morning sun split the horizon, edging the shadowed land with angles as I drove away. I watched the game through my rearview mirror, and in that light, I saw the sweat on one young man show itself as a swath of blood dripping from his forehead, a gash from the accident. He paid it no attention. The game kept on, the clear sound of the kids' voices and laughter suspended in the still morning air.

Willa, 1980

THE FIRST DAY OF Thanksgiving break I wake up early to help Zeb gather his things for his hunting trip. I sit on the floor in his bedroom and wake him by kicking his back with my feet. He groans, then says good morning. "You taking the big tent?" I ask him.

"Only tent we got, Willa."

While he's getting up, I heave the tent from the hallway closet. Dad sleeps on the sofa when he's home now, since Mom's Parkinson's keeps him awake at night. When she can get medication, it gives her what doctors call "dyskinesia," and her trembling turns to thrashing. Without the medication, she's in too much pain to have anyone sleeping near her. So Dad doesn't get much sleep either way, and I try not to wake Dad as I haul the tent back into Zeb's room. "What's Dad like when he's hunting?" I ask.

"Dad doesn't hunt." Zeb sleeps in his long johns so he just pulls his jeans on over them to get dressed.

"I know he doesn't shoot. But what's he like when he goes hunting with you?"

"I don't know. Walks with me. We talk some. Not a lot, but more than we talk at home."

"He doesn't talk at all at home."

"Not a lot. No."

We head to the kitchen and make breakfast together: I break the eggs, get the bacon from the fridge, grate the potatoes, and he cooks it all up. When Dad gets up, he dresses fast and makes his way to the table. He sits next to Zeb, and both of them can barely bend their arms because of their thick clothes. They eat like it's their last meal, three eggs, two glasses of orange juice, a package of bacon between them. "Good thing you'll be bringing back more food for us to eat. Some meat," I tell them. "Not too much left in the fridge right now."

"Mom still sleeping?" Zeb asks.

"Let her sleep all she can today, Willa," Dad says. There's a sadness in his voice, too. It's been that way ever since he's had to sleep alone. Dad hasn't been home much since that change happened, takes as many on-the-road sales jobs as he can get. When he is home, he mostly just sits alone in his chair, staring. He turns on the TV, but he doesn't watch it.

"All right, let's get on the road," says Zeb. He talks just like a man, takes his orange, flop-eared hunting hat from the table, adjusts it on his head.

Dad does the same exact thing, Zeb and Dad moving with the same kind of solid slowness, like hunting is a thing they have to do, when it's usually a trip they both enjoy. Dad walks down the hall and looks in on Mom, then comes back out, no words. He looks out the front window. "Looks like the Thatchers are heading up to the mountains, too," Dad says. He zips his coat.

Zeb turns to the window. The headlights of Chet's Dodge light up. Dolly walks to the car carrying blankets and food while Chet sits waiting in the driver's seat, smoke pouring from the tailpipe. "Chet doesn't hunt," Zeb says.

"They got that cabin they go to anyway," says Dad.

I can see Zeb hating Chet and at the same time, he smiles and waves to the Thatchers right along with Dad. Then he reaches down and thumps my head lightly. "You be good while we're away, Willa."

"That's right," says Dad. "Your mother's really going to need your help around the house." He says it sad but firm, in a way that makes me think he expects me to heal Mom while they're away, or something, like me and Mom are going to be doing housework together, maybe some Christmas shopping, when she hasn't been able to do any of those things for a long time. It feels like that's what he's really asking me to do: to heal her. It weakens me, but I nod and assure him I'll take care of Mom the best I can.

They head out the door. I press my palms against the glass of the living room window, and it is ice cold, and my palm leaves a handprint on the glass. Snow sputters from the grey sky, hitting the ground like tiny balls of hail. I watch Dad and Zeb drive around the corner and disappear.

* * *

AN HOUR OR SO later, the sky turns light. The snow is no longer sputtering, either. It's dropping huge flakes that drift like feathers to the ground, like heaven is made of birds, which makes sense to me. Mom is still sleeping and our house is quiet, and the house she used to live in sits in the field, snow softening its edges. When I'm with her, I can't imagine Mom ever being my age, but while she's sleeping, I can almost see an amber light glowing in the window of that old house in the field, can hear the voices of parents and of a girl who is like me, but who wears dresses like they wore back then on special occasions, like Thanksgiving week. There's something about it, knowing that she was my age in *that* house: I can look at it and feel her there and see her in a way I never have—before she was my mother, before she married Dad, before Parkinson's crawled inside her—I can see all this when I walk on that land. When I'm walking where she walked and fishing in a pond where she used to fish when her legs worked and her body was not bent and stiff and shaking all at once. It feels good to me, even important. It's like the land is a movie screen, and I can see a whole movie of Mom's life there, and it feels like part of my life, and it all rises up from the land in the field somehow, like the place is alive and packed with lives that connect to mine. The walls of the house may have crumbled, but it's not so much the house that matters, anyway. It's the place itself, the given ground.

When I run out there sometimes, I like to see my own foot-prints as I come back. I see the imprint of my own tennies in the mud, and it makes me smile. I think, beneath them somewhere there's the imprint of Mom's shoes still on that land. I'm glad we don't have a paved sidewalk like Chet and Dolly. I'm glad our ground is still soft, and in the future I can bring my kids here and let them leave their imprint too, all of us becoming a part of this land.

But all these images go away when I hear Mom rousing in her bedroom. I hear the bed creaking, and I know she's awake and writhing to get out of it, and I have to go in there and help her. I really *want* to go in and help her, but I can't bring myself to move. I've never felt anything like this before. Like my willpower will not let me do what I want to do, the fear, or whatever it is, it over-whelms me. It has more power than my own mind. I sit there on the couch, as stiff and immobile as Mom. I can't breathe regularly for all the extra pounding my heart thinks it has to do. I tell it to be quiet. It keeps punching my chest like a pissed-off boxer.

Pretty soon I'm just mad, not sad anymore, and then I can finally stand up. Soon as I stand, though, the madness goes away because I have made my way back to Mom and she is in bed and trying to get herself out of bed, and she can't. My mother can't get her own self out of bed. There are medications that could make her better, but we cannot afford them. "No one lives forever," Dad said to me once, explaining the situation, as if explaining would make me feel better about it and not just make me more pissed off.

Now and again, Dad gets enough insurance coverage from work that Mom can get some doctor help, and things are better for a little bit. But the insurance runs out fast, Dad says, and then he loses that job because he takes on a third job that makes him so tired, and when he's home we do things like drive all over the state of Colorado on what we call a *scavenger hunt* for medications. The pharmacy companies give free samples to doctors, and if we can get the doctors to donate their free sample pills to us, we can sometimes bridge the gaps in between insurances and Dad's jobs, and Mom's disease gets better, for a while. But it's not a perfect set up, like Dad says, not a good situation overall.

I can see it's not perfect when I look at Mom. She is fading away. She is twig-thin and brittle and even her head is veiny, and it frightens me. She looks like a baby bird before it has feathers, her head too heavy for her neck to hold up, her bony wings laying useless at her side. I love her, and she scares me.

I know I have to buck up; it's on me this week while Dad and Zeb are hunting. Her care is on me. I take a deep breath, and I walk over to the bed, where Mom is now. We've put chairs all around it so she can't fall out at night, and I move one of those chairs and sit down next to her. "Ready to get up?" I ask.

"Oh, yes," she says. Her voice is soft, not because she is feeling gentle, but because her voice is shrinking away.

I help Mom from the bed, into one of the wooden chairs, and then into the wheelchair where she spends her days now. Her body has folded in two, like a wilted sunflower in a vase, that heavy head on that weak stem, and she can't straighten it up. So I have to prop pillows on both sides of her to keep her halfway upright. But her neck is still wilted so she looks at me sideways all the time. I look at her and feel weak. I don't wonder if she knows she's dying. I wonder if she knows I know she is dying. It's unspoken between us, and I think it's something she thinks I shouldn't know—like not knowing Zeb smokes cigarettes, not knowing about sex, not knowing about Zeb's stealing. It's been too long now that he's said he was stealing to help her. His theft hasn't helped a goddamn thing, and he keeps at it, and it's like he's addicted and he can't stop, and I'm old enough now to make my own decisions and I have quit going with him. I made up my mind firm about that because whatever he's stealing has not made a goddamn difference, because this is my mother, and even if I don't want her to be sick, she is. Nothing you can take or give to someone else makes one bit of difference. That's what I know.

It's a month before Christmas, and in school they asked us to go through a bunch of catalogues and cut out pictures of things we want to give or get as gifts. But I can't understand it. All this stuff—it comes and goes, and there's nothing in those catalogues that you can own. I learned that from stealing with Zeb for sure, but I can't say *that* to the teacher. Can't say, "Everything in this catalogue goes away. Just leave your window open a tiny crack one night. You'll see."

What I want is not in her slick little catalogue. I want my mom back. She's alive with me now, and already I can't remember who she was before Parkinson's wilted her. Give me that back in the fucking Sears catalogue.

I wheel Mom out into the living room, and I put on the TV for her. *Days of Our Lives* is on, but it's about people killing and stealing and dying, so I turn the channel. We settle on reruns of

Alice, a show she used to like, but she stares at the TV blankly. It's different than Dad staring at the TV because Dad looks like he has too much in his head and he's trying to erase it. Mom looks like she has thoughts brimming over, too, but she can't say them aloud anymore. They escape her. She is too tired to speak them.

"Maybe we could take a nap," she says. She's been up about an hour now, but I understand her wanting to take a nap because even though we haven't done anything, I'm exhausted.

It takes another hour or so to get her back into bed, but this time I stay there with her. I take a book she's been trying to read but hasn't gotten too far in. "Want me to read it to you?" I ask.

She says yes. I snuggle up next to her and read about five pages of *The Way to Rainy Mountain* before we both fall asleep.

.   .   .

WHEN WE WAKE, THE window is bright blue, the sky pressing against it, and the sun melts the snow so fast that when I sit by the tiny opening in the window, I can hear crystals of snow popping in the sudden heat. "Let's go outside," I say aloud, though I meant to just think it to myself, but Mom says, "Good idea. Let's."

I can feel myself jittering inside because it's what I want to do, but I'm scared.

"It's okay," she says, as if giving me permission to go out and play, or something.

"It is?"

She says, "Yes. We can go outside."

I don't waste any time. I just start gathering our winter clothes before she changes her mind. I take Mom's red hat from the closet. "The other one," she says.

"What?"

"The striped hat. One you gave me for Christmas a couple of years ago." Her voice sounds almost strong. Parkinson's goes up and down in a body, some good days, some bad, but this is

Mom's first good day in a long time. It has never felt so good to do something so simple as taking a hat from a closet. I slap it against my thigh to dust it off. She asks me for the warm boots she used to wear, too, and I scramble to the far back corner of the closet to find those. With her clothes all laid out, I sit her up on the bed and her fingers grasp my neck so hard as I'm dressing her that my neck feels like clay taking the imprint of her hand, and I'm still jittery with hope. It takes me a good twenty minutes to get her shoes on because her feet are so stiff and she can't muscle her way into the boots, but I'm happy the whole time I'm doing it, and Mom is too. When I take a shirt out of the closet and it has a big stain mapped out across it, because *all* her clothes are stained by now—no way to keep them clean the way she writhes as she eats—she says, "I like that stain. It's modern art." I haven't heard her try for a joke in so long that I crack up hard at this one, and we both keep laughing way too long, and we fold into each other and wipe tears from our eyes and laugh again and again.

Pretty soon she's dressed, and I'm pulling her wheelchair backwards, out the front door, and pushing it across the snowy front yard. "Oh look at this sky!" she says, because it is an excellent sky today, bluer because of the fresh white snow outlining the houses, the trees, the fence, the sharp blue horizon across the snowy field. Her face turns upward to feel the sun's rays, and she opens her arms wide, and they flop there like a rag doll's. They make me laugh because she looks funny and beautiful all at once. Her wool hat has covered up her veiny head, and I remember what she looked like before she was sick, her reddish hair falling to her shoulders, her beautiful, uncrooked smile on her lipsticked lips.

I push her wheelchair down the dirt road, and I see the faces of our neighbors peering out their windows at us, staring. The ones who had their drapes closed part them just enough to peek out, and the ones who had them open look out real fast, then close the drapes so they can't see us anymore. Since Mom is in front of me and she can't see what I'm doing, I raise a middle finger to the starers, hold it up there for a good long time before they can get to the drawcord and close us out.

When we get to the edge of the field, we look at the old house
for a while, then I start to turn the chair around. "Let's keep going," Mom says.

"We're at the end of the street," I tell her, and she asks me why
I can't hold the barbed-wire fence down.

"With your foot," she says, "And pull this stupid chair and me
over it, into the field. Can't you?"

I know I should not be out here like this with Mom, but I
don't care. I'm used to the feeling of doing something wrong, but
usually there's nothing good at the end of it. This time, it feels
right. I wonder for a second if I am healing Mom, like Dad wanted
me to, some magic happening that I can't understand. She's better
than I've seen her in a long time, and she has always told me I can
make anything happen if I want it bad enough.

When I step on the sagging barbed wire and the rotten fence
posts bend inward on both sides, I feel like a cartoon character,
like those fence posts are made of steal and I am bending them
so my mom can cross into the field. I pull her over the wire, and
she raises her hands as high as she can, like a victorious boxer,
and she sighs, a good sigh, like she's home. The grasses that were
tall in summer are folded down over the mud like a blanket now,
and it's easier to push her chair here.

"Look!" she says, and she can't point, but I follow her eyes. In
the gathering of blue spruce trees that used to outline the border
of Mom's childhood backyard there's a flock of bluebirds. They
look like the blue light that twinkles off of white snow, but bigger,
and brighter, and alive. "Mountain bluebirds," Mom says.

"I've never seen them before," I tell her.

"Only a few migrators left this time of year. Now that you've
seen them, you'll see them this summer. They'll be even brighter
blue then." She says this calmly and certainly. The birds flash like
gems in the snow, and then, in one gust, like a bright blue wind,
they rise up from the trees and fly above the frozen pond, then
disappear out of sight. I'm so distracted by the birds that I push
Mom's chair into a dip, and it begins to fall, and it takes all my
strength to keep her from toppling over. It leaves me shaken, and

I tell her we should go back now, and she says, "No." She says, "Take me over there." She tries to point.

I'm getting cold and more afraid. "Where?"

"Can we go one more time to the house?"

One more time? We've never been to the house together before, and I want to go, but for some reason, my teeth start chattering. "It's getting toward evening, Mom."

"It's barely even afternoon," she says.

"And it's hard pushing this wheelchair."

"It's harder sitting in it."

"So let's go back then."

And that's when she says, "I feel so good today. I feel like I could walk."

"You do?"

"Let me hold onto you," she says. She concentrates and arranges her feet carefully and then puts all her weight on my hands and shoulders. She stands.

I see that I've grown to be the same height as Mom. I've never known this before, and it makes me feel like we *can* do this—together. She can walk, with me. "Want to walk to the house?" I ask. It's less than a football field away from us.

She says, "Yes," but her lips are pulled taut with the effort she makes to take each step. Still, she is stepping. We walk together. Nothing matters but this. I'm not cold anymore, and my mom and I walk to the house where she lived when she was my age. The rotted doorway is open, as it always is, and we step inside.

There's a quiet here now. It's almost like the walls are standing again and the roof is nailed back into place, not sagging. Things echo. I walk with Mom over to the rickety rocking chair. I use all my muscles to lower her into the chair, and when she lets go, I feel light again.

Maybe if she felt better she'd tell me stories of her life in this house. But she is quiet. And I am quiet. I remember all the photographs she has shown me of this place when she lived here, anyway. I can see her in it when she was a kid, can hear her voice back then, and it sounds a lot like mine. The stories of her life find me here, on this land. They know Mom. They know me.

Time passes and I don't know how, because everything feels still. But pretty soon she starts trembling again, and she is not feeling well, I can tell. She says, "I worry."

There's nothing to say back to her. I worry all the time too.

"If you don't know you don't have it, you can't know you're missing it," she says.

This is the part of her disease my dad and the doctors call "Lewy body dementia." It's when she starts to go away and not make sense, even though she is still there, sitting right in front of you. Nonsense comes out of her mouth. "People move around all the time now. Nothing to hold onto, nothing to lose, so they think they have everything to gain. They think they want everything. It's crippling."

I look at her, and I realize what I've done. Her muscles are frozen stiff, and her dementia is setting in. The sky dims, and the evening chill comes on earlier than I expected. I stand up. "We have to go back now," I tell her.

She has the fixed gaze now, too. She doesn't look at me. I'm nervous leaving her alone in that rickety chair, but I have to fetch her chair from the distance and bring it back to her side. I run back and get the chair and push it toward her, my teeth chattering the whole way. I'm breathing hard by the time I get back to her. "Come on. Put your arms around my neck." I try to sound calm and confident, but I have never been so scared.

She doesn't move. I pry her gloved fingers one by one from the arms of the wooden chair. They are so cold and stiff. "We have to go back," I tell her. She comes out of her daze a little and almost looks at me. "Good, Mom, good. Move your feet, now please. Move your feet." But she can't move her feet. She is connecting with me now, I feel it in my gut, even though her blank eyes don't show it. She wants to move her feet, but she can't. I have to bend down and place her feet in position to stand.

Her legs are stiff as dried wood. It's hard to believe she's not fighting me, but I know she isn't. The strength is all Parkinson's, all disease. The force of it is never constant. It goes up and down in her, the rhythm of this disease. Her feet are locked into one position. I work up a sweat, and I finally get them under her. I force her arms to my neck, and they feel like iron posts, they are so stiff, and it feels like I'm trapped under the iron girds of her. That's when we both fall to the ground, stiffly. She falls hard, hits her head on the earth, and tears come to her eyes. Fear rushes through me hard, and I feel myself howl, and I lift her in one strong movement into the chair.

Shaking, I begin the long walk back to the house we live in now. I push her chair in front of me, and she sits motionless. It's harder going back than it was coming out. When we finally reach the fence, I stomp the barbed wire down, and the neighbors stare as I walk down the street again. I don't have time to flip them off.

At home, I'm exhausted and cold and I want to feel better. "I can make us hot chocolate," I say, knowing she hears me but will not respond because she can't respond. It pisses me off and weakens me all at once. I take longer in the kitchen than the hot chocolate requires. I turn the stovetop on low so the milk heats slowly. I stare at the red hot coils.

By the time I pour the hot cocoa into two mugs, my shakes have almost gone away. I head back out to the living room, set Mom's mug right by her chair, and she suddenly moves faster than I've seen her move, maybe ever. Her hands grab my face and she presses both palms on my cheeks, hard, and she pulls my face right up close to hers with a strength that feels like Parkinson's, but I know is all her. She says, "I love you." I tell her I love her too, and I try to break away from her, but that makes her grasp my face even harder and she pulls me close to her and she says, "I know. I *know*. And I never, never, never, *never* want that to go away." The way she says it scares me like nothing I've ever felt before. It hollows me out, and I can't feel anything inside. She cries now, and I want to hold her, but I feel as stiff as she usually is. I don't know if this is still her dementia talking, but it scares me to the core. When she finally lets me go, I feel wrung out, like she squeezed every bit of life from me. The room is dark, and I don't get up and turn on any lights. I don't make dinner. We sit, Mom and me, my hand resting on hers.

That night when I tuck her in bed, she says, "Would you help me?"

I want to tell her I am helping her, I will always help her.

She tells me she wants to see me before she goes away. She tells me she is going away, she knows she is. She asks me to help her go away peacefully, so I can be there beside her when she goes. She says she doesn't want to go alone, and she says Zeb can't help her and she can't ask Dad. She says there's only a strand left of her now. She asks me not only to be there when she goes, but to help her go.

There's nothing but fear and love inside me. I can't imagine it. But I tell her, "Yes, I'll help you, Mom." I know what she is asking me to do. I have no other answer. I want another answer. But I tell her yes. When she is ready, I will be there. I will help her. Yes.

That night I'm in bed, alone, and I've never wanted Mom to get better more than I do now. I pray for the first time ever that if she doesn't get better, I'll go before she does. Jesus will snag my praying hands, and I'll just wait for her to join me. When she asked me to help her, I told her yes, and I want time to stop now. I want everything to stop. The house is so quiet it feels hollowed out inside, like the houses after me and Zeb left from a job of stealing. I can't sleep, so I get up, pull my rubber boots on over my footie pajamas, and walk outside. The other house feels safer. I want to be there, in the house in the field where Mom grew up.

It's a quick trek in the night. When I reach the house, I sit with my back against the wall, looking out across the field to the icy pond turned silver by the moonlight. I think of the fish under the surface, protected now by the first thin layer of ice. I learned all about fish in biology class before Thanksgiving break. In winter, they sink to the bottom of a frozen pond or lake, where the water is mudlike and silty, too dense to freeze solid. Swimming in the muck there is what keeps them alive through the frozen winter.

I close my eyes; I imagine them trudging back and forth through the silt with their little fins flapping. It's tough swimming. But they keep at it, hoping for summer.

I feel like a fish.

.   .   .

THREE DAYS LATER, ZEB and Dad are back from hunting. From the kitchen window, I watch them hang the deer, their bodies moving like dark patches of smoke in the wintry fog. Zeb makes a cut near the hooves of the deer, and the ankle turns into a bony eye of a needle. He works thick rope through the hole between tendon and bone to make a loop for the deer to hang from. Behind Dad and Zeb, the Thatcher dog stands at attention in his pen, eyes riveted to the carcass of the deer. That dog has been out there alone for four nights now, shivering.

Zeb uses his whole body, bending at the waist, to hoist the deer up with the pulley system he has rigged over the branch of a tree. When the deer is hung, Dad pats Zeb on the back and they walk inside, Dad's arm around Zeb's shoulder. It looks, at first, like Dad's taking care of Zeb, like Zeb's been hurt. But they come inside, and I see Zeb's fine, and I figure they're just quiet from spending all that time in the woods. They peel off their hunting clothes, and I can smell the woods on them. Their flannel-lined canvas jackets are soaked with snow and the scent of blood, like the meat department at the Piggly Wiggly grocery. It mixes with the salty smell of the pheasant and sage stuffing I tried to make, with a little of Mom's help.

Zeb sits on the couch, staring out at the deer he got. I sit next to him, keeping quiet like he is. "It's a beautiful deer," I tell him, almost whispering.

He nods halfway, like he's tired, even a little bit sad. "And we take all that beauty inside us."

I think about it for a little bit, what he said. Then I ask him, "What about the fear?"

He looks at me now. He's not angry, but he says, "What about it?"

"The deer must've been feeling fear when you shot it. I figure we take that in too when we eat it."

He squints his eyes at me like he hates me, but his look softens right away. He looks back at the deer. "Maybe," he says.

We sit down to dinner as daylight fades to evening. Dad and Zeb are still so quiet. It haunts me a little, makes me afraid that something happened between them up there, like maybe Dad knows about our stealing now. Out the window, Christmas lights glow.

"They're so pretty." Mom tries to smile. I want her to smile like she did when they were gone, and I want to tell Dad that she walked and we spent time in the old house. But it reminds me of the secret between me and Mom now. I want that secret to go away.

A few minutes later I notice the red Christmas lights suddenly fill up the whole window. They pulse against the misty November sky, *red, grey, red, grey*. I stop eating. I look outside.

A police car parks in front of our house. Zeb sees it, I can tell by the way he fixes his eyes, then looks away real quick. It makes him nervous, but he acts all tough and nonchalant. I know what's about to happen, and I want to spill out all my confessions now. I do not want that police officer coming up here and telling Mom and Dad on Thanksgiving that me and Zeb have stolen things. I want to confess before he gets to the door. I wish I had confessed everything before now, but things just kept piling up, and I couldn't tell where my confessions should begin. I open up my mouth intending to spill out everything I know once and for all, and the only words that come out are, "Dad, pass the green beans, please."

Zeb looks at me, even glares. It's that tug between us, and he senses I'm scared and about to tell on us both. The cop lights keep pulsing. I can't tell if the pheasant I roasted is dry, or if it's just that my mouth is a desert and even water wouldn't quench it.

"A toast to the cook," Dad says. His back's to the window, and he hasn't seen the police car yet. So he's cheery, like he always is on Thanksgiving. But this year it's fake. I can see by the way his smile is flat and broad, more like a dog bearings its teeth than a smile. All the same, me and Zeb clink Coke classes with Dad, and we bend down to toast with Mom.

My eyes swing toward the window. The sky is one bruised heartbeat. Then comes the *knock*.

Dad wipes his mouth with his napkin. "Who could be visiting during the Thanksgiving dinner hour?" he says. But his voice is fakey, and he tries so hard to act happy. When he turns and sees the red lights flashing, he falters a little. Then he bucks up like I've seen Zeb do. He stands up, carries his napkin with him to the door, wipes his mouth as he walks. He's still chewing his pheasant as he opens the door. He sees the police officer standing there, stuffs his napkin into the pocket of his slacks and he makes his fake smile even bigger. He sticks out his hand to greet the cop. "Evening, Sir."

I hear only snippets of what the cop says. "We're looking into it. . . . She'll be all right," and so on.

"Are we in danger?" Dad asks.

My thoughts whir. *Dad thinks he's in danger because of me and Zeb?*

"No danger," says the cop. "You could help her out a little at this time."

The cop wants dad to help me out? Why would Dad help me out after he knows I've been stealing with Zeb? I stand to be punished for the rest of my life.

For years I've been rehearsing my confession. I want, most of all, for Mom to understand that I thought I was helping her. I'm ready to tell her now.

Dad sits at the table. He sucks in a deep breath, lets it out in a whistle. "Seems something's happened next door," he says.

The belts? Of all things, they caught us for stealing Chet's belts?

I look at Zeb. He avoids making any eye contact with me. For the first time ever in my life, I see his hand shaking as he cuts his meat.

Right then a knock comes on the door again. Slower this time. Dad walks to the door, pulls it open, and smiles his fake smile. "Officer," he says, sticking out his hand as if he just met the guy, even though it's been less than ten minutes since they last spoke.

The cop pokes his head into the house, and we can all see his ruddy face now. He points with his clipboard to Zeb. "You had some run-ins with Mr. Thatcher in the past, didn't you, son?"

Zeb looks at Dad, not at the cop, and Dad keeps his smile going, and he steps outside. He stands on the porch, talking to the cop for a few minutes. Then he leads the cop around to the backyard. From the window, we can see him showing off the deer that Zeb got. They stand there in the cold, fog billowing from their mouths, and I can see Zeb trying not to watch them as he eats his meal. Pretty soon Dad's back at the table again and his jaw must ache from fake-smiling. The cop car sits in front of our house a few minutes longer. Then it pulls away.

Dad tries to eat his dinner. "Now I don't want anything ruining our Thanksgiving dinner," Dad says. "Who knows how many Thanksgivings we'll have when we can all be together." He tries to smile again, but it weakens every time. He takes a deep breath. "Seems Chet had some trouble up at the cabin," he says. "Dolly's fine. We need to look after her, but she's fine. But Chet, he took his own life."

Mom gasps, and Zeb keeps eating, doesn't look up at all until Dad says, "The gun he used was stolen. They're looking into that."

Dad repeats what he said before, says we're not going to let this ruin our Thanksgiving. He starts eating again, like nothing has changed. But everything has changed. I can see his hands shaking as he eats. I look at Zeb, and I swear I see water coming to his eyes. But he keeps eating, trying hard not to look at me. Mom sits motionless. Along with everything else, I can't stop thinking about what she asked me to do. I am not hungry.

·　　·　　·

THAT NIGHT, MOONLIGHT TURNS the snow bright, almost like daylight. I look out my window at Zeb's deer before I go to sleep. Blood drips from the head of the deer onto the snow, a dark outline. It looks like a map drawn in the snow by a finger I can't see. It looks like the deer is dreaming and its dreams are spilling red out onto the snow.

My dreams are like that sometimes. They're bigger than anything my head can hold. They spill out of me and outline a map of a place I've never seen, my secrets at last as visible as blood on snow.

Zeb—Thanksgiving, 1980

ON THE DAY OF the hunting trip, before light, he wakes up but keeps his eyes closed, stays perfectly still and listens to the house breathing. His bed folds around him like mountains, the way they embrace him and lock him in all at once. He wants to see what's on the other side of them. He tries to imagine a landscape that does not hem him in. He wants his mother to get better. This morning he's half afraid to head into the mountains and hunt, something he loves, but he fears that, this time, he may not come back. The jaws of that ragged skyline might clamp down on him once and for all, keep him there, in the woods, where he knows he belongs, away from people, away from family, away from anything he calls *home*.

But soon as he feels his sister's feet kicking his back, he comes out of it. He knows he could never really live alone. His kid sister sits on the floor and kicks at him to wake him.

"Morning, Willa," he says. He thinks, *Jesus, she's a kid. She's such a kid, and she has no idea about anything.* He lets one eye open just a little, gives her the exasperated brother look. She smiles that giddy smile, and his exasperation falls away. Before he can get out of bed, she's got his tent out, his bags half packed for him, and she's already prepping the eggs and stuff for breakfast. She's such a kid.

When he meets his father in the kitchen, it strikes him how much he, himself, is not a kid. Not anymore. He feels like a man now, like this trip will be the first one where he's in charge and his father's not coming along to make sure he stays out of trouble, but coming along because the two of them need time together. Like maybe he is there for his dad this time, and not the other way around. His mother is dying. He and his father both know this, and his little sister will never really understand it. If she did, it would gnaw at her the same way it gnaws at him, his edges frayed with doubt constantly, when Willa is always so certain and content.

He wants to go hunting, wants it more than anything right now. But it takes all the determination he can muster to get him to walk out that door, leaving Willa and his mother alone in the house. "You take care of your mother," he says to Willa, and she says yes, she will, and he believes her, but it does nothing to make him feel better. Only thing that takes his mind off it all is the headlights out the window, Chet's headlights, because that asshole is heading out for the Thanksgiving weekend, too.

"Thatchers are going up to the mountains, I'll bet," Dad says. Zeb says "Yeah," and he watches them pull away, and already his mind is relieved of thinking about his mom and kid sister, and his brain clicks into scheming a way to get his favorite gun back. He's broken into Chet's house a couple of times now looking for it, but it's never there. He's seen Chet target practicing with it in the field, knows Chet still has it, but that gun is never in the house when Chet is gone. Must take it with him everywhere, he thinks. Until he gets that gun back, Zeb's mind won't rest. He knows where Chet's cabin is, has been there himself once, a long time ago, before his mother was sick and before the whole family knew what an asshole Chet was, when everyone was still friends with Chet and Dolly.

He's the hunter here, not his dad. So he leads the car to a hunting place not too far from where the Thatcher cabin is. "I worry about Mom," his father says.

"Yeah," Zeb says, and it feels sharp in him, and he quits thinking about Chet and the gun for a little bit. But two seconds later it pisses him off that his dad brought up his dying Mom in the first place, out here in the woods, of all places. "They'll be fine, Dad," he says. "Willa's a good kid. She can look after Mom."

"You're right," his dad says, and he hates his dad for saying it because Willa is twelve years old and she can't take care of his mom. No one can. He doesn't bring it up again. He never stops thinking about his mother and his sister, and his thoughts agitate him, keep him constantly on edge. But his dad makes like he's okay with it all. He sits back and starts asking Zeb silly questions about hunting.

"What's it feel like, Son?"

"No way to explain it. Just something I like to do," Zeb says.

"Beautiful animal," his dad says.

"That's part of it. Yeah."

"Well, you're very good at it," his Dad says, finally.

Zeb thinks the word *thanks* to himself, but he doesn't say it out loud to his father. Most of what he wants to say coils up tight inside of him, no reason to uncoil it. He knows his father knows he's grateful. The words are extra. His sister talks a lot. Zeb doesn't.

When they get to the mountains, Zeb directs his father. "Turn left here. Take this dirt road. Head back into the woods." His father follows his directions. Zeb takes them to a camping spot that is less than a mile from the cabin where Chet and Dolly will spend the Thanksgiving vacation while their dog sits in its pen in their backyard, shivering and hoping for food.

Zeb and his dad set the canvas tent up together, neither one of them saying anything more than they need to say to get the thing to a standing position. But it's that small amount of talk that makes Zeb start to feel good. He's camping and hunting with his father, and everything starts to feels okay.

With the tent ready, Zeb lights the Coleman stove, and he cooks dinner by the light of two lanterns. He likes the glow of the mantles that keep the light burning. They look like little fishing nets set afire, burning bright. He sets one on either side of the stove and gets water boiling for one of the newfangled meals-in-a-bag he's not too fond of. But they make it easier on his father, and that makes it easier on Zeb. He opens a can of pork-and-beans and heats that, too. Real food.

When dinner is ready, his father joins him. They sit under the stars, and their breath makes little clouds of fog as they eat the hot food. "Not bad," his father says.

"Wait till morning," Zeb says.

His father looks at him.

"Tastes even better in the morning," Zeb explains. "Longer you're out, the better the food tastes." The stars milk the sky with light like they never do in town. There's more light than darkness in the wilderness night sky, something Zeb longs for in the lowlands, something that eases him here, in the mountains. There are sounds in the trees behind them. Rustling leaves. Hoot owls. Zeb and his dad keep eating. "If we could stay out here for a week, like my Boy Scout troop, a can of beans would taste like a steak!" Zeb says.

His father laughs. "If we stayed out here for a week, I'd be hankering for a *real* steak, I'm afraid."

"That, too," Zeb says. Then he realizes they've never had a beef steak, not even once. It's just a figment of their imaginations. It makes him laugh even harder, and his dad chuckles right along with him—no reason—and the no-reason part of it makes them both laugh even more, when laughing is not something common to either one of them.

Eventually, his father asks him if he has a plan for the next few days. Zeb nods. "I know this area. We'll get a deer."

"All right, then," his father says, and they both stand up.

"You waking me up, or am I waking you?" his father asks.

"Me, you."

The two of them crawl into the tent and sleep soundly. Zeb doesn't think about his mother, about Willa, about stealing. He just sleeps. He wakes up in what seems the middle of the night but is morning, and he tries to remember what hooked him yesterday and made him feel so pissed off. Right now, nothing could trouble him. His father sleeps, and he crawls out of the tent and lights the lanterns. The glow of them does not diminish the thickness of the stars. By the time breakfast is ready, his father is squatting next to the campfire with him. They don't need to talk to know what to do next. Everything falls into place naturally.

When the time is right, they both start gathering gear. Zeb carries his .30-30 in the event his shot comes to him in thick brush, and he lets his father carry his .30-06 for any deer that show up in open fields. Two guns, two different shooting circumstances. "You okay with that?" he asks his dad.

His father nods, and they take off walking into the woods.

It's not long after sunrise when he remembers why he came to this spot for hunting. He remembers Chet's cabin and the gun and it bothers him a little, but what he really wants right now is just to be here, in this place he loves. The anger that hums in his brain, the desire for that gun, that asshole Chet, they still bother him, but he can put them all out of his mind here. When he doesn't want to think about them, he doesn't have to. This morning, all he is thinking is *deer*. He starts following animal signs, doesn't give a shit about Chet in his cabin. He sees deer scat followed by fresh morning tracks, and his mind clears. He bends down, points to the signs, and his father leans over to see. "There's a resident herd here," Zeb says. "We picked a good spot."

His father nods and follows his son.

They walk together into the woods, their feet sinking soundlessly into beds of soft greyish-blue fir needles. Just as the sun tips over the bony backed mountains, they duck into a copse of aspen trees. In that light, the gold leaves, like sharp dots of light in the lifting fog, turn bright enough to hurt Zeb's eyes.

Zeb sits with his back against the trunk of a tree. His father sits next to him, and *this is it,* Zeb thinks; *this* is the life. They talk now and again, neither one saying more than, "Hear that?" or "Deer are taking their time this morning." Time passes like time should pass—rich and quiet and all their own. It's cold, and the woods smell nutty and sweet and dusty, the way hunting-season woods always smell.

About noon, Zeb notices the tall leaves rustling in a particular way, not wind. His posture changes. His back straightens against the tree he's been leaning against, and he lowers his eyes. He listens. His father hands him the .30-06. Seconds later, seven does and one buck spill from the aspen, into the meadow. He can feel

his blood rushing through his ears like little rivers, and then the
sound pours over and out of him, and the woods throb all around
him, and he can't hear a damn thing except a *whoosh, whoosh,
whoosh* moving through him.

He offers the first shot to his father. "No. It's all you," his
father says.

"I'll teach you how to shoot," Zeb says.

His father shakes his head no, and Zeb knows this is his job
in the family. He is the only one who can shoot. He waits perfectly still for that magical moment when the deer stop grazing.
It happens every time. They suddenly sense him, and he sees
them sense him. They become as still as Zeb. Right then, Zeb
smoothly raises the rifle and shoots. The deer scatter like seeds
across the land, and the buck falls to his knees. Then to his neck.
Then to his side.

The click of the gun cocking, the blast, the sound of the buck
falling, and the crash of the rest of the herd taking off are all one
sound. Time layered, no sequence.

After the deer is dead, Zeb snaps back to this world. He feels
as if he's been gone, as if where he's been is not "better" than here,
but it's more real. His father helps him field dress the deer. They
leave the entrails there, steaming on the frozen earth.

"It's hard work pulling the deer back to camp," Zeb says.

"We could tie its legs to a thick branch and carry it upside
down," Zeb's father suggests.

"Dangerous," Zeb says. "When hunters see a deer moving,
some of them don't take time to see if its right-side up or upside
down."

"No kidding?" the father says.

Zeb laughs a little under his breath. His father seems so slow-
minded and innocent sometimes. That's what he thinks to himself.
He wonders if it comes with age, this slowness. He plans against
it right then and there. He vows to never let himself become like
his dad. He thinks about his mom now, wonders if his father were
smarter and stronger, if she could be healed. It pisses him off, the
thought of it, and he forces his mind back to the deer.

He considers making a travois to carry the carcass, but that would mean one man doing all the work. Instead, he cuts two thick branches from a tree, ties them to the buck's antlers, like handles. He hands one tied branch to his father, and the two men start walking together. Their breathing turns heavy and fast within minutes, and their layered clothes smother them. They keep on, working together. "Still don't like hunting?" he says to his father.

His father almost doesn't answer. He looks at Zeb as if he's silly for asking. Then he says, "It's your sport, Zeb. Not mine."

Zeb admires his father now. He hopes he would be like this if he ever has a son.

They've been pulling this deer together for a good fifteen minutes when they hear gunshots nearby. "Hey," Zeb calls out. "Got hunters here, not deer!" They both let go of the deer and crouch close to the ground.

The father follows Zeb's lead now. Zeb stays low, but tracks the sound and looks that direction. It's not just one shot, and then silence. It's one shot after the other, like target practice.

"Hunters target practice during hunting season?" the father asks.

"No," Zeb says, firmly, pissed off. He calls out again, "Hey! No deer here. Stop shooting!" Both men are still breathing heavily, the adrenalin rush of pulling the deer mixed with the situation they have now.

"Let's get out of here," the father says. Zeb can see that his father wants to leave for good. He wants to stop hunting altogether and regrets coming with Zeb. It pisses Zeb off, how moments can be stolen like that. He can see his father thinking of Willa and his mom back home. His father says, "Who knows what this guy's up to? Let's just move on out, Zeb."

"Exactly," Zeb says. "Who knows what this jerk is up to? It's not good hunting practice to move on without telling him." Zeb has it figured out now. It does not come to him like a memory. It's like an entire world drops down around him, and he is back at home suffocating with all the anger he feels there and the way he hates Chet and Johnny and the people around him who are not part of him, who do not help him or his mother or his family, when he knows they could. He remembers with his entire body why he led his father to this spot so close to Chet's cabin, and he adds things up in his head, the arrogance of Chet, the stupidity, the handgun, and Chet's idiotic target practice that he does in the field behind their house. He can barely hear his father's warnings now. He forgets about the deer and starts walking toward the shots. His father walks with him until they see a cabin in a clearing and a man standing alone, in front of the cabin.

"Chet," Zeb says.

"Look! Our neighbor!" his dad says, cheerfully. There's a happiness in his voice that Zeb cannot stand. He thinks his father is like Howdy-Doody, a man who thinks only the best of people, even when they have never deserved it. The father waves like a real pal. "Chet!" he calls out. But Chet can't hear him over the shots. That's when Zeb loads his rifle and fires a shot into the air.

Chet stops cold now. He stands in the clearing, turning in a circle, looking for the source of the gunfire. Zeb walks toward Chet, his rifle hanging at his side. "You fucking asshole, it's the middle of fucking *deer* season and you're fucking *target* practicing?"

"There's no need for that kind of language," says Zeb's dad, and Zeb is too angry to even laugh at that Howdy-Doody response. He looks behind him, sees his father waving at Chet, saying hello like a friendly neighbor.

Dolly comes running out of the house now. She's got her frilly apron on, and her hands are white with flour, and she's cooking Chet a fine meal, no doubt. She waves toward Zeb, smiles like she's greeting the president himself into her home. Chet hears her voice, turns around, and tells her to get back into the house. "I'm target practicing," he says. "You shouldn't be out here. It's dangerous."

"Oh, *now* it's dangerous," Zeb says. "Two seconds ago me and my dad were ducks in your fucking shooting gallery. But *now* it's dangerous. Good thing you couldn't hit a goddamn elephant two feet in front of you."

"Your boy's got a mouth on him," Chet says, to Zeb's dad.

"Better watch it, Chet. That's my son you're talking about." Zeb hears his father's voice like a cyclone rushing through his head.

"Better keep a leash on him," Chet says.

"Now, Chet," Dolly says, admonishing him while at the same time smiling at Zeb and his dad.

She doesn't have time to know what hits her when Chet turns on her, grabs her arms so tight that his fingers dig through her sweater and into her flesh. He pulls her close to his face and says through clenched teeth, "I said get back in the house."

"Get your fucking hands off her," Zeb says.

Zeb can see his father stepping aside now, half-stunned, still trying for the friendly smile, anger and confusion spilling out of him, and that's when Chet turns back to the two men. He lets go of Dolly and points the pearl-handled handgun at Zeb. Right then, Zeb sees his own father step toward Chet, asking Chet to stop, and Chet has the gun.

And then Dolly walks up to Chet and says, "Who are you kidding? Put that thing down. You look silly. That's the Robbinses, honey. That's our next door neighbors, Zeb and Hal Robbins," and she walks right between Chet and Zeb, no fear of the gun. She takes Zeb and Hal by the hand, saying, "Come on in. I've got coffee and cookies inside," and that's when Chet does his favorite trick. He grabs her by the hair, almost lifts her off her feet. When he lets go, he slams her to the ground, her bones crack, you can hear them, and Chet doesn't see that Zeb's up on him now too, doesn't see that Zeb is about to take that gun back from him, and his father is still back there trying to be a good neighbor, but Dolly is on all fours, blood streaming from her nose and hands. Zeb catches sight of the blood now, and he elbows Chet in the face, grabs the gun, and the stupid sonofabitch wrestles with Zeb. He knows Zeb already beat him, he *knows* it, but he keeps coming at Zeb and calling Dolly a bitch and saying he's going to teach Zeb a lesson, and that's when Zeb stops. He takes the handgun and presses it to Chet's head. He pulls the trigger.

* * *

IN THE AFTERMATH THERE'S just silence. Zeb can't hear anything now except his own breathing. He wants to kneel down, to beg forgiveness from Dolly, but Dolly seems a part of it all. Her eyes go wide and she looks scared, and it's like she has absorbed some of Zeb's guilt, his bad feeling. She is the first one to move. She bends down and holds Chet's bleeding head. Tears come. She holds her husband's lifeless body. "I'm sorry," Zeb starts saying, and then he can't stop saying it, and he realizes he's not saying it aloud anyway. It just plays over and over in his head. Then Dolly stands up. Tears slice her plump and reddened cheeks, and she starts walking in circles, then she beelines for Zeb. "Give me the gun."

Stunned, Zeb does what she says. She takes the gun and rubs it in the snow. She hands it to Zeb, places it right into his gloved hand. "Put it in Chet's right hand," she says.

"What?"

"Put the gun in Chet's hand." She commands him. She is suddenly stronger than all of them, and Zeb does what she says. He bends down and wraps his hand around Chet's hand. This is the hand that beat the dog, that beat Dolly, the hand that he has killed, and it makes him want to throw up. He stays stoic and strong, but in his gut he wants to puke. He knows what Dolly is doing. He doesn't know if she's protecting him, or if she's thinking about how many years she's been beaten. It doesn't matter. Zeb wraps his own hand around Chet's and let's go of the gun.

"He's been shooting that gun all day," Dolly says. "No one will know, Zeb. Know one will know. Now leave," Dolly says. "Get out. Both of you."

Zeb and his father stand motionless. Then Zeb grabs his father's shirt sleeve. "We need to help her," he says. "We need to help Chet."

Dolly steps up close to him. Her entire body shakes, and she seems bigger than Zeb can remember her being. "Go. Now," she says in a whisper that is so strong and threatening that both men move away from her, Zeb leading the way.

A few minutes later, Zeb hears footsteps. He does not have the gun and Dolly does, and he hears footsteps and he turns. She is behind him and his knees weaken. She comes at him strong and she is sobbing now. She hugs him. She squeezes his whole body tight and presses her sobbing face into his chest. Then she backs up, pushes him away, and walks back toward Chet's body.

"Son," Zeb hears his father say, but it's like a dead hum that goes nowhere in him. "Son!"

Zeb keeps walking. By the time they get back to the deer, the father has quit calling to Zeb. Zeb knows he has to leave his home now. He knows this is the last time he will hunt with his father, that this is the last time he will have Thanksgiving with his family, that if he sees his Mom and sister again, it will be the last time he sees them. The deer is heavier now, even though it is hollowed out. It feels weighty and full of guts and heart and blood and bile, even though it has been relieved of all those things. He looks back at it as they walk. Zeb and his father carry the deer through the woods, back to camp.

two

Wolves

U NDER THE CIRCUMSTANCES, no pack was stable. Pack
members disappeared sometimes like vapor in the desert,
like the dust devils that started up and turned to ghosts in the
same in-out breath of the land. Sometimes new pups were introduced and accepted into a pack. Centuries of tradition in their
clans had been fractured. They would change, adapt, or they
would die off forever.

There was something about the word *forever* that they could taste.
They could smell it in the smoke trailing from the fireplaces of new
suburban homes built at the edges of the wild, in the star-hazed sky
that turned cold sooner than it had in centuries past, the winds that
shredded the same lands they once caressed, the earth itself frayed at
the edges, pulsing like a wound, and fighting to survive all the same.
They could taste it in the bony meat of a dozen scrawny rabbits and
the fading memory of the heft of a single elk, in the scraps of the elk
kill they had traditionally left for scavengers. It was in their nature
to feed what remained around them, what depended on them, the
same things they depended on.

In this climate, within these confines, only the alpha female
and the alpha male would mate, and there was room, on this

slender ground, for only one of each. Their survival depended
on scarcity and proliferation, simultaneously. Every pup must be
strong. They killed to eat, and in that act, encouraged life in their
habitat to flourish, a paradox like proliferation and scarcity held in
one human fist.

With their loping canine gaits they feigned ease, even arrogance, as they crossed the earth, all four paws leaving the ground
for an instant with every stride. But within that split-second sus-
pension lay the solid desire to return to earth, the dirt beneath
their feet, the ground that gives rise to all life. They followed
the deer and elk, kept the animals on the move, which let the
land beneath the hooves of their prey replenish as they all moved
together with what fed them, a relationship of understanding, a
simpatico of survival.

Mornings, Ciela and Hector would rise from the horizon like
smoke coming up over a desert ridge, you could see them, their
doglike heads familiar, almost human in their gaze, their awareness. They had this working for them and against them: their doglike appearance to humans, half-familiar, wholly wild. They were
the essence of evil on the one hand, and on the other, the only
animal humans saw as able to take in and raise children, the myth
of the wolf-child. Their coats were tufted here and there, clumps
of grey fur making them look scrappy, lean at the haunches, bony
and almost hunched at the shoulders like silhouettes of the buffalo
that once grazed the land with the elk, the shadows of everything
that had come before cast over them now. Their evolution had
narrowed the set of their eyes even closer together, their line of
sight designed for the tunnel vision of predators, not the wide,
two-sided eyes of prey, the softened gaze that can see the world
as two wholes coming together at the center. Like humans, the
wolves had the eyes of hunters, set forward in their heads, with
only a slight sense of periphery.

Ciela and Hector swung their heads low as they loped, the
pack following the two of them, their gaits becoming one, a
weave of long, scrawny legs looping the horizon like threads that
entwine and connect, their very presence blanketing the land.

Ciela had been with this pack since birth, born in the wild, and she took over the place of the alpha female when the former lead female was poached. Hector had come from the Sipapu pack into the West Canyon pack a few months later. He easily fought off the old alpha male who now stayed on the periphery of the pack, alone, and by doing so, Hector kept the Sipapu pack from invading the territory of the West Canyon wolves. If there had been more territory, the invasion would have gone on without question. But knowledge came to them through their noses, and they could smell devastation, and they could smell their own land curling up and pulling in at the edges, shrinking even as the rest of the world expanded. They knew without naming that resources were limited. They sensed things and lived within their means.

But they had no sense of imposed boundaries. For years they had been shot and killed if they crossed over an arbitrary line that cast them outside the Días de Ojos National Forest. Their home territory, historically, was huge, covered most of the North American southwest, and with their instincts they could read land like a story, the earth itself reciting a narrative over and over again, one of survival and balance—and now, of warning.

These days the elk had grown slow. They stood with a lazy confidence that eroded their wildness, grazing for months in one meadow or copse before moving on. Without large predators to keep their senses piqued, their animal minds had grown sluggish, cattle-like. They lived on the seam of domesticity. Human hunters would come once a season and take the strongest of the herd, and through this kind of unnatural selection, their overall stature had diminished. Smaller elk remained to mate when the leaders were taken.

But the wolves were constant, like weather, and they took the weakest, leaving the strong to proliferate. It would balance out, said the narrative of the earth. It would find its middle ground.

The wolves were constant. That is, until they weren't. Until the families they'd chosen and formed and fought for and loved grew fragmented and estranged, the fabric of them fraying from the outside, in. Ciela and Hector couldn't succumb to that kind

of imposed loss. Ciela and Hector had led their pack into a new
territory, outside the bounds of the one provided for them. They
had slipped unseen and unmonitored past Días de Ojos National
Forest boundaries. They had found a way to survive.

Willa

TO GO BACK TO the place I was born. Time had never drained
it from memory. The black highway I'd traveled to get here was
the tangled umbilical cord I'd tried to sever decades ago. They say
there are no geographical borders drawn on a place itself, that the
buildings and landmarks are the only things that make it readable.
But I could have traveled a buildingless landscape and still found
my way here. It was the feel of the place beneath it all, the way the
grit of this terrain grasped my gut.

I pulled off the highway, and I saw a Dairy Queen where
Mom's childhood home used to be, a Taco Bell in the exact place
where Zeb and I used to fish. I parked the car, walked in, and
ordered my ninety-nine-cent burrito. I could feel every story this
land had ever told, the most vivid memories rising up like night-
dreams, the way those kinds of images never really found their
way to words. They haunted around inside you like spirits looking
for form. But no words could embody them.

I trashed the rest of my burrito and walked out to my truck.
I sat for some time before I turned the key in the ignition. The
house I grew up in was a block away. My father had remained all
these years, though he had not spoken to me and would not return my calls. By all accounts, he'd stopped talking to everyone.
Still, I drove the block to see the house where I'd grown up. Chet
and Dolly's rose bushes were still there. Every house had a green
lawn now. Still, the houses looked even smaller than they did back
then, more rundown. The whole neighborhood looked as if it had
always been an afterthought, a quiet violence seething beneath it.

I pressed the gas pedal and drove away. At the stoplight
in front of Johnny's, I pulled to the side of the road. I felt a

desperate longing for Magda and Cario, for my home with them on the mesa where I lived now. I picked up the phone and dialed Magda. No answer. A lump ached in my throat. I fumbled with my phone, flipped it open, then closed it, then opened it again and checked for messages. None. This time not even Christina had called. It felt like a small stroke of genius to me when I remembered I could call Raymond. Raymond always answered his phone.

"Hey, I was just about to call you," he said when he answered, and the connection felt like a lifeline. "Taking the day off work tomorrow. I'll be visiting our wolves bright and early."

"Good, good. Thank you."

"Not doing it for you, my friend. All due respect. I'm doing it for our wolves."

He made me smile. "Those wolves haven't killed livestock, you know. I mean, not by habit. They hunt."

"Hey, is the sky blue?"

"What?"

"While you're telling me things I already know, I thought you might answer that."

I laughed a little and so did Raymond. "Just make sure Andy knows those wolves are good wolves."

"Andy," he scoffed.

"Well, he's the only one who can protect them."

"Oh, that's right. He's the man to trust the wolves' lives to. He's the head of the agency that's rehabbing them. Same agency that's killed more than half of the same wolves they paid to rehab and re-release. Good system your people have there."

"Is the sky blue, Raymond?"

He laughed. "Just sayin. Anyway, I'm on my way right now. Like I said, they'd have to step over me to get to those two wolves and their pack. You know that."

I could hear him walking to his truck, the outside air crackling through a bad cell phone connection. His voice was all static, and I heard him saying, "Hello, you there? Can you hear me?"

and then the line went dead. It felt like being dropped from great heights. I was alone again.

I sat in the truck, remembering what I had wanted to say to Raymond, a thing I had never told anyone.

Three years after Zeb left home, with no medication to soothe Mom's pain and Dad working three jobs to try to make life better for all of us, I helped Mom, like she had asked. I was there with her to the end, when the last sky she ever saw was the last sky she would ever see; when her breath turned quiet. I did not want to let her go. I wanted to hold her face in my palms and pull her close to me and tell her I never, ever, ever wanted it to end. But she asked me and I said yes and I helped her; I honored her choice. I gave her the pills she had asked for because she could not hold them in her hands, and she could not drink water without my help, and I sat with her and waited and held her hand as the life went out of her.

My father knew. It was something he figured out on his own. He covered for me like he had covered for Zeb. But he never forgave me. In the final years when I lived with him, he talked less and less to me. By the time I left home on a college scholarship, he had pretty much quit talking altogether.

I wanted to tell him I did not understand what I was doing at the time. It was a thing I wanted to take back as soon as I had done it, another act I didn't see the whole of until it was over and the permanence of it came clear. It never faded. It just kept playing clearer and more vividly through my mind across the years, something permanent in the face of everything else that was not permanent.

I wanted to tell Raymond that. I wanted my own confession.

Brenda

BRENDA STOOD IN THE gravel lot, wind kicking up grit from the ground and blasting her eyes that were turning pink along their tender edges now. Peterbilts and Macks rumbled, idling, checking in from the road, rolling out. She looked up at that asshole

Mike, six-feet-plus and every jean-flannel-clad inch of him made of pure sonofabitch. "You got me or you got nothing, Mike. Zeb is not available," she said.

"You telling me you're driving his rig? You got a license?"

She handed him Zeb's papers with his name whited-out and filled in with her own, and a delaminated driver's license with her photo jimmied into it to make her look legal sitting in the cab of a sixteen-wheeler.

Mike studied the paper and the license. And then he smiled, his deeply pocked, ruddy face creasing around the mouth. "Not bad, not bad." He handed the documents back to her, nodding his head and patting her on the back like an old friend. "All right, fine. Let's see what we got for you, Bren."

Mike walked inside the building and came back out with a set of keys, handed them to Brenda. They walked together across the lot. "Look, I don't know what's going on, but if Zeb wants to let his woman do his work for him, it's fine by me."

"You gotta make the check out to me, though, Mike." Brenda could feel herself shrinking in his presence, something she had not felt for years, something that ate at her.

"Check?"

"Look, Mike, I'm filling in for Zeb. He's not around and I gotta get paid, you understand. I need Zeb's check. I need to get by."

Mike waved his hand like he was blocking the grit from the wind. "I'm not saying I won't pay you. I'm a man of honor. I'm just saying I'll pay you the same way I paid when I fucked you. When we all fucked you." He swept his arm over the whole lot. "Whatever's in my pocket when you get back, that's yours."

She gripped the keys so tight the jagged edges nearly split her skin.

"You know I'm good for it, Bren. There's never less than a big, fat hun-dun sitting right here in my jeans." He patted himself just to the right of his bulging zipper. "Take it, or leave it, sweetheart."

The shiny toes of his cowboy boots stood directly across from her tattered work boots. She could feel the hate for him grinding in her jaw, and she wanted to be drunk. But she wouldn't drink.

Not today, not tonight. Not tomorrow. She looked at him square. "What am I driving?" she said.

He chuckled. "Yeah, just as I thought. You'll take whatever you can get." Then amused, and half to himself, "Once a whore, always a whore." He patted her on the back again. "Okay, well, you're taking the same route Zeb had, up to Boulder, out to California, back through Arizona, driving the meat wagon."

"That's shit, Mike. Zeb didn't drive no goddamn meat wagon."

"Welp, Brenda, the route we got open today is a meat wagon. That's it. You drive the dead head up to Boulder, visit most of the plastic surgeons up there, fill the trailer up with body parts, few other stops in between before you drop them body parts off at the bio hazmat dump in Arizona, then head out to shaky town, drive all around Hollywood picking up more body parts, and you drive all that body fat right back to that toxic dump—you know it. It's right around your own homeland there, your Indian reservation. Then you come back, check in, and make the circle all over again." Mike was getting a big kick out of himself right about now. "Who knows? You could be hauling some movie star's lipo-ed hips, some rock star's nose. It's a good gig, Brenda, a glamorous gig." Self satisfied, he took off across the lot.

"Fuck you, Mike," her words a whisper as she climbed into the cab. And then louder. "Fuck you, Mike."

He turned. "Say what?"

"This is a goddamned twin stick."

"Most guys'd kill to drive that vintage beauty. Zeb's rig. One he drove most often."

"Zeb's been driving a single stick for years."

Mike shrugged, and she knew she'd get nothing out of him except sheer satisfaction if she complained for one more second. So she shut up, walked around the truck, checked the lights, the tires, the brakes, the radio, then hopped in and turned the key. The rig shook like a small earthquake when it started up, and with all the shaking already going on inside her body, she thought she might be sick to her stomach. She held her gut tight, swallowed hard, and jammed the main stick into what she thought was reverse. She checked all three mirrors, let the clutch out, and the rig leapt forward a few feet before she could slam the clutch, hit neutral, and try again.

She could see Mike standing in the lot, his back arched, his head tossed back, gut jiggling with laughter, and she was glad her windows were rolled up tight so he was rendered a flat-screened, silent movie. Fuck him. She'd driven with Zeb before. He'd taught her how to drive, and she had taken the wheel for him more than once. That was back when they were younger, when being on the road meant being so pumped full of white cross speed that they came in fast on almost every trip, too early to log in, and so why not take some time for some fun on their own? So what if they were a little more tight-skinned back then and hard times slid off them like oil off rubber? She had it in her still. She knew how to work hard and have fun doing it. She knew how to drive.

She slid the clutch in—the only time she would have to use the clutch till she stopped again—and the gears ground, then finally engaged. As she backed up, the curved mirrors turned Mike small and contorted, like a circus clown, something that pleased her more than anything on that goddamned day. He was still laughing as she drove past him, and she had a hard time not turning the wheel toward him and watching him flatten into a cartoon cutout beneath the ton of metal she was driving. He blew her a kiss as she passed. She blew him one too, straight off her middle finger.

*   *   *

BRENDA FELT THE FIBERS of every muscle in her body frayed. An electrical quiver ran just beneath the surface of her skin. She'd made it safely up to Boulder, picked up several Tupperware like tubs full of human waste, and now she was heading back through Denver, then south, toward the state line. She dialed her cell with one hand, double-checked with Tommy, the kid down the mountain she had hired before she left, making sure he'd take good care of the animals. "There's pay in it for you if you do a good job," she said, and he promised, and she trusted him. He said he didn't need any pay for doing what he loved to do. He was Frank's son, after all, and Frank was one of Zeb's long-time friends. "We're looking after him," Tommy told her. He didn't know too much more than that. But "We got his back," Tommy said. It was something Brenda needed to hear to allow her to keep going. That no matter what they had Zeb on this time, someone was looking out for him. She held back her desire to turn around and head home, just to see Zeb again. But it was the least she could do for him, to take over some responsibility now, to keep on. The night pressed black against the wide windshield of the truck now, and the silence collected her thoughts.

"Son of a woolly bitch, what a day," she said in a whistled voice. It was a curse at Mike and the cops who had invaded her cabin, and it was a longing for Zeb all in the same breath. She remembered the way Mike had come at her, over and over, back in the days when she turned tricks on the lot for cash, and though she'd never liked him, never once put her lips close to his, she'd done her job, and that was that.

But Zeb was different. The first time she saw him at the truck stop, she was standing with her back pressed against the office window, the work of the day and the heat of a midsummer night wilting her. She was looking the other way, not pressing a trick, when she felt his leather-gloved finger tap her shoulder. "Hey, Miss," his voice low and calm.

"Not working tonight," she said, not looking at him.

And he squinted to look at her, moving in closer for a second. Then he pulled away and leaned his back against the window with her, standing side by side. "Hot night," he said. He took his driving gloves off, slapped them against his knee, then folded them and stuffed them into his back pocket. She didn't move, didn't have anything to say to him, and they both stood for some time in that silence before he said, "Been a long time."

It was a line she'd heard a thousand times before. She'd heard every line. She didn't turn. Something familiar in his voice strummed her memory, but there was no trusting memory. To her, it was just a story the mind started telling at its most desperate times, wishing for a soft place to land, a quick and easy comfort.

He stood there a good while longer, till his presence began to itch at her and she started to move away, and he said, "Never thought we'd see you again, me or Willa."

She was pushing thirty by then, her days with Willa so far behind her they seemed ghosted, mere figments. But when he spoke, she could hear something real behind his voice, and in it, she heard the memory of Willa's voice calling out in Mother-May-I and hide-'n'-seek. When Zeb spoke, she remembered the evening settling over the field on a hot summer night just like this one, but full of innocence and hope, and the memory of those two things weakened her, and she stopped walking away from him. "Zeb?" she said, and she saw him, and her question turned into certainty. She looked at his adult face, his smooth, tanned cheekbones lit by the dim light coming from inside the office, the other half of his face shadowed.

He took her home with him that night, no romance between them in the beginning. They both knew how their lives had fractured long ago. It wasn't a nostalgia of place and time, really, as much as it was a recollection of something that had belonged to them. It was fragile and at the same time, indelible. There was no way to put a finger on what they had lost back then, no way to tell what, if anything, had belonged to them to begin with.

They sat in Zeb's cabin that night, drinking Jack Daniels straight, and that simultaneous fear and attraction she'd had around Zeb when she was a kid turned to comfort now, a deep familiarity. She'd had her own transgressions by then, had seen the ragged edges of life, had no time for the smoothed-out bullshit of too much privilege and ease. Zeb knew her. They shared something she could not share with anyone else.

Come time for sleep that night, Zeb curled up on the couch in a sleeping bag, gave the bed to her. It wasn't until then that he said,

"She missed you, you know. A lot. Wherever she is right now, my guess is, Willa still misses you."

"You haven't seen her, either?"

He shook his head. "Not since the day I left." There was a thinness in his voice. They slept separately that night.

.   .   .

SHE'D MAPPED OUT HER route: She would cut the top off of New Mexico, then wind her way into southern California through Arizona, rehearsing the same route she'd have to take on her return. That was the plan she'd made. But there was so much going on in her head that she drove half-dazed. She didn't follow the highway signs correctly, and the shitty GPS Mike had tossed into the truck called out, "lost satellites" in a fucking computer robot voice every time she turned it on. With the holy bullshit of the last few days barreling through her throbbing head and no alcohol to numb it, her limbs were shaking, and her life was coming at her vivid and strong, the presence of it, the past of it. By the time she gathered her wits again, she realized she'd followed some off-trail scent she knew too well to forget, though forgetting is exactly what she'd wanted. She had sniffed her way by habit to a place that was unfamiliar, but at the same time felt like home. She shifted the main stick, then the second stick, gears grinding, the cab trembling, the constant tremor of it all like a hand of some god shaking her to remind her that what was happening now was real. The tires rumbled on the dirt road, lurching with every shift, the truck moving huge as a dinosaur on what she finally knew was the reservation road that led to her father's house.

Well, she was there now. And though she hadn't really intended to be there, because she hadn't intended much in her life up to that point, she made the decision to carry on with it. The decision felt good. She drove to Raymond's place.

There it was. The place she'd dreamed of when she was a kid. The place she had found, and then left. She killed the engine. It lurched and grumbled once, then sighed. Then silence. She dimmed her lights. The hounds around the place started a clamor so loud that the noise blurred to nothing in her mind—just blended with the howl that had been screaming through her own head the past few days. A couple of hounds ran at the truck, their long legs unfolding like the legs of giraffes as they ran, then backed off, frightened by the size of the vehicle.

The slats of the house were so loosely bound that light shone through them—sunlight creeping in during the daytime and lamp-light leaking out at night. In this darkness, those cracks made the whole house glow, a square of jagged brightness in the midst of the dark desert. She remembered Raymond, the father she'd dreamed of being with before she met him, the one she'd idolized so much from a distance. When she finally met him, she could not tolerate any contradictions in him. If he was not all good, he was all bad. And when she learned that he had done some things he was not proud of, some things that had gone against everything he believed, she could not comprehend it. It was the reason she'd left Raymond's place and set out on her own when she was eighteen. It was a child's mistake she knew now, but too many years had engrained it and set her decision in stone. She remembered Raymond's stature now, his huge bear hugs, and she missed him. She stared at the tiny hut unable to fathom how a man of Raymond's size could live there, how he even squeezed through the bright turquoise doorway. It was right about then that she saw the shape of him, his blue jeans and silver belt buckle clearly lit by the lamp inside the house as he passed by the window. A few seconds later, the door opened, and he stood there, on the threshold, looking out. With the flimsy wood door flapped open behind him, no screen, he lifted his huge hand and waved to her.

Did he actually see her? Could he recognize her from where he stood? Or was he just waving, Raymond being who Raymond was, helpful to any traveler, a wicked smart ass, but a good willed man to the core. Her father. He waved. And it was reflex. She turned the key, tripped the clutch, and floored the pedal. The truck lunged in huge hiccups away from the place, a dinosaur lumbering down the road. She felt the strain of it, her whole body aching and relieved as she drove away.

The trailer of the truck snaked behind her cab. She drank coffee, praying for some mental focus, some emotional calm. She wanted to do this job well, to give Mike no reason to keep her paycheck. She hadn't intended to get off track so early on, and she needed to make time now. Her mistake made her body ache for a drink, and she was glad she was on the reservation without any booze for sale for miles. Knowing she could not have a drink gave her the shakes, and she knew it was right, even though she gritted her teeth against it.

Somewhere down the road, breathing hard and still not catching her breath, she caught sight of something that calmed her: the graceful figures of two coyotes loping across the desert. She looked closer, remembered seeing coyotes with her father long ago, something beautiful to watch, the way they loped in a straight line, like wild animals almost always do, knowing their way, their purpose. She watched them run, and as they stepped near to the shoulder of the road, she realized her lights were still dimmed from when she'd pulled up to Raymond's, and she moved to turn them brighter, and the first coyote stepped into the road, and she lifted her foot from the pedal, slammed it toward the brake, hoping she was fast enough. She swerved and felt the heft of the trailer rock behind her, and she wrestled with the wheel to steer clear of that soft, narrow shoulder, and she felt a few seconds of confidence when she righted the truck. She stopped, took a few seconds to breathe. After that, she set off steady down the road again. She glanced in the rearview mirror and saw the silhouette of one four-legged figure make its way across the road. She hoped the other animal would follow. She waited, keeping an eye on the rearview mirror. There was nothing.

With time already lost to her senseless detour that took her to Raymond's, she pressed the pedal even harder now, kept the truck roaring forward, focused on what lay ahead. But her eyes kept drifting up to that rearview mirror long after she'd seen the coyotes. The thought of them crossing the desert alone, and of her crossing the same land, too, and the way their paths had intersected—it hovered in her mind. She knew she had seen one coyote make it to safety. She was sure of that. But the other coyote? She wasn't sure.

It gnawed at her like every single other goddamn thing gnawed at her, every little mistake and every bad decision, but she had no booze to drown out her conscience now and so *fuck it*, she was going to do the right thing, right now, which meant doing the wrong thing as far as Mike was concerned, but *fuck him, too*. She hit the brakes and took the next left onto a dirt road. She maneuvered the rig with what turned out to be about a twelve point U-turn that took up the whole road and the trailer rocked when it hit the soft sand, but she stuck with it. She turned that goddamn rig around and headed back down the road. She would check. That's all. Just five minutes more off schedule. She would check.

She saw her own skid marks in the stretch of her headlights and pulled to the side of the road. Already the sun was beginning to rise and the new light outlined the sandstone monoliths, and she scrambled her way up a small embankment, the scurry of lizards scraping the sand now and again, the hollow calls of sunrise birds sketching their song into the morning sky. She was out of shape, and by the time she crested the small hill, she was out of breath. The leftover night still shadowed the land, and it looked as if the heap of an animal slept at the base of every sandstone pillar. But those were just illusions, made more real by the tangible form she saw to her right. It was straggled and awkwardly laid out, not heaped neatly at the base of the monolith. She took a deep breath. She walked toward it.

It was like glimpsing a sliver of her past, the time she'd spent with her blood-father. She had helped Raymond reintroduce animals to the wild, one way to heal the land he loved so much. She didn't second-guess herself now. She knew what she was looking at, what her truck had struck. And she knew it was no coyote. It was a wolf, the only wolf indigenous to this territory,

the most endangered mammal in North America. She played
the instant back over in her head. She thought she had braked
before she crossed paths with the two wolves. Her rig had come
to a complete stop by the time she saw the first wolf cross to
safety.

But even the slightest graze by a truck like the one she was
driving could do it. And now, the wolf was here, seemingly lifeless, and it had been her doing. There had been no other car on the
road between now and then, and the animal she was looking at
had not been lying there motionless very long. She had helped her
father rehabilitate these wolves when she was younger. She had
left the reservation when she was younger because she'd heard bad
rumors of her father betraying these wolves, and it was something
she couldn't stand. Now, she may have helped kill off one of the
few remaining in the wild.

This new thing she was feeling was more addicting than most
anything she had tried before—and she'd had her share of so-
called addictions (though she preferred to call them *tools*). But this
was more addicting than anything, this new exhilaration of doing
the right thing. There was no room for fear or self-blame and pity
anymore, not in this situation. And it was liberating. Her own
weaknesses didn't matter. She had to go back. She had to knock
on Raymond's door, tell him she was the one who'd woken him
in the middle of the night. And she had to tell him she was the
one who had hit this wolf. The rumors she'd heard didn't matter
now. If there was anything to be done about this injured wolf, he
would know.

She walked back, turned the key in the ignition, and ignored the gentle rumble of the truck. She headed back toward
Raymond's.

Raymond

BRIGHT MORNING, THE KIND that made Raymond want to put
on his oldest cowboy boots, ones with the hole in the right toe

and the heels worn down so far they made his too-skinny legs
bend outward like a hunting bow strung taut. The wear of those
heels pitched his posture back a little like he was always walking uphill, kept him moving slow and steady, the way he liked.
He could smell the crisp desert sky before he even opened the
front door and stepped out, red dirt welcoming him to the day,
sandstone rocks looming like gods on the horizon, no hand-built
Stonehenge here, the whole landscape carved by weather, nothing
holier, something he prayed to daily without saying a goddamn
word. The crooked heels of his boots sunk into the sandy earth,
and he walked out to the road. He'd never seen a semi truck on
this scrawny strip of tar before, was surprised the width of the road
even held the rig. Red sand crawled up from the soft shoulder so
far you could only see a few feet of black asphalt underneath it.
What the hell? he thought. What the hell was that hulking thing
doing parked outside his place, and why did it take off just as soon
as he came out to greet it? That unfriendly scoundrel was sure as
hell not a skin.

He shook his head. Strange things happening on this land.
Strange spirits rising up, or maybe it was some friendly State
land manager making sure Raymond was behaving himself and
not bringing in what they called "foreign wildlife." Or maybe
it was some other law official making sure he was not protecting
existing wildlife that was not supposed to be protected, according to their bullshit rules of what got saved and what got shot.
Raymond himself had been known to shoot over the heads of
the shitfools who brought packs of greyhounds out to the desert just outside the Navajo border, to hunt coyotes for sport, for
instance. The shitfools set their dogs loose, and when the hunt
was over, they took the coyote carcasses home for trophies and
left their own injured hounds out in the heat of the desert to
die. This is how he'd ended up with six of them pointy-nosed
racing dogs, and the truth was, he did not shoot *that* far over the
shitfools' heads.

"It's not your business to keep those coyote hunters off that
land," the officials had told him. And he'd told them that land

was not a *business* at all, that was their first mistake, and he would kindly show them exactly *how* he'd aimed his gun very close to the fuckers' heads if they wanted to test his patience much longer. But sending a semi out to check on him was a new trick, stupid even for them, nothing stealth or sly about a semi rumbling by your door at midnight.

He scratched his head, then slicked down what was left of the grey-black strands on his scalp. He hooked one arm back inside the house, reaching for his cowboy hat, closed the door, and then headed out. His hat touched the ceiling of his Chevy mini-truck as he drove, a feeling he'd come to like, the height and bulk of himself hunched in that little cab. He was a ship in a bottle, he joked; no one could figure out how he got in that mini-Chevy or how he could get himself out. The local radio station played a mix of traditional Indian music and singing, some political talk, grassroots activists rallying the community, American country music, gospel, rap, reggae, Jesus-talk from preachers, and drumming, the same mix that had been jumbled around inside his head since he was born; it made him smile. Commercial-free, his station was, but all the same the sponsors came on in between just to inform the listeners that the coffee was good and the breakfast burritos were cheaper than usual at Maria's burrito wagon this morning. He appreciated that kind of information.

That morning, he'd taken the day off to keep his promise to Willa. He had it planned. He would head down south to the land, track the wolves, and see what they'd been up to since he'd last tracked them. He thought of stopping by the store to make sure Simon was feeling okay about working there alone on such short notice. But on second thought, he knew Simon would be okay. He'd told Simon all along that the only thing most tourists who visited wanted was to have a look at a real Indian so they could go back home and speak of Indians and "Indian spirituality" in an enlightened and accepting way. "Don't worry about it, Simon. Just ring the customers up and give them change," he'd said, when he called in sick for the day.

Simon had complained, but it didn't matter. Raymond was not heading into the store today. He had made a promise to Willa, and he was keeping it. And right now he had a narrow open road stretched out before him, and some cold brews sitting in the Coleman cooler waiting for him in the back of the truck, and there was nothing like an extra-hot autumn day in the high desert, the last days of summer perched on the promise of winter—*nothing* like a day like that to make a man feel like he just might live forever.

He took off his hat, used a paisley blue bandana to swab the sweat from his crown, put the hat back on, and hunched his shoulders, both arms draped over the steering wheel. A few minutes later, though, he straightened his posture and squinted. A heat wave already turned the morning air fuzzy in his sight, and it blurred the semi truck moving toward him, made it seem almost like it was crossing the middle line, coming right at him. He swerved a little, swearing at the crazy sonofabitch, looking back over his shoulder and trying to make sense of it all. But he kept on driving.

It was not far after that when he saw a set of black skid marks on the road. Skid marks weren't rare in these parts. Enough Indians raced these streets at night to engrave the entire stretch with streaks of rubber crisscrossing like braids. But these weren't the tread marks of bald-tires on low-riding Impalas, or the skittering imprints of decades-old trucks that had seen better days. These treads were thick and heavy, doubled up like the footprint of at least a twelve- maybe a sixteen-wheeler. This was the goddamn spore of his crazy late-night visitor, and according to the sign it left behind, it had been traveling the other direction. Now that same sonofabitch had turned around and was making his way back toward Raymond's house.

That was it. Raymond swung his truck around in a quick U-ey. Far as he could see, that crazy fuck was just two steps away from being escorted off the reservation in a proper manner. It was curiosity more than anger that had snagged him, but either way, that driver was not getting away without a formal introduction to Raymond, so to speak. But as he made the turn, his tire caught on the sandy shoulder, and he spun out just long enough to catch sight of something indistinct, but out of place, just up the small, sandy hill. He stopped, looked closer. He knew right away he was letting that driver get out of sight. And it irked him. But he'd seen something out of place, and to a tracker, something out of place was an irresistible mystery that had to be solved. He stepped out of his truck.

Heat seared through his thin cotton T-shirt, prickling his back. He felt the morning sun scorching his neck and arms already. He opened his canteen, poured ice water onto his bandana, and wrapped it around his neck. His leg muscles thickened as he climbed the short but sandy incline into the sage and cactus.

What he saw next thumped him like lightning, made any thought of that driver leave his mind and left his chest hesitant about breathing, unsure the next breath was his right.

He saw sign first, just sign: small tufts of grey fur clumped together at the base, the memory of skin still holding that hair together, coarse at the tip, downy soft underneath, dozens of clumps caught on the tips of sage and cactus plants, fluttering across the desert like butterflies might in more hospitable land. This was the distinct fur of a Mexican wolf. He crouched lower, but kept walking steadily forward.

Then he saw the heap of her curled up next to a tall spire. "No…" His voice a harsh whisper. "Holy Jesus, please, no," higher now, strained into disbelief. He walked closer, then knelt by the wolf's side, the empty morning quiet enough that he thought he imagined the sound of her breathing, a soft in-and-out, like the sigh of the land itself.

Life turns to nothing fast in the desert. Heaps of muscle wither tight around skeletons overnight, skin ripped and shredded to striations of red muscle by scavengers, picked to the bone by the beaks of corvids, the teeth of coyotes. The wolf hadn't gone that far yet. But he feared he was witnessing the beginnings of it: her return to the earth. He looked at her, then took a chance and rested his hand on her side.

Usually, he was one of those guys who believes hope is the greatest form of pessimism. To him hope was just the sad inability to see and appreciate what's right in front of your face in the moment and move forward positively from there. But goddamn if he wasn't filled with hope when he touched her, and goddamn if his hand, resting on her chest, was not rising up and sinking down in a rhythm that felt like breathing. Stressed breathing. Fast breathing. But still, this wolf was taking in air. This wolf was alive. Respectful as he was of the damage that a wolf could do to him if she decided to wake now, he crawled closer to her, looking for signs of how and where she'd been hurt. He saw the scrawniness of the back leg that had been injured long ago, her identifying mark. He let himself recognize her now. "Ciela," he said, the name tumbling from his mouth, gentle as touch.

He walked back to his truck, turned the engine, and drove that rickety thing onto the sand, up the short hillside as far as the vehicle would travel, several feet from where Ciela lay. Humming a prayer as he got out, he grabbed a heavy tarp from the bed of the truck.

By the time he returned to her, Ciela was still dazed, still motionless. Still, as he approached, she let out a low siren growl, a haunting whine, sensing his presence. Yes. This wolf was alive. And this wolf was pissed. Now, if he touched her, she would attack, a reflex of survival. He knew that, and he knew the attack would be weakened by her condition. But still. Years back, he'd have had tools in his truck, something that could calm Ciela long enough to get her to a safer place. But he'd been stopped by cops too many times, frisked and relieved of his "wildlife importation tools." He couldn't afford to replace them time and again, and now he had nothing. Except an injured wolf and the need to get her to safety. He ran through the years of training he'd received from Andy and the folks at WWA back when they were on speaking terms. He had taught them a few things he knew about handling wildlife, and they had taught him what they knew, too. Handling a wolf under the best of circumstances was risky. But the best of circumstances rarely existed in the wild. Ideally, this type of situation required tranquilizers and a team of people. But he was fighting time and struggling with the fact that Ciela already had a death note on her head. For Halvorson and the WWA, this injury could be just the reason to let nature take its course with her—one less wolf and no one to blame. He knew what he was up against, knew the risks, and made the decision anyway.

He walked around toward Ciela's hind flanks. Mexican wolves are smaller than their Yellowstone cousins, and Ciela was slight, even for a female—just over sixty pounds. Raymond weighed in at two-hundred-plus, and right about now he felt every one of those pounds quaking from fear. No matter. The task had to be done. In a slow but certain motion, he lowered the heavy tarp over her body, and when she turned her head to attack, as he knew she would, he leaned his weight in and held steady. He lowered his body firmly but calmly over hers, tightening the tarp over her eyes, muzzle, and head. His breath stuttering with fear, he shimmied his arms underneath her body, felt the sand scraping the skin on the backs of his hands and forearms, and he lifted and loaded Ciela into the bed of his pickup. He prayed two things simultaneously, each one cancelling the other out: He prayed Ciela would come out of her stunned daze and rise up out of the bed of his truck and become a shadow disappearing into the desert again. And he prayed she would stay right where she was, too, that she'd let him take her home, examine her, see if there was some way he could prolong her chances of survival. He knew from his falconing days that a wild hawk that spent even a short part of its life in the human world would usually live twice as long as a hawk that had never been caught and released again. Unnatural as it seemed, sometimes human intervention *did* help. He wanted to give Ciela that chance. She was injured now, and he wanted to go against nature this time, to reverse what had happened. He wanted to give her the chance to heal.

With one hand on the wheel, one arm reaching back through that little window between the cab and the bed of the truck, he held tight to the gathered end of the tarp. He cursed and prayed, settled on praying for a bit, then went back to cursing because what the hell was that semi truck doing there in the first place, and who had sent it out driving on this godforsaken road? He drove the highway back home. The desert sun, high and hot, made him dizzy and turned him even more optimistic.

Soon as he pulled up to his place though, there it was. That goddamn semi truck sitting no more than a few hundred feet from his house. He shook his head in disgust, told himself he would take up his grievance with that gentleman later. For now, he went straight to his backyard. Greyhounds yapped and jumped on him as he rummaged through old tires, paint cans, doors of old cars, all strewn on the land around his place. The rays of the midmorning sun were still hitting him like razors, soaked his shirt and pants with sweat, and he took his shirt off, and a few seconds later he cursed the sun and took off his jeans, too, his whole body shiny and damp. Working in just his cowboy boots and bright red boxers, he uncovered the large dog crate he'd come for. "Hold on," he whispered, even though Ciela was out of earshot. "It's gonna be fine, Ciela. Just hold on, please." He had this hope clinging to him like mold now. He sang softly, working slowly and carefully, as he pulled the crate out from under the pile of junk, carried it to the truck, then stood looking at Ciela, figuring the best way to get her inside that contraption.

The heat was truly beginning to play with his head now. It turned his thoughts as delirious as the heat wave he'd driven through earlier. He heard the sound of a voice, soft at first, and he felt a presence. He didn't turn to look because the voice sounded like his daughter's and that's exactly what hope can do to a man. Let a little of it in and all hell breaks loose, and you start dreaming impossible things in the midst of doing something important. He unlatched the top of the crate from the bottom and split the thing in two. He heaved the Coleman with the Coors in it out of the truck. Concentrating, working fast, he walked into the house, came back out with a bucket of water and a flank of frozen venison. He placed these in the bottom of the crate. "Yeah," he whispered to himself. "I can lift her right in there."

"I can help," he heard, distinctly this time, and he turned with fists at first. But that changed. Raymond was a big man, he knew that, but at this particular second even the immensity of his body felt too small to hold everything he was feeling. She was standing there in front of him, Brenda, and the wolf he was trying to save was there, too, and he had to keep working and Brenda saw that, too, and without speaking a word to one another, the two worked together seamlessly, the father lifting the lower half of the crate into the truck, and the daughter moving with him to grab a corner of the tarp where Ciela lay. "Careful," he said to her.

"Is it alive?" Brenda said.

"Name's Ciela. She's alive and snarling like a banshee, yeah."

There wasn't time to smile, and Brenda's relief was more than a smile anyway. Raymond cinched the tarp tighter and worked his way around to the most dangerous part of Ciela, her head. He gripped the tarp, and then signaled with his head to Brenda, and the two of them lifted the wolf over the edge and into the crate. Without stopping to think, he secured the top to the bottom of the kennel, reached inside and slipped the tarp out, heard the wolf wake and snarl again, and it exhilarated him to the bone. He turned and hugged his daughter.

They held each other like that for a good long minute, maybe two, neither of them speaking. "You're my late-night visitor," he said.

"I'm sorry," she said.

He placed his entire hand on her face, covering her mouth and letting his fingers outline her cheeks and eyes. "Never sorry," he said.

"For leaving. For the wolf," she said. Then she whispered. "You sure it's alive?"

"You heard her yourself. She's welcoming you home." His words released something in her, like the air going out of her and a brand new breath being taken in. The two of them stood facing each other, Raymond in his boxers and cowboy boots, Brenda with that semi truck looming behind her. "I want to sit with you, to talk. But I'm working against time," he said. He shifted his eyes from Brenda to Ciela.

She gestured to the truck. "I'm on a route."

He laughed. "You're driving a route now?"

She didn't laugh. "Not really. Long story." Now she smiled. "I'll tell you on the flip-flop."

He pointed at her, all that hope swelling like a storm in him now. "You're coming back this time," he said. It wasn't a question.

"Yes," she said. "I'm coming back." It was simple and sure.

Raymond couldn't stop looking at Brenda, but he knew he had to get the wolf to his vet, fast. He walked back to the house, grabbed his cell phone, didn't take even enough time to pull on a pair of jeans.

When he came back out, he handed his phone to Brenda. "Call yourself," he said.

"What?"

"Call yourself on my phone, then I'll have your number and you'll have mine." He pushed his phone her direction, and she plugged her numbers in fast and heard her cell ringing, and it made her look at the truck, a place she did not want to be.

"Drive," he said. "I'll do the same." He hugged Brenda again. He wanted to ask her one more time to promise him that she would come back. But he knew it would mean nothing and that the only thing he had now was something he'd never trusted: hope. He hung onto that slippery trickster silently, fiercely now.

He watched Brenda grab the rearview mirror and pull herself up in the rig he'd cursed the night before. "Sonofabitch," he said to himself, this time gently, this time with awe. His little Chevy drove off in the opposite direction of that huge rig that held his daughter.

He drove Highway 264, his hand-beaded *jish* sitting on the seat next to him, his heart pounding so strong he had to roll down the windows and sing as loud as he could, drumming a steady beat on the steering wheel as he sang. His voice was strong, and the mixed-up emotions resounded like a twister in his chest. The highway snaked out in front of him, curves only when curves were necessary, which was not often in this terrain. He drove and sang like that for who knows how long, his head emptying itself of daily thoughts, turning itself to old times, to Brenda, to the belief he had in everything he claimed he didn't believe in. The beat of his own drumming moved through his body like the rumble of a Harley he'd ridden across the Sonoran Desert when he was eighteen, rode that bike all the way up into Osoyoos, Canada, a place he'd been told was the northernmost tip of the Sonoran Desert, even though the story was just a myth. That land was part of the Great Basin, a good enough place on its own, and nowhere near the Sonoran Desert. But he loved finishing the last leg of his trip in a place based on myth. The entire way, that engine had reverberated in the cavity of his torso, like he was the engine it-self, making the Harley run. The beat of the drum was like that, and his love for his daughter was like that, too, the throb starting inside him, moving outward from there.

Driving fast, he came almost bumper to bumper with a rickety old VW bus patchworked with bumper stickers, rumbling down the highway. The hippies driving the VW heard him singing and started singing right along with him, and they waved when he passed them, and he waved back and kept singing loudly, drumming hard.

He would not have noticed the red light flashing behind him if the state patrol hadn't whooped the siren a few times, too, and he wouldn't have heard the damn siren if he hadn't had to take breaths between his singing. He kept up his song and pulled to the shoulder of the road. He leaned out the window. "Hey, cute outfit," he said, to the cop.

The officer was a young guy with a scrawny build for a cop, and his uniform looked all too baggy. He smiled as he spoke, but he put on an overly stern voice that did not belong to him. "Are you aware you were traveling a couple dozen miles per hour *over* the speed limit?"

"I am." Raymond was still humming loudly.

"Twenty-seven miles over, to be exact."

"Impressive. No arguments. Just write out the ticket." He held out his palm to receive the summons.

The officer leaned in closer, showed Raymond the readout on the speed gun, and caught a glimpse of Raymond's red boxers and cowboy boots. "Cute outfit," he said.

Raymond chuckled, giving him props for his quick wit, but he nudged his palm closer to the cop, urging him to speed up writing that ticket.

"Got something in the back of the truck?" the officer kept on.

"Pretty clear that I do."

"Mind if I take a look?"

"Why you waste your breath asking when you know you're going to do it no matter what?" The cop nodded to Raymond now, giving him his props, too. Raymond's foot tapped the gas pedal, testing his restraint.

The cop walked around to the back, lifted the tarp, and leapt back a few inches. "Holy shit! You got a vicious dog back here."

"Yeah, that's what it is. It's a dog. And it's vicious as hell, and I need to get it to a vet, fast."

"You can't take a vicious dog to a vet!"

"Everything's vicious when it's injured."

"What's wrong with it?"

"Stunned. Badly. Maybe a leg injury. Maybe more. Like I said, she needs help."

The cop inched his way closer to the crate that held Ciela. She was stressed and more awake than she needed to be now. Raymond could hear her snarling, and it made him smile a little. When the cop came close to the kennel door, Ciela lunged, and that ungodly whine-like howl permeated the desert quiet. "Holy moly! That a wild dog?" the cop said.

"It's just—it's my dog, yeah. She's mean as a jackal. You checked everything out now? Want to look in the cab here, too? I got nothing to hide." He opened the glove compartment and emptied it of trash and papers.

"You in a hurry?" the cop said.

"As I said. Yes." Raymond reached out the window and pointed to the back of the truck. "That animal's counting its last few breaths and you're using up a couple hundred of them jawing on and on to me."

The cop walked closer to the cage now. "That's not a dog. That's a frickin wolf," the kid cop said.

"Very likely it is, yes."

His eyebrows went up. "Is it really a wolf?" He was excited now in the way that people who usually don't care become excited once they see a wild animal for themselves.

"She's one of about forty-nine of her kind left in this country. Which is about to become forty-eight because of your chattering, and I'm about to take off without waiting for your very belated permission."

"You can't have a wolf. Even Indians. You guys can have feathers. And certain psychotropic plants and paraphernalia like that. But you can't have wolves." He pulled a ticket book from his belt loops. "Would you say it was endangered? Are you endangering an endangered species?"

"Endangered? No. I'd say it was fucking massacred. I'd say this wolf and all her kind are on the brink of forever, and forever's a bad thing, not heaven and streets paved with gold and eternity where all the special people go. The eternity I'm talking about is a fucking bad thing. Because when this wolf and her pack are gone, they're gone forever, and if you don't quit jawing on and making your lists and checking them twice like Santy Claus, it's gonna be one less wolf for eternity, and that one less wolf is going to be your fault." He took a breath. "Sir."

After a few confused seconds, the cop said, "So you trapped and caged an endangered species?"

Raymond let a thin stream of air out through his lips, ran his hands over his balding head. "Whoo, that's fresh. Look, mister cop, I gotta get this wolf to someone who can care for her, and that means—"

The cop's radio shredded the air with static. He talked into it, ignoring Raymond, then pushed the kill button and asked Raymond to step out of the vehicle.

Raymond knew now. He sat stone still in the driver's seat, shaking inside with anger and frustration. His past, one dedicated to restoring animals and land in all the wrong ways, at least according to the law of federal and state animal management, would do him in again. He had been arrested for importing animals in the past. He had a choice now, between this wolf and his own life. Between this wolf and the possibility of ever seeing his daughter again, of having a chance with her again. It was a position he'd been in too many times before, and he hated every choice available to him now. Staring the cop down hard, he stepped out of his truck, felt the handcuffs on his wrists, walked slowly to the officer's car in his cowboy boots and boxers. "Look, Officer, you gotta hear me. That wolf'll die unless you get her where she needs to be," he said.

The officer nodded. "We'll take care of it."

It was a puny response. "You sonofabitch," Raymond said, but he felt his powerlessness consuming him. He fell back in his seat. "Sir. Call Andy at Wilderness and Water. Tell him it's Ciela, Willa Robbins's wolf. Tell him the wolf is—"

The young cop was not listening. He was absorbed in radio talk and paperwork.

Raymond watched his truck and Ciela grow smaller in the side view mirror. He felt his chest caving, and he sang against it. He tossed back his head and started singing again, consumed with desperation. He opened his mouth and let his voice boom like a Harley going a hundred and fifty on a desert road on a summer night. The sounds came out of him like a drum, like his skin was the head of the drum and there was nothing but rage pulsing through him. "You sonofabitch, you make that call," he said. "You get that wolf taken care of."

The cop radioed for help. Raymond sang.

Willa

THE FALL PLUMAGE OF the aspens with their stark white trunks turned the mountain air even brighter. In the clearing sat Zeb's cabin, small as I'd imagined, but it also looked so domestic, not like the Zeb I knew. Late-blooming pansies still spilled over the sides of old wine casks sitting around the place, and scraps of Zeb's iron and wood projects scattered the land.

The place was dotted with police cars—two painted with silver police badges on the door, two others that were solid black. From what I could tell, they were waiting for me *inside*

Zeb's cabin, and it felt like an intrusion to me, though I had no claim to Zeb's property.

I waited in the car, imagining Zeb here, living the day-to-day life he'd built for himself alone throughout the years. I tried to remember my own home out on the mesa. My home, the mesa, it all felt like an illusion to me now, as if while I was driving here, the mesa had transformed into an island too far out to sea for anyone to reach. I felt it drifting farther and farther away from me. I needed to know Cario and Magda were there, that my house still existed, that my life in New Mexico was still real, not something I'd dreamed up.

I grabbed for my phone and dialed Cario and Magda. I redialed three or four times. Then I remembered where they spent their days, even when I was away. I dialed my own home phone number. "Bueno," Magda said. It was a salve. "Buenos días," she said again, into my silence.

"Magda." Her name felt so good to say.

"Willa? Dulce Niño Jesús en un pesebre con burros y la Virgen María ¿dónde estás? ¿Qué cosa loca te has ido y—"

"Magda—"

The cell phone crackled with static, and then her voice came through again. "Estamos esperando por ti aquí con Chile verde y tamales que hice hoy frescas en su casa, estamos esperando por ti y—"

"Magda—"

"Mija, where are you?"

"*Magda*," I said, loudly. She stopped talking. "I miss you. Te echo de menos." I waited for her calmer reply. But after a pause, she set off on another string of words about food and fresh roasted green chilies and how my house was falling to shambles, and then Christina's voice came on the line, a surprise not because she was there, but because hearing her voice calmed me even more than Magda's. I heard her, and my home felt like my home again, solid and certain. "It's all okay here," Christina said. "Magda's just being, you know, *Magda*." We both laughed.

I could still hear Magda in the background telling Christina to hand over the phone, and then I heard a door closing, and

Magda's voice went away. I heard jays and ravens calling. "Beautiful day here," Christina said.

I imagined her outside with that New Mexico land and sky wrapped all around her. I wanted to tell her I missed her, that I could not wait to be home, but what came out of my mouth was, "Is my house really falling into a shambles?"

She laughed. "The TV was out. Cable line. That's all. I came up to fix it for them." She asked me how it was going in Colorado, and I wanted to tell her I wanted to be there, with her. But the words didn't come to me. I sat silent.

"You coming home sometime soon, or what's up?" she asked.

"I don't know," I told her. "I just needed to hear your voice . . . I mean, Magda and Cario's voices. I needed to know everything's okay with them and my house."

There was a pause on the phone and then Christina said, "They're fine. Magda and Cario are fine. Your house is fine."

"And I guess you're fine, too?"

She paused. "I guess so, yeah. I'm fine, too."

I could hear hurt in her voice, and I wanted to change the way I talked to her, but there was something holding me back. A man in a rugby shirt tucked into his well-pressed black slacks walked out of Zeb's house. He wore a radio receiver on his belt and waved to me officiously, all business.

"Good," I told her, but when I hung up, I kept staring at the phone, wanting something more.

"Polo," the man said, extending his hand to me before I could open the door of my truck. I stumbled to greet him, and before I could say my name he said, "And you're Willa Robbins," not a question. I nodded and tucked the phone away. Polo, a tall, lean man with a round, boylike face that seemed too big for his body, patted my back with his wide palm. "Come in," he said. "We're glad you're here."

I tried for a firm handshake and a convincing smile. "This is Zeb's home, right? We're meeting *in* Zeb's house?"

Polo cocked his head as if the answer was self-evident. "It's the investigation site. The place your brother fled from.

Sonofabitch, we had him right here." He pointed at the cabin and let out a high-pitched chuckle. It disoriented me. I half expected him to know I'd come here because I thought they had something on me. But I saw now that Polo honestly thought I was in on it with them, that I had agreed to help them because I was on his side and wanted to bring my own brother in. He called my brother a sonofabitch to my face. "He's not a sonofabitch," I told him.

The man stopped short of opening Zeb's front door for me. He was still smiling. "What's that, Miss Robbins?"

"My brother. Zeb. He's not a sonofabitch."

Polo kept up the chuckle. "Hell, we've been trying to pin something on that guy for one helluva long time. You know that? This or that, here or there, I'm telling you, that sonofabitch gets around, man, steals and lies and never leaves a trace, which is how we know. Where there's damage done and no trace left behind, we know it's Zeb Robbins."

"You know it's him when there's no proof left behind?"

He nodded.

"That kind of evidence hold up much in court?" I asked.

He shook his head with a twisted kind of admiration. "Can't get the sonofabitch *into* court. He's a slick one, all right," he said, and then we were inside the cabin.

I could smell part of the story of Zeb's life now: the scent of tobacco, wood, leather, fire, wool, something beneath those earthy smells, too, something sweeter, everything mingling with the distinct sharpness of whiskey. Polo introduced me to three other men, and they shook my hand, but their words were a blur. Here was the kitchen table where my brother had eaten his meals over the years, the tile counter, the window that looked out on the mountains he had always loved. I decided to take a chance and interrupt the blur of sound behind me, the men making plans about how to track Zeb. "Hey, guys, could I maybe have a second? Just a few minutes to look around the place, alone?"

They all stood up in unison. "Sure, sure," one man said. "Study the place. Get a sense of the man. Sniff him out. Good idea."

Sniff him out? He spoke gibberish, far as I could tell, but I nodded, and the men quieted down, and everyone but Polo headed outdoors. I walked from room to room, looking at signs of my own brother's distant life. There was a full set of dishes in the kitchen, pots and pans for more than one person. Woolen throws hung haphazardly over the sofa. After the living room, I walked into a small workroom jam packed with a table saw, some leather working tools, wood scraps here and there, and a pack of Zig-Zag rolling papers on the handmade workbench. I lifted the Zig-Zags, pressed them to my face, then tucked them into my pocket. Tiny brown curls of tobacco lay next to them. I pressed my fingertip onto the tobacco pieces. They were so fresh that they stuck to the pad of my finger. He'd been there recently. It came clear to me now. I was on the verge of seeing my brother. Whatever obligations I had to Polo and his men, there was also this: I would get to see Zeb again.

I moved on to the bedroom, and I could tell right away that the workmanship of the quilt on the bed was not Zeb's. The edges were not straight, and the stitching was machine done. I looked through a few of the dresser drawers: handmade elk-skin clothes, Lee jeans and flannel shirts. Along with that, Lee jeans for a woman, some cowgirl blouses.

I opened the top dresser drawer and found a sachet of rose petals. They turned me stock-still and silent, my heart sore with memory. There was nothing else in the drawer—no linens or pajamas to be sacheted, just the rose petals in the bare drawer. I lifted the petals in my cupped palms and brought them close to my face. They were dusty reddish-brown, fragile enough to flake in my hands. Even in their aged discoloration, I saw that none of them had any white at the tip. I inhaled their sweet and acrid scent, then lowered them back into the drawer, slid my palms out from under them, scraping the backs of my hands on the rough wood. On the wall there were two photos: one of Mom and Dad when they were young, the other of Raymond surrounded by his greyhounds.

I heard the faint sound of Polo's men talking outside the window. Slowly, I stiffened up and walked back out into the kitchen. Soon as I entered, Polo sat down at the table again, and, like a

sudden blast of instinct had overcome them, all the other men
came barreling in from outside to join him. One man offered me
his chair. I shook my head no, choosing to stand. "Someone else
lives here," I said. "Along with Zeb."

Polo chuckled. "You're good," he said. "They said you were
good, and you're good."

"His wife?" one man said.

"Nah," Polo said. "They're shacking up is all. Who knows
how long. But the damn hippies never tied the knot."

"But they're *together*?" I asked.

Polo nodded. "The old lady's in on it with him, too."

I had a hard time putting my memory of Brenda together with
the words "old lady," and an even harder time putting her together
with Zeb. "I'm tracking her too, then? Zeb's 'old lady'?"

"No, no. She's got some kid from town caring for those animals
out there," he said, pointing toward the paddock I'd seen driving in.
"She took off, who knows where. We got nothing on her. *Yet*."

"Aiding and abetting," one man said, brightly.

Polo shook his head. "Aiding and abetting a bunch of guys not
doing their goddamn jobs, letting a guy who *confessed* to murder
get away. Not sure we could make that one stick."

"I don't see what makes you think the charges against Zeb
will stick anyway. Hell, anyone could confess." I took a risk
that surprised me, testing to see if they knew about my own
past. "I mean, *I* could confess to killing someone. That's not
evidence." I felt the uneasy sound of my own voice pinched in
my throat.

Polo's cheery face turned serious. "*Did* you kill someone, Miss
Robbins? " He pretended to wait for an answer, then he laughed.
"See, that's the difference. You're innocent. He's not. Look, we
pretty much have this sonofabitch bagged. It's just a matter of
finding him and taking him in."

"So." I shoved my hands in my pockets and waited, stunned
into submission by his joke.

"So we get started at the crack of dawn." Polo reached behind
him and tossed me a stuffed duffel bag. "Here's your gear."

When I told him I had my own gear and preferred to use it, he shook his head. "Nothing but what we issue you goes on the trek with us. You can leave all your high tech shit in the car."

"High tech shit?"

"You're tough. You don't need that shiny new REI shit." He tossed his arm around my shoulder. "We share everything, you and me."

"I prefer to work alone." I told him "And the bigger footprint we go in with, the less chance we have of actually finding Zeb."

Polo let out that laugh again, the annoying one that sounded like a flock of starlings. "We already lost your brother. We're not losing you, too. Anyway, I'm looking forward to working with you, myself. Learning tracking from a master tracker."

"I'm far from a master tracker."

"Chance of a lifetime!" He patted my shoulder, then peeled his arm off my back. "Crack of dawn. See you then." I took my police-issue gear and headed out to set up my tent.

*   *   *

I PASSED BY THE animals, gave them an evening round of hay, and followed the stench of what smelled like death to the far side of the stables, part way up the mountainside. From a distance, I could see the mound of something almost like earth itself. Then the softened shape of a horse came clear, its lose skin folded as if shaped by erosion and weather. As I walked closer, the arc of rib-cage and bones protruded like fingers of eroded white rock, some-how making even death seem beautiful on this landscape. I stood next to the carcass of the horse now, covering my nose against the smell. I turned my head, but could not help looking closer.

The horse had been killed by a lion, the scrapes of teeth and claws still visible on the bones. The tracks also told this story: The hungry lion had circled the horse's carcass, but had been held off, at least for a while. The signs showed that Zeb was vigilant about protecting something that no longer needed protection. The horse was already dead. In tracking, the human body (or a wild animal's body) tells its story to the earth. Neither is capable of lies. Zeb cared for this horse. He hung onto it even after death. That was the story the signs told. Here was the imprint of Zeb's capacity for love, the vestiges of the desperation that caring for something this much had left in him. Zeb's gentleness and grief had always looked like anger and strength.

Prayer had never been my way, at least, not as an adult. Words, especially those that pleaded, had come to seem unholy to me when compared to silence. So I sat quietly beside the horse without praying, without uttering a word inside my head. It was the best way I knew to honor a life. These remains, more than the house and all it contained, told the story of my brother's life in my absence. I knew Polo and his men were awake and watching me. Even so, I sat there by that stinking horse for some time. I listened to the night coming on.

When the time felt right, I stood up and made my way to the tent site Polo had selected for me. It was only a few feet from him and, thank god, it was upwind from the horse. I set up camp while Polo and his men sat talking, the murmur of their voices a soft buzz, the embers of cigarettes lighting, then going dark, pulsing like tiny red police lights in the night.

I crawled inside my tent, and lay there, waiting. Screech owls and great horned owls carved out tunnels of sound in the wooded silence. My body shivered—the cold earth on my back, or the fear inside me, not sure which. I hadn't counted on Polo insisting to come with me as I tracked Zeb. It would take every bit of skill I could muster to find Zeb before Polo woke in the morning. My breath fluttered as I closed my eyes, hoping for rest, but not sleep.

· · ·

IN THE DEEPEST PART of the night, when no seams of daybreak or sunset lightened the horizon in any direction, I set out. I opened theft   · 151

the green canvas duffle Polo had given me, pulled on his government issue thermal shirts and flannel lined coveralls. I hated
putting them on. They smelled of mothballs and dry-cleaning
fluid. The chemical stench of the clothes alone could have announced to any animal that I was approaching. But I knew I had
to follow Polo's directions exactly. And when I turned my mind
to tracking, I no longer noticed the stink of my clothes anyway.
The night landscape turned intensely lucid. Even from inside the
tent, I could smell the change in the weather. I could smell snow.
When I unzipped the fly, I saw the huge flakes drifting down, the
earth dusted in white. I looked at Polo's tent. No flashlights, no
cigarettes, no lanterns, no sound. They had tracked Zeb day and
night at first. But time had worn on. They knew their chances had
grown slimmer. They were sleeping fast and hard now, counting
on me for their last ditch effort.

I felt half animal now, like I'd drawn the short straw when I
was handed my opposable thumb and my too-heavy brain. I tried
to shut off my mind and to let my sense of smell and hearing take
over. I closed my eyes and listened. Owls calling. Hares moving through the brush. I knew that animals in the wild sounded
bigger than they actually were, that people unused to the wilderness will sometimes report the "loud sound" of a "huge animal,"
when it turned out to be just a bird flitting from branch to branch.
Still, every sound grabbed my attention. The relative quiet of the
night amplified everything.

I felt like a cat as I walked up the hill, the way cats keep their
haunches flexed with every step so they can walk on the earth
without making a noise. Under the moonlight, the trees seemed
to move. Their trunks were thick and humanlike, and as I walked,
they seemed to bend with me. Maybe they *did* bend with me;
maybe it was something I'd just convinced myself was impossible.
You have to believe it to see it. Raymond had always said. He believed
boulders, trees, everything in the wilderness had its own mind.
That was how it felt to me. Like everything could move, was alive.
Like maybe this kind of magic happened all the time and we overlooked it in our daily lives.

When I tracked the wolves back home, the most important thing I did was to think like a wolf. I gave up my logic and let instinct take over, at least, as much as I could, given the limitations of my human brain. Same thing here. I had to slip out of my skin and into Zeb's. I remembered the scent of him when we were kids—either the metallic, greasy smell of a car shop, or the outdoorsy smell of dried grass and hay. I remembered the sound of his voice, his unpredictable anger, his reticence, his concentration—a fish underwater, I used to say, and no pulling him out if he did not want to come. I tried to put those memories together with the story his cabin told, a gentler life than I ever imagined him living at this age. I tried to fathom the fierceness I'd seen in how he'd cared for that horse. That's when reality kicked in. I was here tracking my own *brother*. I was no longer afraid that Polo and his men might be looking for me or that they planned to use my own past against me. But I was here, tracking Zeb. I had no plan, no way out. Once I found him, I could not turn him in, and I could not let him run. There was also this: In his mind, his trackers would never find him. So what if *I* found him? What if he reacted violently to being found before I had a chance to tell him who I was? I remembered his fights with Chet. I knew Zeb always carried a gun. I thought of the story he used to tell over and over, the one of the fox he wanted to set free from that trap.

He was on his way down from a backwoods trip in the San Juans near Creede, Colorado, lagging too far behind the Boy Scout troop he had spent the weekend with because he wasn't ready to come out of the wilderness and go home yet. He spotted this fox from a distance, and it was late September, and the animal was fox-red on the gold aspen leaves, and the blending colors made it hard to see the animal at first. It was lying down, resting, till it set eyes on Zeb. When it saw him, it leapt to its feet and ran at him full speed. But just as quick as it started running, it stopped. It put its butt up in the air, front paws flat on the ground, like a dog asking him to play.

Zeb walked closer. The fox bolted the other direction. But it only ran about six feet or so before it turned back around, bolted at him, then stopped short, just like it had done before. The way it was circling, Zeb thought it might have been rabid. He thought of calling to his scout troop, but *Fuck 'em* he said. If he had to spend the rest of his life there, in those beautiful mountains, looking at that crazy fox, it would be better than going back to his home in the suburbs.

Then he saw the look in that fox's eye. Zeb told the story the same way every time. He said as soon as he looked at that fox, he knew it was going to attack him. So he started figuring what to do. "I felt for the knife in my pocket, almost took it out," he said. That's when he saw the end of the chain and the trapper's post in the center. One of the fox's paws was clamped down in the metal teeth of that thing.

It was one of the few times I'd seen Zeb cry when we were kids. He said, "I could've tossed my jacket over that fox, held it tight while I uprooted the post of the trap. Could've held its head in the crook of my elbow while I loosened the clamp from its bloodied paw. I could've done a dozen things to save that fox."

While he watched the fox turn itself weak and winded, he cursed the guy who'd set the trap, fox meat not good for eating, and the pelt the only reason for killing it. "And the fuck who set the jaws of that trap was probably sitting comfortable and warm in his house while that beautiful animal died slow." That's the way Zeb put it.

He had to make a choice. To take a risk and try to save it, or to move on. He moved on. But the picture of that fox stayed with him. He was halfway down the mountain and the fox was still running in circles inside his head.

He'd heard sometimes an animal will chew off its own foot to get itself free from a trap. He wanted that fox to do that, to free itself. It was just a thought at first, but then he couldn't stop thinking it, and the thought kept gnawing at him, and he had to go back and see if that fox had had the guts to set itself free.

He went back up the mountain.

That's the part of the story Zeb had always told people. It made me proud of Zeb, the way he cared about that fox. But the whole story didn't end where he always ended it.

Zeb went back up the mountain, saw the fox, still trapped. He watched it run in circles for a while. He coaxed it and tried to calm it. He ran with it in circles for a while, tried to tire it so he could maybe get in there and release the trap without the fox biting him.

The fox just kept at it, never wore itself out, even as it was dying. "Gnaw your foot off," Zeb hollered at the animal. The fox licked at the wounds already there from the clamp. It bit down on the steel chain.

"Gnaw it off," Zeb yelled, again, and he started throwing rocks at the fox, maybe get it mad enough to release itself. But the fox just turned meaner toward Zeb, not toward the trap. Zeb was crazy as the animal, running in circles with it, screaming at it to set itself free. Then, without thinking, Zeb took out his knife. "All of a sudden I was right there with that fox, and I didn't know how I got there," he said, and he had the fox's neck pinned in the crook of his elbow, and he was still hollering for the fox to set itself free, and the thing turned more and more vicious toward Zeb, and instead of freeing the fox like he wanted to, Zeb stabbed it, over and over, till the fox turned limp and bloody in his arms.

He lay there in the aspen leaves, the trapped, bloodied fox still attached to his chain, dead on his chest.

That's the part of the story Zeb had told me only once. I came to know it in the same way you remember dreams, how sometimes the most vivid images never find their way to words. They haunt around inside you. It was not because Zeb had threatened me or told me not to tell, like he'd done with other things. That was not why I kept it a secret. It was just that there was something about him that made me want to keep his dark-side secret. As I sat there, the reality of my position stunned me. I knew what Zeb was capable of when he felt trapped.

Just like when I was a kid, I knew that the best thing to do would be to leave, bow out of Polo's search now that I knew the cops had nothing on me. It was time to let Zeb go once and for all. But it was a decision I could not make. I could not bring myself to leave my brother there, to let him be caught, maybe even killed, by these men. I could not leave my brother. I was what Andy and the guys at WWA called "entangled." The rule was to never fall in love with your subjects, whether you were studying them in a lab or tracking them. I'd never been good at it, had always named my subjects and felt connected to them. I'd been heavily entangled with my wolves, Ciela and Hector. After years of fieldwork, I even began to feel them in my mind and spirit, and sometimes when I moved, I could feel them in my body, even when I was not tracking them. I'd hear a sharp sound and turn my head with animal-like vigilance. I was moving and acting wolf-like.

I might have been able to live up to what Polo had called me—a master tracker—if I'd had better boundaries, if I could have ever taught myself to care and not to care. But I had never succeeded, even with animals unrelated to me. Now I was tracking my brother; I'd been entangled with him since I was born.

I was unsettled in a way I never had been with the wolves. I heard Raymond's and Magda's words—that my brother may have changed, that he may be violent now, even toward me. Shaken, I stumbled as I walked, tripping on the smallest twig. It was one of those clumsy moves that sent me straight to the ground, and when I landed, I saw exactly what I needed to see to keep me on track.

One of the first things you learn about tracking is the simple but relentless awareness of something, *anything*, out of place. Those out of place things were the keys to the story unfolding. What I'd stumbled upon was miniscule: the twigs of a dried chamisa bush trimmed at an angle that meant a rodent had eaten them. The cuts were recent, and I'd have overlooked them if I hadn't stumbled. And they led me to notice a tuft of brown hair mixed with white hair caught on the same plant. A few hundred feet from there, tufts of that same hair were scattered across the ground, skittering on top of the fallen leaves and snow, pushed by a slight breeze. I picked up one tuft. It was the fur of a snowshoe hare midway between its winter and summer coat. It was clumped together by skin at the base, not just snagged on a bush, which told me it had been killed by a predator. The skin was still supple; the kill was recent. Beginning trackers looked for blood, but blood was almost always the last piece of evidence that mattered.

Across a clearing in the forest, I saw scratch marks left by a mountain lion after urinating. They were fresh enough that the scent of the urine lingered. It was the musty but frequent smell that day-hikers usually turned up their noses at without ever knowing how close they were to a lion.

I sensed I was onto a mountain lion now. And some instinct told me the lion and Zeb were connected. I thought about the horse I'd seen, the story it had told me of Zeb. This was the heart of tracking, a game of connect-the-dots that became so intense that it felt as if the constellations of the night sky had fallen onto the earth. Only the constellations on earth were not stars outlining the stories of ancient gods. They were the tracks of animals and people, an undiscovered mythology waiting to be told. If I could keep connecting the dots, they would complete the story I needed now.

I kept walking, following the tracks of the rabbit and the lion, and they began to frighten me. Shortly after the tracks of the hare ended, the tracks of a human started up. There were no other tracks in the area except those of the mountain lion and those of a man. The man, I had to presume, was my brother. But that alone wasn't what scared me. It was that the tracks crisscrossed and circled one another in this sort of chaotic pattern. It was as if the mountain lion knew the man was there, and the man knew the lion was there—and they were both conscious enough of each other's presence to tease, lure, and then avoid. It was as if they were entangled.

I was into the deepest part of the night now. It was no longer snowing, but balls of snow tipped the branches of trees, leaving the trunks inky, barely distinguishable from the darkness. The moon dipped behind the mountains. In that light, everything was black and white, and the tracks themselves, like the boulders and trees, seemed to move. There was a dizzying feel to it. But everything stilled when I saw the outline of a handgun lying in the snow. It had been dropped there recently. I could tell because the snow had stopped falling only ten minutes earlier. No new snow had fallen on the black handle of the gun.

Zeb was nearby. My chest heaved—with excitement, fear, joy—I couldn't tell. But when I bent to pick up the gun, my legs turned to rubber. I felt twelve years old again. I felt tricked. The gun was so out in the open, so blatantly placed that it had to be a set up. My brother would never drop a weapon like this. I opened the clip of the gun and saw bullets lined up there. It didn't make sense. Zeb was arming his trackers. His mind had always been a weave of contradictions. But this seemed beyond even his usual extremes. I knew him, not just in my memory but in my blood. I heard the warnings again. "He may be dangerous, even to you."

About another hundred yards from the gun, a pocketknife lay in the snow. Like the gun, it had been dropped recently. It sent a chill through me when I ran my fingers across the engraved initials: ZPR. Zeb was setting up his trackers. He didn't know I was among them. Whatever plan he had for them would be the same plan he had for me.

I wanted to turn back, to tell Polo I quit. I craved my safe home on the mesa, the loved I shared with Magda and Cario and Christina. I wanted my life back. But I had not seen or heard from anyone in my blood family for so long. And my brother was *here*. As far as I could tell, he was entangled with the mountain lion. And I was entangled with him.

Zeb

IT HAD BEEN A kind of meditation, the mulch of the hut wrapped around him, the warmth in there, the smells of the earth, the complete quiet. It felt like home to him, like his body was already becoming earth. It felt good to him, and he knew he was ready. This had been the time he needed to solidify his choice. He knew it was the right decision, but he had not let it sink into his body— not all the way. Now he let it consume his muscles, his heart.

At twilight, he left the shelter he'd built. He destroyed it, scattered the rubble around, even strewed some into the trees, and then he left. He had with him the handgun he'd tossed to himself as he fled his cabin, his wallet, a pocketknife, the clothes he wore, nothing more that he could name.

What he felt first was harder than he imagined it would be: the letting go. If life had ever made sense, it would have been a slow and steady letting go from beginning to end. But it was the opposite of that. It was a constant piling on, a weave of love that knitted its way more permanently into him daily. The absurdity of it had drained him and confused him—this intense love he'd been born with living side by side with the fact that no connection ever satisfied him. If he'd sometimes avoided connection, it had been because he craved it so much, and it was never enough.

He walked deeper into the forest and farther from the place where he had spent so many years with a woman he cared for, living on a patch of earth that had grown to feed and hold his tangled roots. As he walked away from it, he could feel the roots snapping, his life falling away from him. It was as if the mountains folded around him like huge hands, and as he stepped, the hands clasped around him and cut off any access to where he'd been. There was no turning back. Everything behind him grew dark, and what was in front of him grew more visible. Eventually, and for the first time since he was a kid, he had only the present in front of him, no past. To get there, he had to let go of the cabin; he had to let go of Brenda; he had to let go of his life.

With the twilight wrung from the horizon now and the inky night saturating the frayed edges between land and sky, he began to feel his life as his own. Like springing a lock on his ribcage, his entire body felt open, and it felt right. He could hear better, see better, smell better. His senses were so keen it felt as if he could smell and even taste the mountain lion every time he inhaled. It was the one connection he could never sever.

He kept on toward the rocky outcropping just below the cliffs where he knew the cougar had claimed a cave as her own. In the past, she had waited for him at his cabin. Now he would do the same: meet her where she lived. If she was out, this is where he would wait for her when she returned. If she was in the cave now, he could track her from there. Either way, he would find her.

Anything that had comforted him in the past felt heavy now. First, there was the weight of the gun he'd taken with him. He tried but could not remember when or if he had ever set foot in the wilderness without a weapon of some kind. He didn't think about the men tracking him. He had not forgotten they were there, but they didn't matter now. He took his gun from the deerskin pouch he'd made and he let it fall. When it hit the ground, his body felt different. Not better or worse. But new and deeply familiar all at once. He kept on, and he felt himself craving the lightness he'd felt when he'd let his gun fall. He took out his pocketknife, the one Brenda had given him long ago, engraved with his initials: ZPR. He let it fall, too.

Without his knife and gun, he had to pay more attention to things moving around him. His naked awareness was his only protection now. It made him a better follower of the cougar, he thought, the attention he had to pay to every sound. He spotted three snowshoe hares, one right after the other, weaving so fast through the trees, white on white and barely a shadow cast by the waning moon. In the new snowfall, any scat was easy to see and identify. The place was alive with what had been left behind, even if no animals were visible at the moment. He saw the prints of the lion in the snow. They crossed with the snowshoe hare prints, and his heart thrummed. His mind blurred with desire, and he crossed the tracks of the hares, and he traced step for step the prints of the cougar. She was nearby and she was silent, watching him. He could feel her, but he couldn't see her; not yet.

His bad hip caught on the craggy spur in his bones, and he made his way to the nearest fallen tree and rested for a second on the trunk. Then he stood back up again, began walking. He was about five hundred yards from the base of the cave where his mountain lion wintered. Recent traces of her encircled him now. Every one of his senses piqued. He would make his way up to the mouth of the cave. In his mind, he had an appointment with the lion, a mutual agreement to settle something with her once and for all. He could not see her. But he would wait.

Brenda

SHE DROVE TIRED AND exhilarated through the sunrise-colored sandy hills of the Painted Desert. It was a beauty she felt she'd never seen before, though she'd seen it several times when she'd passed through, driving with Zeb. But there was a difference in her now, something settling even as it swelled in her. She didn't know what was happening with Zeb, but she knew he had always wiggled his way out of trouble, and she knew her time with him up till then had made all the difference in them both. Whatever they shared—call it love, call it understanding, call it history—it had made a difference in their lives. Without the whiskey soaking her mind, she knew this. She wanted to see Zeb soon. She wanted him to see her now, to introduce him to her father, to Raymond; maybe she even wanted to start over.

She looked at the outline of her route, saw addresses of about a dozen hospitals and private plastic surgeons where she needed to pick up wasted body parts and haul them back to the desert where they'd swelter in the sun and seep into the earth while the people where she lived worried about how to best recycle things like yogurt cups and toilet paper rolls. She noticed that the absurdity of it didn't piss her off like it usually would. It even made her laugh a little.

When her cell phone rang, she looked at the caller ID, saw the area code, and smiled. Raymond calling already. She hit the answer button. She didn't even give him a chance to speak before she said, "Damn, I miss you already, too. I can't wait to get back to see you again."

"Can you make that sooner rather than later," Raymond said. "The coming back part?"

"Love to. Soon as I finish this route," she said.

"Understand," Raymond said. "But I have a situation. I need your help."

"I don't know, man. Best I can do is make it an overnight," she said. "I have—"

Raymond's voice grew uncharacteristically forceful. "I understand," he said, again. "But this is not something I'm asking for me, Bren. It's something I'm asking for the wolf."

She stopped and listened now. He explained the situation to her, how he'd been taken in and she was his one phone call. "There's no telling when or if someone will get to that wolf," he said.

There were no words between them for a while. She knew Raymond had been here before. It was the reason she'd left long ago, and he knew that. She heard him sigh on the other end of the line. "Brenda, call Simon. Please. He'll tell you everything you need to know," he said, "He'll tell you he doesn't know shit about animals, but he knows a helluva lot, actually. He knows that wolf—Ciela—has got to be in a cool place, not sitting in my truck in the middle of the damn desert. He knows what to feed her. Tell him you can help. Tell him there's no other choice right now. Because there is no other choice right now, Brenda."

She listened to him explain that she needed to go back, find his truck and Ciela parked along the side of the road, get Simon to help her take Ciela to the *Snack-n-Pump*, and then release her into the store. "Just till I get back," he said.

When she told him it sounded crazy and like a jacked-up idea that only he could dream up, he said. "I know what you think of me, Brenda. But you gotta believe me this time. You have to help that wolf, just till we can get her some medical attention."

"How about I take her to Wilderness and Water? She's a part of their reintroduction project. They'll know what to do with her."

"Good idea, Brenda. Take her to the place that's arguing in favor of shooting her. Take an injured wolf to them. See what happens."

She heard her own sarcasm in her father's voice, familiar and direct and comforting.

"Look, WWA is technically not supposed to be managing these specific wolves anyway. These are outside their territory. These are *our* wolves. Can you do it? Can you go back and help her?" he said.

The possibilities of what could happen if she went back and did what her father was asking her to do played in her head. There was nothing legal about it, she was pretty sure of that. And she was saddled with this new obsession she had with doing the right thing. She wanted to get back to Colorado, collect an honest paycheck from that asshole, Mike, to figure out what the hell was happening with Zeb, and then make her way back to the reservation, to spend some time with her father again, really get to know him this time. She was ready for it.

She held the phone to her ear in a kind of stupor of emotion. There was no figuring it out logically, no answer that was right or wrong. She had only her instincts to guide her. "Okay," she said, finally. "I'll go back. I'll help the wolf."

This time she made that twelve-point U-turn in less than ten. She headed back to the reservation, and by afternoon, she was on the road where she'd left Raymond earlier that morning. She was praying, as Raymond had taught her to do when she was younger, which meant she was singing softly to herself as she drove. Prayer like that makes things possible, Raymond had told her. She needed to believe that everything was possible right now. She needed to believe that Mike would pay her, that the wolf would still be there when she got there, that the sun would not have gotten to Ciela, that Simon would meet her and help her. She needed to believe she had the confidence and the craziness required to get this job done.

She dialed the number Raymond had given her, introduced herself.

"Brenda?" Simon said on the other end of the line. "You're back? I had no idea that's why Raymond was taking the day off. That's good. That's a damn good reason."

"Raymond's not here," Brenda said.

Simon made a whistling noise. "Well don't talk to me before you talk to Raymond. You gotta go see Raymond first."

"I've already seen my father. I need your help with something," she said. She told him that she'd spoken to Raymond, that he'd been arrested. Then she outlined the wild-ass plan her father had laid out for her and Simon.

*   *   *

A FEW MILES SOUTH of Raymond's, she saw her father's truck sitting by the side of the road, desert heatwaves trembling around the crate that held Ciela. She ramped up her prayer now, the song rising up in her as a way of burning off the fear that frayed her edges. She swung down from the truck, felt her breath catch in her chest, and walked fast to the crate. She looked inside. Either way it happened, it would feel the same to her—if the wolf was alive, if it was dead—she was scared as shit of both options. She stood, now, at the back of the truck, looking in. There was no telling what lay in front of her, if that heap of animal was sleeping and breathing, or if it had quit living. The crate turned everything dark, outlined by the blinding sun. "Shit," she whispered, to herself; then she took a step closer. When there was nothing, she leaned in toward the metal bars of the crate and blew lightly, and just then the entire crate jolted forward toward her, and the sound the wolf made was nothing less than a scream so humanlike it could have been a child, the sentient quality of that cry. She leapt back, stumbled almost to the ground, and it was okay. It was even good, this fear she felt, because it was something. It was tangible and real and goddamn if she was not there, on the reservation, doing something good for her blood-father. He had not disowned her when she left him before. "They're the most bonding creatures on earth," Raymond had said to her, long ago, speaking of wolves. She understood now what he had meant by the power of the bond that is family. She understood that it had far less to do with blood than she'd imagined when she was a kid. It had to do with love. Raymond, this wolf, Zeb—these had created the family she chose.

Brenda stood a distance from the crate. She knew that the other wolves would be nearby, that they would stay for a few days, waiting. There was no way she'd be able to lay eyes on them, but she knew they were around, watching her, maybe even counting on her to come through for Ciela. She felt somehow dedicated to them. It felt good, that responsibility.

She leaned on the truck, waiting for Simon now. When she saw his red El Camino come lumbering down the road, she flagged him down. The size of the car made Simon look even smaller than she remembered him, but that didn't keep her from wrapping her thick arms around him and smothering him with a huge hug. Simon blushed, and the white stubble on his chin brightened. He laughed in the same way he used to laugh years ago. He had a hard time breaking that hug with Brenda. Eventually, he patted her on the back and let go. Then the two of them set to work.

It took some maneuvering of the vehicles to get things started. She had to drive her rig to Raymond's place, leave it there, pick up Raymond's keys, and drive back to Ciela with Simon. "You sure we're up to this?" she asked Simon.

"Doesn't look to me like we have a choice, does it?" Simon said. "We can leave Ciela here to die in the sun. We can take her to WWA, where who knows what'll happen to her. Or we can do what Raymond told us to do."

"There's no vet we can take her to?" she asked.

"It's illegal," he said. "Working on these wolves. There's one guy who works with Raymond. *Just* with Raymond."

"Hell," she said. "This is crazy."

Simon laughed. "You've been away from the reservation too long if you think *this* is crazy." She laughed right along with him this time. Because Simon was right. Things happened here, absurd things—like carrying a wolf in a crate to a *Snack-n-Pump*—but somehow things felt right, not absurd, not on this land. She listened to the jumble of voices on the radio stations Raymond had preset in the truck. She couldn't help but laugh a little more.

In the parking lot of the store, she pulled the truck into the only sliver of shade, a knifelike strip cast by the building itself. There wasn't too much to say to Simon now. There was just work to be done. So Simon and Brenda took to ripping down the racks of Slim-Jims and bison jerky that Raymond had so tidily organized and priced several nights earlier. They hauled most of what could be eaten into the stock room and into the men's and women's bathrooms. Then they locked the front door of the store.

The *Snack-n-Pump* was far from empty now, but it was as cleared out as Brenda and Simon were going to get it. The last arrangement Simon made was to take a couple of big buckets from the shelves and fill them with water. The two stood looking at each other now. "Well," Simon said.

"Okay," Brenda said.

They walked to the bed of Raymond's truck and tossed a thin tarp over the crate to blind the wolf to their presence. After that, they scooted the crate with Ciela in it onto the open tailgate. Already, Simon's worn cowboy shirt was wet with sweat, and Brenda was now wishing she'd gotten a drink of water when they filled the buckets in the store. On three, they lifted the crate and waddled awkwardly to the back door, breathing hard and grunting. Once inside, they stood on both sides of the crate. The door could swing open on a hinge, or it could be lifted like a guillotine. With her hands covered by the tarp and her heart slamming to remind her she was doing something important, Brenda reached down and unlatched the door. The two looked at each other, counted breaths, and on three, they pulled the tarp up and the door open.

If she was healthy enough, Ciela would step out, and if Simon and Brenda hauled ass enough, they might make it out of the store before the wolf knew she was free, or at least, free enough to shop at the *Snack-n-Pump*. Brenda was the first one out the back door, and she held it for Simon. When he slammed the door shut behind him, the two of them collapsed against it. "Shit," Simon exhaled.

"Holy shit," Brenda said, and the two of them wilted at the knees.

·   ·   ·

THEY SPENT THE NEXT few hours sitting in front of the store, staring through the smudged plate glass window, waiting for any sight of Ciela. If tourists came by, they shooed them away. "Inventory," Simon explained. "We're closed today for inventory."

"Inventory usually takes place *inside* the store," one businessy-looking traveler said.

"It's Indian inventory," Simon said. "It's different."

The guy looked down at Simon, confused, then walked away.

"Try and call Raymond," Simon said, after hours of seeing nothing but the cash register and the half-cleared aisles and no sign of Ciela. "See if they let him out yet. Tell him what's going on. It's worth a try," Simon said.

Brenda dialed and then clicked the end button when Raymond's voicemail came on after one ring. "Shit." She hung up the phone. "We need Raymond."

"If she was well enough, she'd have left the crate by now," Simon said.

Brenda shook her head, disbelieving. "Could've broken her leg. Something simple like that. Something that keeps her from walking out of her crate, but not from living."

"Could be something like that, sure," Simon said. They both kept looking through the window. After a while, Simon said he was heading home for the night.

"I think I'll stay," Brenda said, and she watched Simon drive away. Come midnight, she curled up in the cab of her father's truck and slept, the smell of sage wafting through the open windows.

·   ·   ·

THE NEXT DAY BROKE more fall-like than the days before it. Sunrise harbored a gentle chill, and the red clouds didn't seem so much full of fire as they were plump with the colors of autumn. Still, by eight o'clock, the back of Brenda's neck was sweating and she was thirsty and ready for something to eat. She checked the store one more time, saw nothing out of place.

There were no words that made her feel better now. Not her usual swearing at nothing, not her usual complaints. It was just silence, this kind of blind optimism that she would not let die, not this time.

As she turned the key in the truck engine, she had to admit that her optimism was beginning to flicker out. She drove the stretch she remembered to Raymond's favorite burrito wagon. Maria was still running the place, and Brenda ordered without introducing herself, taking a quiet pleasure in her anonymous return. There was just no celebration in her right now, so when Maria handed the Styrofoam container to her and thanked her like a stranger, Brenda just said, "Yes, thanks," and plunked two quarters in the empty tip jar.

On the way back, she tried Raymond again. Nothing. She called Simon. Nothing there either. And then she parked the truck and got out.

Standing in front of the store were six people she'd never seen before: four kids, two adults, their faces pressed against the glass. The kids were excited about something, and Brenda had a feeling it was not Slim Jims or red licorice. "Store's closed," she called out, hurrying toward them.

But the man turned away from pressing his face onto the plate glass. "You know what's going on here?" he said.

Brenda's back straightened. The man had the look of awe on his face, not the look of wanting to use the restroom or buy a Coke. He said, "We've been trying to call someone," he said.

"No," Brenda said. "There's no need to call anyone. *No.*" She pushed her way through to a front row position at the window and there, in the store, sitting under the swamp cooler on top of an end-cap display of Coke, sat Ciela. She was curled up, head resting on her haunches in a way that let Brenda know she was probably not feeling well. But when anyone at the window would move just a little bit, that wolf's lip would curl into a beautiful snarl. *Good wolf,* she thought to herself. *Holy shit,* she kept saying inside. *Holy, holy, holy shit.*

"It's okay," Brenda said. "We're not open for business, but it's okay."

"This some Indian ceremony or something?" the woman asked.

"Yes, it's an Indian ceremony," Brenda said. "It's a private ceremony, though."

"Bullshit," the man said. "There's no Indian ceremony in a frickin gas station store."

"We try to keep up with the times," Brenda said, echoing a line she'd heard her father say a dozen times when she used to help him in the store way back when. Whatever she said to them, it worked. The people straggled slowly to their car and moved on.

She couldn't stop looking at Ciela. That wolf was sitting there like the *Snack-n-Pump* was her new territory, these aisles of road maps and 10-40 oil her new home. Those cold coke cans probably felt good on her injured hip. Brenda opened her phone and called Simon. This time he answered. "Come up," she said. "You gotta see what I'm looking at."

Willa

IT CAME OF A sudden. It always worked that way in tracking. Following imprints left over after the animal had disappeared was like reading a story, each imprint a word left on the earth telling a tale that, with any luck, I could step into and become a part of by the end of the story. At home, it was the wolves, the sudden appearance of them across a landscape. Here, it was my brother. He'd risen up from the two-dimensional tracks: my own flesh and blood sitting on the edge of a precipice. Even from a distance I could see his body, as angular and lean as it was when he was a kid. I wanted to sit back and watch for a while, to savor this time before he discovered me, before he understood the reason I was there.

I was scared. I was excited. I was terrified. But it was like we were connected again, like that hook I'd felt back when we used to fish together was still in me and the line between us was unbreakable. I walked toward him, making my way through the wooded land below his cliff. The area was rife with mountain lion sign, no lion in sight at the moment, but fresh sign all the same. The snow fell lightly. I walked. Occasionally, I lost sight of the cliff where he sat, the trees obscuring my line of sight. But he stayed in that one spot. He had set up some kind of camp on this overlook. It seemed like an exposed hiding place for a fugitive, and his decision made the kid in me smile. He had never been predictable.

His hair was longer than I'd ever seen it, past his shoulders. It was the coldest part of the night, the sun rolling around somewhere on the other side of the globe, leaving us to the frozen darkness here, and even so, as far as I could tell, Zeb was not wearing a shirt. I had the urge to keep him warm and protect him. I needed this time with him. I missed our connection.

The trees thinned out, and I was at the base of the granite cliff where he sat. From there, I had to scramble on all fours to reach him. The rocks were jagged, and my gloves were too thick for me to get a good grasp, so I took them off, and the icy granite stung my fingers. The only way up was a twisted route behind the face of the cliff. Occasionally the climb turned to flat sections where I could rest. I sat with my back to the wall and closed my eyes, trying to sort it all out before I met him again. Nothing came but tears.

That's when I felt his presence. I didn't hear him until he sat next to me, on the cliff, and I opened my eyes, and I said his name. "Zeb."

He didn't say anything at first, just wrapped his bare arms around me and held me. He said, "It's been so long, so long, so long," not really talking to me, just letting these words spill out of him. "Willa, it's been so long."

I wanted so much to be able to let my arms wrap around him, too, and I did, but not with the openness I'd hoped for. There was this stupid grudge straight-jacketing me with the promises he'd made long ago, promises I'd believed: that he was going to heal mom, fix the family, find a way out for all of us. They were all just kid's dreams that were never real anyway. But he dreamed them with such violence and desperation that they seeped over into me, and I dreamed them right along with him, believing. He made me believe, goddamnit, and there he was now, again, making me believe that his arms wrapped around me were real and strong and good and that this was not just a passing thing, but something I could depend on. He kept holding me and rocking me and saying my name, and eventually I felt myself holding him, too, and it felt good and sad and confusing, and I felt myself letting go of my age-old grudge. There was nothing now but us: my brother and me.

When he finally let his arms drop, I knew what it meant to be numb. It began in the marrow of my bones and radiated outward. It was not that I felt nothing. It was that I felt everything all at once, and I couldn't name anything except two huge feelings: this utter numbness; this love. I didn't want to think about Polo. I wanted the reason I was there to go away. I wanted to sit with my brother forever. That was everything.

For a little bit, that's exactly what we did. We sat with our legs dangling over the granite ledge, looking out across the meadow. The snow had quit falling now, but crystals still drifted from the branches of trees.

"How'd you know it was me?" I asked.

He laughed a little. "I always know what I'm looking for," he said, just like he used to say about stealing, aware of everything inside a house before he even broke in. "And because you're my sister," he said. "And because those are some smart guys down there, bringing in a tracker like you."

Nothing he said made sense, and all I could think about was the fact that he was shivering. "Aren't you cold?" I asked.

I touched his bare skin, and he took my hand away and assured me he was warm. "It feels good to me out here," he said. He opened his arms slightly to the sky.

I had so many words piled up inside me, but my feelings stifled anything I wanted to say, except, "I've missed you, Zeb." I wanted to tell him I'd had no idea how to reach him over the years, but that was a lie. I had never really tried. There was no way to explain this to him because I was so different than he was: What I went in for, what I wanted most, was always the same thing that made me back away. He had always called it smart and cautious. I only felt it as fear.

So for now, we just sat silently. The snow had stopped, and there was a window of sky that was clear and round and shiny as a black widow's abdomen, stars like little red hourglasses splattered across it. In the distance, I saw a lantern turn on in Polo's tent. I shivered, pulled my shirt tighter around me.

"Yeah," he said. He laughed a little. "They actually sent you."

"What do you mean?"

He smiled the same kid-smile he always did under similar circumstances.

"You telling me you knew they'd send me, Zeb?"

He shook his head. "I didn't *know*." He held out a little longer. "I did what I could. And then, I hoped. I really hoped they'd send you. Didn't think they would, though," he said. "Didn't think they were smart enough to find you. I never could."

"What do you mean? You tried finding me?"

"Every chance I got. Truck stops, late night, sitting at the computer tables. Other guys looking at porn or whatever, and there I am, Googling my little sister." He laughed, making fun of himself. His life over the past years came clearer to me now. He had a mundane job, lived a responsible life; he was an adult, something I never could fathom he would actually become. "And— I know you're a tracker," he said. "That much I know. That's why I hoped like hell they'd send you when I ran. But I kept reading about you tracking wolves somewhere in New Mexico, and I could *not* figure out where that place was. If I could've, I'd have been there, Willa." He looked down and shook his head, and his long hair fell over his bare shoulders. "I'd have been there."

His words tugged on me. I looked for a response that made sense. All I could say was, "Yeah, they keep it pretty quiet, the place I work. It took them years to show me the compound. It's a kind of halfway house for the wolves they plan to release."

He laughed a little. So did I, but neither one of us knew why we were laughing.

"Well, you do good work, Willa. You've always done good work." There was a silence between us, and then he said, "So, you going to turn me in?"

"No." I said it quick as a reflex. "I never had any intention of that." I was too tense to smile with him now, too serious. "I came because I was scared," I told him. "And to see you."

"Scared?"

"That this was a set up."

"It *is* a set up. They're here to take me in."

"No. They're not going to do that, Zeb."

He laughed.

"No way," I said.

He gave me the big brother look that told me he knew more than I could begin to fathom. He shrugged. "Anyway, why the hell would *you* be scared?"

My guts quivered. "I thought they knew something about what I did back then," I said. "I thought they had something on me."

"Ah, Willa. Nothing you ever did was bad. It was all me. It was always all me."

It was all I could do to keep from holding him and making him warm now. I didn't want him sitting next to me and shivering so much in the cold. My throat ached, and the words felt impossible. Our past enveloped me, and I was shivering right along with him, like when I was a kid. And then I said, out loud, for the first time ever, "I was there with Mom, Zeb. I helped Mom on her last day. I helped her die. She asked me to, and I did. It was the same thing you did to Chet, Zeb, but she was my mother, our mother. I killed our mother."

His back stiffened in a way I remembered from when we were kids, and he took a deep breath. "Christ," he said, through his teeth. It frightened me. "Does Dad know?"

"I never told him. But he figured it out."

"That's why—"

"That's why he shut down, yeah."

He stared straight ahead, trying to make sense of it all.

"You talked to Dad since you left?"

I shook my head, my teeth chattering and my head pounding with a spinning ache. I wanted him to hold me. But he sat staring straight ahead, saying nothing. Finally, he sighed, a huge sigh as if he'd been holding that single breath since I last saw him. "My god, it's not the same thing, Willa," he said. His voice was firm, but not angry. "You were helping someone. I wasn't helping anyone."

"Dolly."

"No. It's like instinct in me, something that won't go away once it turns loose in me. It's not the same thing at all. *Not at all.*"

I couldn't hear his words. They blurred all around me. "You don't know."

"I *do* know," he said. "There's a lot I don't know. But I *know* that. It was not the same." His arm was still around my shoulders, and he pulled me closer to him. "I can't believe I left you to do that. Alone," he said. His voice softened. "What—what did she say to you? What did Mom say?"

"She asked me to help her. She didn't want to go, Zeb, but she was barely living, and there was no way to change it or make it better or—"

"No. On the day she died. Did she say anything to you, like something to help us now, you know, something to keep us going?"

I wanted to answer him, but I couldn't remember anything about the day itself, just the last breaths my mother took, how there was no separation between us at all, and then there was only separation. A kind of permanent separation I'd never felt before and had not stopped feeling since. I felt myself growing smaller and smaller and pretty soon, I was curled up in Zeb's lap. I cried until everything turned grey inside me and there was nothing left. He didn't move, didn't say a word the whole time. He just sat with me.

"I'm sorry," I told him. "I'm so sorry."

He shook his head and pressed his finger to my lips. Then he sat perfectly still and stared at nothing, blinking deliberately and slowly, as if each movement he made, even his breathing, came from a clear decision. He stared for a long time, and after a while, he took out his Zig-Zag papers and rolled a smoke with that same slow deliberation that had become his way. He didn't light the cigarette, just licked the seam of it, and held it in his hands. "My god. We were so . . . small," he said.

"We were kids."

"No. We were smaller than kids. We were nothing." He was not speaking to me, just speaking out into the air. We sat, my brother and I, in the night, in the mountains, the place we'd always dreamed of when we when we were kids. I always thought when we met again we'd have so much to say. But instead, there was a deep quiet between us. It was not the same quiet as the distance we'd been stuck in. It was comfort. It was home. We sat for some time saying nothing. After a while, I asked him, "So you were smart enough to think they might bring me here. What now?"

He didn't respond.

"You always know. You always have a plan. Tell me you have something, some way out of this for us both."

Still nothing. There was this understated way about him now, something I'd never expected of him, not when he was a kid. All that agitation he'd had, it seemed to have evaporated like so much mist. He didn't fidget when he had nothing to say. If he wasn't ready to talk, he just sat quietly. It was unnerving in almost the same way his fitfulness was when he was younger. Eventually, he tried to answer me, but the sentences came out flat and plain and had nothing to do with the plan I needed to know about. "Everything was broken," he said. "You go back and look at it now—it's all broken up, that field we played in every day, the place we lived, the house where Mom grew up, our lives, everything—sounds like a small thing, like nothing, really. But it got to me somehow." He said, "It made me crazy, Willa. It didn't mean a thing to anyone else, that land, but that was our lives there."

I couldn't help but be concerned about the cold on Zeb's bare skin, but when I drew attention to it again, he brushed me away. But I kept at it, offering him my jacket and begging him to keep warm. My insistence broke his stare and his rambling. "Leaving was all I could do," he said clearly now. "I was scared about killing Chet, yeah. But that wasn't everything. That wasn't the only reason I left." He explained how he'd hidden out for a long time, five years or so. He'd lost track of the time during those years, so he was not sure. He was barely seventeen years old, and he'd squatted on some land in the mountains, lived in a tent year round, sold cords of wood in the winter, done odd jobs for families, and worked illegal trades now and then when nothing else came through. I tried to imagine my young, scruffy-Elvis brother living the life he was telling me now. It felt distant, and at the same time, it got under my skin; I knew the images of him struggling like this would never leave me. He told me he'd sold pot and had run other drugs. He'd gotten to know truckers this way, had made connections, and had friends scattered all the way from Maine to California.

Then one guy, Mike, a major drug runner he didn't much care for, but one who owned a legitimate trucking fleet and had enough dirty cash to pay his drivers and mechanics under the table, offered him a job. A few years later, when everything felt cool and his past felt distant enough, driving turned into a steady gig, paycheck, taxes, all the fixtures of a regular American life. He took the legal runs Mike offered and started a career. "'Bout that time," he said, "Is when I ran into Brenda."

I could still smell the rose petals from the drawer, feel their fragile age in my palm. I rested my hands on my knees, the scars where I'd scraped them on the sidewalk year after year with Brenda, making smooth and shiny circles beneath my jeans.

"She misses you," he said.

"Brenda?"

He nodded.

"She never liked you, you know." The words fell out of my mouth as if I were twelve years old again.

He laughed. "Well, some things never change, I guess."

"She coming back? To the cabin? Does she know your plan?"

He shook his head and shrugged. "Neither one of us have ever been much into planning things." He looked up at me now. "If she figures out you're here, though, she'll be back, for sure."

"It's been a long time, Zeb. I might mean nothing to her now."

"Everything means nothing to Brenda. It doesn't keep her from loving it strong."

Through the trees, I saw a lantern come on in a tent in Polo's camp. A man stepped out of the tent, smoked, then walked back in.

"Don't worry about them," Zeb said.

"I *am* worried. I've got a lot on the line here, Zeb. So do you." I looked straight at him now. "I'm not losing you again. Not this time."

He pressed his hand on my leg to settle me. He kept talking, steady and slow. "Brenda still talks about you, tells old stories. Hell, they make up half her storytelling collection."

I was distracted now, looking down at Polo's tent. "Yeah, I think about her, too. I talk to her father. He misses her."

"Her old man?"

"Yeah. Whatever I didn't learn from you about hunting and tracking, I learned from him."

"What're you talking about? Her father's dead."

"I mean her blood father. Her Indian father."

"Kabotie?"

"Raymond, yeah."

"Raymond Kabotie's working with *your* wolves?" he said.

"Yeah. I mean he's not formally employed, but I couldn't do the work without him. He knows more about those wolves than—"

"Kabotie's not helping you," he said. "He shoots wolves."

His words jolted me. They didn't make any sense. This whole thing felt like one of Zeb's lies, like when we were kids and he was trying to trick me into something he wanted. I wanted it to go away now. "I don't believe it," I said.

He tilted his head and shrugged.

"All right," I said. "So tell me. What do you know? How do you know it?"

"I know what Brenda told me. I know he shot wolves for ranchers. They can't have the blood on their hands. Too much at stake if they get caught. So Kabotie tracked them, damn good tracker. And then he shot them. That's why Brenda left. She couldn't stand it. When she found out, she left."

Stars dimmed and went out in the east, and the faint outline of the mountains became visible. Soon, Polo's men would be waking. There was no taming the mix of emotion that stormed me now, and no outlet for them either. What I needed to know right now and what I was learning were two very different things. I needed to know Zeb's plan, nothing else. But Zeb was telling me this bullshit about Raymond. I thought of the times I'd been with Raymond, the singing and praying he'd done for the wolves, his absolute connection to them. *That howl*, he said to me sometimes. *It's a direct line to our evolution, something we think we've forgotten, but we haven't. It's in us. It's a part of ourselves we can't name. It's sanctified.* "You're wrong about Raymond," I said, finally, plain and simple.

He kept it simple, too. "I hope I'm wrong," he said, then he let it go. Nothing phased him or shook him these days. It was like when he was younger, when he faked calmness to appear strong. Except now, his calmness felt real. Nothing seeped into him. As if we'd never exchanged a word about Raymond and the wolves, he wrapped his arms around his own torso, rubbed his hands up and down his bare biceps. "Anyway," he sighed. "I don't really have a plan, Willa. I just—" He paused and looked around, as if tracking something with his eyes, but there was nothing there. "I'm thankful for having this chance to see you. Yeah. I'm so thankful about that."

Sounds of the morning started up, a few nuthatches peeping, the occasional cries of scrub jays. I had minutes with Zeb before Polo woke. I took the gun and the knife I'd found out of my pocket, held them out for him to see. "You want these back?"

His eyebrows raised slightly in surprise. Then he shook his head, no.

"You want to tell me about the lion you're tracking?" Even this didn't jar him. "What's going on, Zeb? It's freezing cold and you've got nothing. How did you even make it through the first few days out here?"

"I've been dancing," he said. "Went into town and danced at Gnarly's, something I never did enough of in my life." He had this smile that I remembered, one that got under my skin for all the lies it told.

"You really don't have a plan?" I asked again.

The moonlight caught the water forming in the corners of his eyes. "You should go back now," he said

"I'm not leaving."

"Look, if I tell you what's going on for me, it makes you complicit. I don't want that shit. I never wanted that shit. You never stole anything without me telling you to do it, Willa. What you did with Mom and what I did to Chet, they're different. You gotta know that." He took a deep breath. "But it's going to be okay now. Everything's going to be okay."

The sunlight bent over the horizon. I figured Polo and his men must have been on the verge of waking. "So you *do* have a plan?"

He wrapped his arms around me again in answer. He held me close, and I could feel warm tears from his face dripping onto my neck. He said, "It'll be fine. Everything will be *fine*." Before he pulled away from me, he wiped tears from his cheek, and when I looked at him again, his eyes were clear brown and innocent, as always.

"All right. I have to go back now," I told him. "Promise me you'll come find me, Zeb. If we don't meet up." I tried to walk away like when I was a kid. The tug was still there. "I have so much I want to show you. The wolves. My friends. My life."

"It'll be all right," he said.

There wasn't anything left for me to do. For both of our sakes, I had to go back to camp. As I walked away, he said, "Willa," just my name, said it soft enough that I knew it was mostly to himself. I didn't turn and look back at him.

•   •   •

I WALKED BACK TO camp. There was nothing else I could do. I crawled inside my tent, a thin tremble of sleeplessness running throughout my body. I pulled my sleeping bag up around my neck. The earth was frozen hard, but it felt familiar and comfortable. I closed my eyes, hoping to rest. But the sleep that came was deep and fast. When I heard Polo's voice outside my tent, I woke up disoriented, my head full of images of Magda and Cario, dreams so vivid that I could hear their voices, and I almost reached out for Christina as I woke up here, in this cold place with this strange man's voice coming through the tent at me.

Polo called again from outside the tent, and I asked him to give me a second. The acrid stench of their Marlboros tainted the snowy air. They talked, and I could hear them moving around, and pieces of last night with Zeb fell into my memory. I was half giddy, elated to have seen him, scared about where he was now, but I had to pull it all together for the day with Polo. I had to fake it good. I knew where Zeb was. I could lead them away from him now. *I could lead them off track.* I unzipped the tent, and the reddish-pink snow of dawn flooded the ground, and then it hit me. I saw it in him now, the same look in Zeb that I'd seen in Mom. "Fuck!"

"You say something, Willa?" Polo asked.

I unzipped the fly of the tent, stood next to Polo, and slapped his arm. "Let's move," I told him. "Let's get on the trail. We've got to find him. We've got to find Zeb now." Polo stood there confused, and I took off, hoping he'd follow. I'd lead him right to Zeb. I would not let him go through with his plan. I would not let go of my brother this time.

Zeb

HE HAD IMAGES IN his head. Who he was, who he'd wanted to be, and who he had become. They were layered one on top of the other like transparent playing cards, the ace landing on the king, the king on the nine, the nine on the deuce—a blur of luck and strategy that no longer interested him, this life. Now he carried an image of this: He would walk into the woods. He had an appointment with the mountain lion. That's what it felt like to him. They had agreed on something, and a hunter keeps true to his word. And so he would walk, and he would find her tracks. They were always there, had become part of the landscape he read daily, a story he had written himself into long ago. He didn't plan on killing her. It was not revenge. It was just a matter of loose ends he had to tie up, of letting go of something that had twisted and knotted itself around the coils of his mind.

As he walked, he felt the tug of the world falling away. He thought it would be difficult. He thought walking away from everything like this would undo his regret. It was a decision he'd made with sadness, but as he walked, it transformed into the deepest elation, this shivering cold, this giddy laughter that followed. And then there was a kind of peace.

The letting go grew easier from then on.

He had planned this much: to face the lion as any animal faces another animal, no protection, no weapons, unencumbered. The night wrapped around him, and he walked bare chested, and then barefooted, and the colder he got, the more he felt the illusion of heat. The snow ached against his feet. He hadn't felt that kind of pleasurable pain before, not that he could remember, not like this. It felt as if his bare feet rooted him to the earth and lifting them tugged at the sinews of his legs, a sharp sting that had always been there but had been shielded.

In his mind, he saw himself tangling with the lion barehanded. He'd seen this on TV when he was younger. He'd read it in stories. He'd read the myth of the man who had been punished by the gods in Greek mythology, the one whose chest had been split open for eternity, buzzards plucking at his heart, and he had wondered why that was a punishment, when it felt to him like the only way to live in the world. He longed for his own sternum to split, for the air to touch his open chest, his heart pumping and alive. It was how his sister had lived. He thought he'd seen this in Willa, her innocence and openness, compared to his sutured life.

The air chilled to icy blackness, slick and sharp and smothering his skin. He imagined himself meeting the cougar. He sat at the entrance to her den and waited. They had made several appointments in the past, and she had kept every one of them. This would be the final one. He savored the couple of hours he'd spent with Willa. But he felt his ties with her loosening now. He let them sag. He let her go. After a while of sitting and shivering, he started walking, no longer waiting, but now actively tracking the lion. There were the usual signs, old and crusted over, unreadable if you didn't already know they were there, vestiges of what had already been left behind. There were newer tracks, the ones he'd come across earlier. He kept on through the woods. His head tangled itself up with images of what it would be like when he met the lion. He would face her, and they would lock gazes. That in itself would be a challenge to her, would make her attack him. It's what he wanted. He imagined her leaping and saw her tawny-furred underbelly as she leapt, claws unsheathed, sinking into his flesh. He felt the full weight of her. He was strong enough to give her a good fight. He felt her claws hooked into him, and he didn't dream of surviving. It wasn't about survival. He had been done with his life for some time. If you listened, he believed, you could hear the moment when your life let go of you. The rest was just hanging on.

For one glorious moment, before he died, there would be his body and hers wrapped around each other, his belly pressed close to her wild body as they fell to the ground together, and they would be bound into a whole until her jaws clamped down onto his neck, teeth to bone, and then a snap, and his life would be over. He wondered if he would be able to feel her dragging him away. If, like Rosalita, the snowy earth would be the last thing he felt on his skin. He wondered if he would feel her devouring him, as they said of deer, that the deer were still living as the big cats tore their flesh and opened the rib-caged cavity of their bodies.

Everything was a story. And the story he told became the only truth he knew. The farther he walked, the more the night chilled. His body shook with cold. There was no glory in this. He knew what it felt like now, this shivering, this craving stillness beneath his skin and no way to turn off the shaking. His bones felt more alive than his skin now, the way they chattered to hold onto life, the way they would not let him sink into the earth.

And then the cold seeped inside him, and he quit shaking. The skin of his feet looked charred, his toes completely numb now. It felt as if the inside of him was crystallizing, his heart shattering off into facets, his blood slowing like mud. He felt warm, even hot. He stripped down to nothing but his boxers now. The lion was nowhere, at least not that he could see. His thoughts had turned to dreams. His thoughts became the images he'd seen, the ones he'd dreamed of for himself. His body lay on the snowy ground now, and dreams leeched his mind. It was not how he'd expected it to be, his last moment of life. It was not glorious. Or wild. It was something altogether different. He wanted to turn back. He had not expected that, but there was no undoing it now. His body was no longer his, and his thoughts had become ghosts. He had already become memory in the minds of those he had loved.

◦ ◦ ◦

WHAT HE LEFT BEHIND as he walked told the story of him letting things fall away. The imprint left by his footprints grew lighter and lighter, the weight of him lessened with each step until he turned too light to leave any spore at all. Polo guessed it was intentional and directed at him. "The sonofabitch's last defiance," he said. "A fucking suicide mission, a fucking waste of my time."

Willa didn't see it that way. By the time they found Zeb, later the following evening, his limbs were swollen and black as a lightning-struck tree, the rest of his body frozen and stiff, skin on his chest blue as new-fallen snow but muted and fleshy and horrifying in its utter objectness. If it had not been her brother, the sight might have sickened her. But she knelt by Zeb's side, and she cried. She looked at his body, then she lay down on the snowy earth and held him close to her. She sobbed, and it felt like oceans inside her, the uncertainty that Zeb had taught her, the constant way he'd made her question everything, all of it turning still now, turning permanently. She felt Polo standing above her, and she said her brother's name softly to herself: Zebulon Pike Robbins.

By the time she let him go, she knew Polo was wrong. Zeb wasn't defiant at all. He never had been. He'd been devoured by some story he'd never even read, some dream that had seeped into his bones without him being able to name it, the tracks of that story leaving an imprint on him that he could not name and could never trap or escape or revise to make it his own story. The beauty of the animal he had hunted and consumed, this time, had been himself.

After

By evening, Polo and Willa had made it back to camp. They didn't have too many words for each other. "So what's this all mean to you?" Willa asked, before they parted ways. "Why did Zeb matter so damn much to you?"

"Sonofabitch didn't have the guts to face me," he said. "To come in to the office and do his confession there. To come in and face me and own up."

Own up. The words made Willa laugh. What was owned and what was lost. There was a thin line between the two notions, and each one canceled the other out. What remained was what could not be taken away, the final imprint of a life, a track blown away by wind, perceptible maybe by some trained eye somewhere. But even then, it was never certain.

.   .   .

Willa walked inside the cabin, lifted a few of the rose petals from the dresser drawer into a nylon stuff sack. When she returned back outside, she asked for information about Brenda. Polo said he wished he could help, but he knew nothing.

"Tell her I was here," Willa said. "Tell her I'd like to see her. If you see her, please give her my contact information." She handed Polo a piece of paper.

Polo agreed, and she figured he'd honor his word. He had at least that much to prove to Zeb, even now. As she cleaned up her campsite and tossed the issued gear back to Polo, she thought of walking back through Zeb and Brenda's cabin one more time. But it felt meaningless. She had no idea when and if Brenda would be back to the cabin. What was in the house had little to do with Zeb. She'd had years with him, and they had left their mark on her, and she'd had a couple of hours with him before his death. That time, those hours: That's what she would keep.

As for the mules and the horse that remained, they were hers now, Polo said, next of kin because the marriage between Zeb and Brenda had never been legal. "Here's the name and address of the boy in town who's taking care of them," Polo said. He handed her a sticky note.

She stood outside the cabin, looking at the closed doorway, and said her goodbyes. Then she climbed into her truck, and the engine hummed. The icy pathway pitched the wheels this way and that, and the gouged road reminded her of her home on the mesa. She wanted to be there. With Christina. With Magda and Cario, too. Instead, she followed the map Polo had drawn (not much to map in this town: a gas station, a gun shop, a bar) and pulled up to an old wooden house, tawny paint peeling off the sides like birch bark, just off the state highway, behind Gnarly's Tavern. She knocked on the door, and a tall, bony man with a long, hollow face and a crooked-toothed smile answered. "Help ya?" he said.

"I'm Willa Robbins," she said. He stared. "Zeb Robbins's sister."

He smiled, bent forward a little bit, and his lanky arms dangled for a moment before he palmed her on the back and invited her in. "What can I get you? Whiskey? Beer? You name it."

She shook her head. "Thanks, no, I'm on the road and—"

"What the hell's happening up there with Zeb?" He ignored her words and folded in the middle like a suitcase as he plopped into a sunken La-Z-Boy chair. He leaned forward, chin on his hand, squinting and engaged. "That goddamn crazy Zeb," he said, before she could answer. He shook his head and laughed. "Must've been something growing up with him as a brother."

"It was something."

He stretched out his arm, but from where he sat, she couldn't get there fast enough to shake it before he absently recoiled it and resumed shaking his head. "I'm Frank," he said, still rambling on. "Yeah, that goddamn crazy Zeb, he's the only news we get around here, you know. Don't see much of him. But we sure hear a lot."

She nodded.

"You know, they put parking meters along the highway here once. Like a half a dozen meters is all. So Zeb come down here one night and sawed the tops off 'em." He laughed. "Didn't leave a trace, but there those meters were, just naked posts with their heads chopped off. They'll never catch him," he said. "No way, not unless he wants to be caught. Well, hell, you know that. You're his sister, probably got some of his ways in you too, right? You sure I can't get you a drink?" He stood up now and poured himself a Crown Royale, showed the bottle to her. "Special occasion, right?" He poured her a shot over a single ice cube, and she took it and sat it on the side table made of an electrical cable spool. Finally, he sat back down again, and he listened.

"I'm looking for Tommy," she said.

Frank craned his veiny neck over the top of the chair and hollered his son's name. A teenager with a Mohawk that swept down his back like a skinny black river came in from outdoors. He wore muddied boots and had a tree tattooed on the side of his head, the roots of the tree crawling down his neck and spreading like fingers gripping his throat under the collar of his black thermal shirt. He didn't say anything, just stood there, a tabby cat curled up in his arms.

"The mules and the horses you been taking care of for Zeb and Brenda. You got a place to keep them?" Willa asked Tommy.

"They already got a place," the kid said. His voice was like a hiccup, restrained and way back in this throat, choppy and hiding its own kindness.

"You like those animals?" Willa asked.

"Chey, that horse. Best horse I ever rode. Zeb favors Lita. Me, I always liked Chey."

Willa looked at Frank. "I'll send you money to care for them." She looked back at the kid. "If Brenda doesn't come back in a couple of weeks, they're yours. You take care of them."

The kid's eyes widened. He looked at his dad.

"That's Zeb's property, Ma'am," Frank said. "Can't be giving his shit away."

"Zeb won't be needing them."

Frank leaned in toward Willa. "Dad," Tommy said. He tried not to sound desperate or excited. But he needed to know. "Can I?"

Frank's long body sunk back into his chair. He stared off. "They caught him? They finally caught Zeb?"

"My brother's dead," Willa said. She felt the words in herself, and they numbed her and split her open at the same time. She didn't hide the few tears that started up, but sat straight and looked at Frank, who buckled over in his chair now, not sad, but angry. "Did you know my brother well?"

Frank looked up, his face red. "As good as anyone knew him, I guess. Liked him. Liked him a lot."

Willa looked hard at Frank as if trying to see some of Zeb in him. "You know the woman living with him?"

"Brenda." Frank laughed. "Oh, hell yeah, everyone knows Brenda."

"Think she'll be coming back for those animals?" She looked at Tommy. He looked like Zeb at his age, living on an edge sharp enough that it toughened his own skin but left his insides shredded and vulnerable and tired because of all the effort he put toward refusing everything.

"Brenda? Hell. No telling what she'll do," Frank said. "She wouldn't knowingly hurt them animals or leave them out there all alone. But she might not be back. You just never know about her. She's got her own code."

Willa stood up and handed Frank a hundred dollars. "That'll take care of them until we know if she's coming back. And if she comes back, I'm counting on you to tell her I want to see her. I'll

write you a bill of sale for the animals in case she doesn't show."
She looked at Tommy. "I'm leaving them to you, you know, not to
your dad. I'm sure he's a fine man, but I am leaving Zeb's animals
to you, Tommy."

Frank agreed. Tommy said nothing to the people in the room,
but he whispered something to the cat, and he glanced at Willa
and then stepped over and shook her hand. If he'd talked, she was
sure he would have never quit talking, never quit saying thanks
to her for this small gesture. But he stayed quiet. "I'll send money
regularly for their care," Willa said.

"Like hell you will," Frank said. "I got Gnarly's over there.
I pull down a good wage. We don't need no money being sent
in from outside." Willa wasn't in the mood to push it. She
thanked him and then headed toward the door. "That's it?"
Frank said.

"What else is there?" She stopped with her hand resting on
the doorknob.

"No ceremony? No service for your own kin?"

"I have some business to take care of back home, then I'm
coming up to arrange it."

"No," Frank said.

Again, Willa was not in the mood. She opened the door and
started out.

"Where is he?"

Willa tried to hide her clenching jaw, her reddening eyes. She
stepped back inside. "My brother?"

"Where's Zeb?"

She squinted to understand what she thought was one rude
and dim-witted question. "Like I said. He's passed. I imagine he's
right where they left him."

"That mountain lion take him after all?"

"No."

"Well then there's something left of him somewhere."

"They're taking care of it," Willa said.

Frank stood over her now, and when she said this, his back
curved like a hook. "They?"

"The people that set out looking for him."

"No," he said, before she could finish. "It's not right."

"Well, they've got—"

"They got no right. He's your brother, man. Those son-sabitches, they got no notion of what Zeb asked to be done with his remains."

Frank was beginning to make a bit of sense to her now.

"He doesn't want that shit, that ceremony, that formal crap."

Willa stopped short of saying what was on her mind, that Zeb had finally quit wanting anything. He'd done so much stealing he'd realized there was nothing he could own anyway. But Frank's anger had fingered its way into the guilt of her, and into her heart, too, and she felt friendship and love coming out of every word Frank spoke about Zeb. "What're you thinking?" she asked.

He pulled on a thick flannel shirt-jacket and opened the door. "Look, I have to at least open up over at Gnarly's. Ody can take over for me once I get it opened," he said. "You got some time to talk?" Willa stood up and followed him on the short path up to the highway where Gnarly's was located.

She sat on a bar stool while Frank started a fire in the wood stove, opened the cash register, and did whatever he had to do to get the bar ready. She didn't know if there was a spirit to be passed on, but if there was such a passing, she felt like it might be now for Zeb. While she sat there with Frank, clinking glasses and cutting fresh limes, it was as if Zeb were there, talking with her, telling that same story about the fox.

But this time, when the story came to her, Zeb's life had ended. She remembered the whole of it now, how the fox lay bloodied on Zeb's chest, and her picture of his life shifted. Her picture of her own life growing up with him shifted too, the differences between her and her brother and how they viewed the world. The connection they'd shared remained. But she was different than he was, had been since the beginning. The choices she had made with her mother were not the same as the choices Zeb had made. She understood that now, and she had learned it from him.

From then on, whenever she told the story of the fox, she'd tell it all the way to the end. Because she understood now that it was not true that you can't change the past. You tell a story different than you told it before, you tell it without any gaps or omissions or parts where you make up your own twist at the end, and the past changes. You tell it true, and it changes the present and the future, too. It changes your life. Like freeing a fox from a trap.

.   .   .

WHEN FRANK FINALLY CAME over and sat next to her, she was already remembering Zeb differently, more honestly than she had over the decades they'd been apart. Maybe more honestly than ever. His contradictions were final now, and she embraced them wholly.

Frank was a jittery man. Nervous energy poured out of him, accounting for his lanky frame. He was a kind man, but he had these jitters, even when he seemed otherwise calm. He sat next to her, his foot tapping the bar stool as he spoke. "They haven't taken his body away yet, right?" he said.

"Right," Willa said.

He convinced her over the next half hour that he knew what Zeb would have wanted. It was out of the question for Zeb to leave a will or any directions for burial. "But he sat right here less than a week ago and pretty much said what he wanted," he told her. "He was telling that story, knowing, *knowing* he was going to die," Frank said, "He knew what he had planned. Right? He was saying how that roadie had been loyal to Parsons. He was asking the same of us. Right?"

He said it was a friend's duty to oblige. Wild with some kind of adoration for Zeb, Frank was set on some crazy idea, and there was nothing she could do to stop him. She was not convinced she should try to stop him anyway.

She told Frank where Zeb's body had been found, under the cliffs where the lion had sometimes been seen. "But it was hypo-thermia," she told him. "Not the lion."

. . .

SHE DIDN'T KNOW HOW long it would take Frank to make his way up the mountain, or even if he would actually make the trek. She didn't know what Frank would find, if anything.

She spent the night in a roadside motel with six rooms. She slept late the next morning, exhausted from the days before. In the afternoon, she headed out. The road twisted downward, and the mountain silhouettes loomed in her rearview mirror.

three

The Return

*I*DON'T THINK ANYONE ever does someone else's dying right. There's no telling if we do our own right, and my guess is that matters less anyway. On the highway heading south, I rested my hand on a note Mom had written, something she left for all of us before she died, something I'd carried with me ever since. I don't know why I never showed it to Dad and didn't tell Zeb about it, even when he asked. Maybe I felt like he was looking for something that would answer his questions, and I knew the nothing and the everything that this note answered.

I have to leave now, but please know I'll be with you always. When you hear meadowlarks in the spring and see geese flying across the field in the fall, think of me. But please don't be sad. I always wanted you to be happy. Remember I will love you always. There were so many things I wanted to do still, so many things left to say to all of you. I wasn't afraid of dying. It was just leaving all of you that was so hard. We can't see beyond, but this much I know: I loved you all so much, and it was heaven having your love in return.

I think because of the meadowlark I buried, because of the stealing and the broken promises, I wanted to keep this one thing for myself. It's selfish. If I'd known Zeb was dying, I would have shared it with him. That's the story I'll tell now, because revision is always cleaner than the first pass. But the perfection of it, if we could live it, wouldn't leave any grit in the wound to remind us of what we had lost. Right now, driving, I don't believe we ever really want to heal. We just want to move on, carrying our wounds with us, imperfect and moving ahead.

Before I head home, I drive one last time past the field where Zeb and I grew up, where Mom grew up before us, and her parents before that. Any imprint we had on this place is lost now, buried under so much of what we don't need. But that matters less than the imprint it made on us, and I'm grateful for that now. Without the grit in the wound, I might be able to forget it. But it stays with me, the whole field and the stars and the meadowlarks and the green-sweet smell of new grass in summer and the musty scent of the wet-and-dead grass in winter, and the fish swimming in the muck in January and jumping like praying hands out of the water in June. None of it is lost. None of it can be stolen.

I drive past the field and to the house where Zeb and I grew up. The drapes are open, and I can see my father sitting in his chair. This is the only way I have seen him since I left home, through the window, sitting in his chair. I park the car, take the note Mom wrote, and carry it to the door. I knock. I wait. I want to peer in the window from this closer distance, but it feels like an intrusion. And so I wait.

There's nothing. No answer. Not even footsteps. I take the note from my pocket, and I wedge it between the seal on the door. I walk away.

I imagine my father finding the note. I imagine him being alone when he learns of Zeb's death, of reaching out to me when he understands what happened. For a moment, I even imagine seeing him again, talking with him.

I drive my truck away from my home and take the highway south. I drive through the open prairie where pronghorns graze and the Air Force Academy is having some kind of practice. Low flying planes strafe the land, and helicopters sputter overhead.

Occasionally, a skydiver, or a group of skydivers, floats down to the prairie. Their floating doesn't look like practice for war. It looks almost beautiful, the way the soldiers hanging from those gliders seem as if they have chosen this falling, this landing back on earth. It takes so much machinery to ascend, and so much grace to return to land.

I wait for the moment when my own life will return to me. When the permanence of Zeb's loss will shift the way I live now—will shift my life permanently—but will also send me back to my day to day life. It happens when I hit the New Mexico border. I know it will happen in layers, but the first shift I notice takes place when I leave "Colorful Colorado" and enter "The Land of Enchantment." I know there is a life waiting for me here and that the life will look different now than it ever has before, and it will remain different, thank god. I wait for the tectonic shift to lock into place inside me, to form some new continent I can stand on. But for now, all I feel is the shifting. I want to return here, to my home. *I want this life.*

The thing I notice: When a part of you empties out, it feels hollow, for sure, but it also feels good, the wonder of what will fill that place, in a different way, but all the same.

By the time I hit the border, stars fill the black sky, and I feel three strands of my life pulling me home: The first is Magda and Cario. They are my everyday, the ones I take for granted and who take me for granted because there is something necessary in this—the assumption that, yes, they'll be there, no matter the misunderstandings or the offenses between us. I don't know them well. I don't know their pains and their losses. What I know is the path they walk daily and what they do to pass the time day-to-day. They walk to my house. We cook. We share a meal and some conversation. It is glorious, this passing of time without worry, without meaning. Having some unscrutinized part of my life makes life not only worth living, it *is* living. Maybe it's the heart of it all. The scrutinized life is overrated.

And then there is Raymond. I could turn the opposite direction on this road and see him. I think of what Zeb told me, that Raymond has killed wolves. I want to forget Zeb ever said it. I don't know which is more important, the truth, or the love that the truth could destroy. For now, I'm betting on the love. I'm trusting in Raymond. But I'll wait and see.

The third strand is the wolves. I need to know they have survived. What they have become to me—I can't put a finger on it. They are every strand I have ever lived all woven into one long braid of time. They are, like Raymond says, a connection to a past that goes beyond my own past. They are wild, and they are completely dependent on us, on our every decision. The only truth they know is hunger; their only right or wrong is survival; their only belief is the day as it comes to them. It's not how I want to live. But I need them to live that way, to remind me that everything beyond this is gravy.

I pick up my cell phone, and it feels foreign. Even still, I see the familiar icons that tell me Cario and Magda called nineteen times while I was out on the mountain, looking for Zeb. They never call me on my cell phone, except in emergencies. It's a difficult decision to make, given the attachment and loyalty I feel to the wolves. But regardless of what Zeb said, I *know* Raymond will take care of the wolves. What I want most is one of Magda's enchiladas smothered in chili verde with some homemade chorizo, frijoles, and plenty of empty conversation. Maybe some silence. Or some stupid TV to annoy me. I want to be annoyed by something meaningless. I consider going to Raymond's first, but instead, I take the turn toward the mesa that is my home.

I hit the dirt road that winds up the side of the mesa just as the moon slips out from under some clouds. *Holy shit.* I had forgotten the feel of *this* gravel popping under my tires, the sound it makes as it rumbles through the truck and up into my chest, jostling my breathing in the most beautiful way. The smell of sage has never been my favorite, not in and of itself. It smells, to me, like a closet of sweaty clothes, and I've complained about it to Cario and Magda. But right now, it is the sweet and welcome stink of home. There is the shadow-red mesa pasted flat against the indigo sky. A few coyotes yip.

I dim the lights and pull the truck into the U-shaped piece of land where I will park it, and it will sit naked and stark in summer, covered with snow in winter. The slopey-topped mountains of New Mexico—so unlike the craggy ranges in Colorado—diminish my truck to a Tonka toy sitting beside a Monopoly-sized adobe hut on the mesa. I want to live my small life here forever.

I turn the key, and the truck rumbles to silence. I walk into my home—no key, the door left open, no fear of anyone stealing anything. I'm the only trained thief I know.

I take a few minutes and sit alone on the couch. I imagine Zeb being here with me. I wanted that. I wanted to show him the life I've come to love, the life that is possible. Not special, not "free," as he would call it (a term I have never understood). Just possible.

As I'm sitting there, late night, my phone pulses. It's news from Polo about Zeb—that someone set the hillside on fire intentionally, kept it contained as long as they could, then fled the scene. It was the exact spot where Zeb's body lay. "Looks like someone had it out for Zeb," Polo says.

"Something like that," I tell him, knowing. Thanking Frank.

"There was very little left of him," Polo says. "This was definitely directed at Zeb. Looks like he had more than a few enemies." I listen, knowing that what was left of Zeb was more than Polo could ever imagine, that the fire was part of Zeb's own doing, his friends looking out for him, even still.

When I hang up, I try to imagine going back there for a traditional burial ceremony. It seems an affront, in the aftermath. I'll find my own way to say goodbye. I dial the phone and call Frank at Gnarly's, knowing he'll be there till two AM, at least. I tell him I probably won't be back.

"Sure thing," he says. He tells me they're having a party in town, "Starting now and ending when we can't dance anymore," he says.

I thank him. "You let me know if you hear from Brenda."

"Sure thing," he says. Then he tells me Tommy is a good boy. He tells me how much Tommy cares for things, how much he loves animals, and, "He loves working hard, as long as it's outside." He says, "He doesn't come off that way, you know. But you gotta get to know him. He's a good boy. Hard worker. A responsible kid. He does a good job."

"I understand," I tell him. I understand hardworking kids who haven't found a way to make their kind of work valued in this world. When I hang up, I know my last visit to those mountains will have been my last visit to those mountains. I bid the field farewell, too, the neighborhood all grown up around it now, and the quiet history of the land still whispering beneath it all.

I sit there for I don't know how long—until my skin twitches like chiggers from lack of sleep. I stand up, look out across the mesa, and see the bedroom light in Magda and Cario's place turn off. Soon as I see a sign of them in their home, I feel like I can finally sleep.

When I get to my room, I find Christina sleeping in my bed. She wakes, groggy and bleary-eyed. "It's you," she says. The way she says, "you," as if there is no other *you* in the world. I tell her, yes, it's me.

"Magda and Cario were worried. They called you nineteen times," she tells me. "They asked me to come up here." She starts to get up to go home.

"I know." I crawl into bed and pull her back, next to me. I tell her about Zeb. She listens. When the story is done, I say to her, "Stay?"

Though she has never spent the entire night with me before—some fear on my part—she doesn't question me now. She just holds me, and I hold her. I can't think of words to say to her, but my body has a hard time letting go. So does hers. We sleep.

I wake a few hours later, early morning, the smell of hot peppers and chorizo filling my nostrils, the sound of Magda and Cario arguing in a whisper in the kitchen. "Go," Christina says, and pushes me out of bed, laughing. "They'll be crazy excited to see you."

It's hard to leave her, to get out of bed. But I do it. I stand in the doorway of my room for a minute, just watching them.

Some people *buzz* around the kitchen. But Magda and Cario *bumble* around the kitchen. There is nothing fast about the way they move. They bump into each other intentionally, as far as I can tell. They kind of waddle. They seem to enjoy this kind of kitchen wrestling, but they complain to each other each time they touch. "Estás demasiado gordo para esta cocina," Magda says, even though Cario is the thinner of the two. He shrugs and keeps cooking, and then they both turn and see me. "Santa Madre de Dios está en casa," Magda whispers. She whips Cario with her dishtowel, and they both open their arms to me. Their warm skin feels so good when we embrace. "Christina, she's been here waiting for you," Magda says. "Go see her. Go now." She pushes me toward the bedroom.

"She's been worried," Cario says. "She's been here every night."

"You didn't call and ask her to come up here?" I ask.

They look at each other and shrug. "No," Magda says.

"I thought you didn't like that we were more than friends."

"You go see her. Tell her you're home. Now." Magda chides me. When Christina comes out of the bedroom looking scruffy and tired, it does nothing to make Magda stop. "Holy mother of Mary, you two," she says. "I don't understand you two." She makes a sound of disapproval, but she sets four plates on the breakfast table, and we all sit down together. Magda and Cario don't ask any specific questions about my trip. They say, "You're back," over and over again. They say, "You never should have gone. I told you so. They did not need you. We needed you here." Finally, Magda asks if it is over now.

"Yes," I tell her. "It's over." Like I said, we don't know each other well. We know each other like family.

After breakfast, I walk Christina out to her car. I have a hard time considering leaving this place, even for a few hours. Through the front window, I see Cario sitting in my living room, the TV blaring, while Magda walks back and forth in the kitchen.

"Come with me today," I say to Christina. She looks at me as if she doesn't know me. I tell her, "I don't want to leave you."

"It's secret, the work you do. Where the wolves are. You've told me a hundred times. I can't come along."

"These wolves, they've crossed the Días de Ojos border," I tell her. "They're expanding their territory. WWA has got nothing to do with them this time. Come with me."

She smiles. "I could call in to work, I guess."

It feels like a gift, and I hug her, and she laughs at me, not with me. We drive, listen to the radio, talk, and it feels right being with her.

I turn on to the final stretch of road to Raymond's place, and the sun is muted by winter, softer around the edges than in summer, but the desert land is still stark and clear. The outline of a huge semi truck in front of Raymond's place is new to me. Its back doors are flung open wide, as if someone's been packing or unpacking, maybe getting ready to move. I can't imagine Raymond driving that thing, can't even imagine one of Raymond's rare, and most times raucous and belligerent girlfriends driving it. And the one thing I know for sure is that Raymond would never move away from this land.

Christina and I walk together across the bare yard. Raymond's door is unlocked and cracked open as it almost always is when he's home. Still, I tap it lightly with a few knocks, and it swings wide open, slowly. "Raymond?"

No response.

From the threshold we can see most of the inside of the house, but no one's there. Dogs are barking, as usual, but they're not running in and out, no music is playing on his duct-taped boom box, no coffee is brewing, and no beer can is popped open and waiting on the kitchen counter. "You go ahead," Christina says.

"No, come with me," I tell her. "It's okay." I take her hand, and we walk inside now, through the tiny living room and peek into the bedroom. Also empty.

I look out the small window, and I see the greyhounds are kenneled. It's unusual for Raymond to kennel his dogs like this, especially during the day. "What the hell?" The words fall from my mouth, and I can see they spook Christina, which spooks me, in return. There's no reason to kennel the dogs during the day. I've never known Raymond to do it before, and it seems cruel, to me. I worry about what Zeb told me, even though Raymond's dogs have nothing to do with it. It's just, he made me fear some side of Raymond that I might not know about yet. If there's one thing Zeb taught me it's that all facets of people are never seen from one angle, but one angle is most often all we get. I don't want to believe what Zeb told me about Raymond. But I also don't want to believe that one of the last things Zeb said to me was a senseless lie.

Christina sees my hesitation. "It's okay," she says. I keep on walking. Together, we step to the back door and tap it open.

In the backyard, crouched down, I see Raymond and one of his lady friends. They're hovered over one of the dog kennels, and the kennel is covered with a blanket.

"Raymond," I say softly.

He turns. He walks to me in slow motion, and his huge arms wrap around me, and he holds me, and he weeps. Unashamed, huge Raymond just weeps. It's not the first time I've seen him do this. He says "You're back, you're back," maybe five or six times, whispering it, and squeezing me close to him. After he hugs me, he embraces Christina, too. Though he's never met her, he gives her the Raymond hug. "You must be Christina," he says. He lets her go, and I introduce them formally, saying yes, this is Christina, and yes, I happen to love her, which makes Christina's eyebrows arch up and makes Raymond hug her again.

I step outside and nod to Raymond's lady friend. She looks at me familiar-like, and I nod again, awkwardly. "Another injured greyhound?" I say, walking toward the kennel.

"Willa, meet my daughter, Brenda," he says.

She turns to face me, and I feel twelve years old again. I can't recall if I ever hugged Brenda when we were kids, but we hug now, a tight and fast embrace that feels like healing. I can smell the rose bushes and see Mom living and breathing and standing on her own, and I can see Chet, too, seething at the edges, and I can smell the field and the ponds. I can hear the meadowlarks.

I remember Zeb, as a kid. So much taken away and so much given back.

When we finally let go of one another, I see that Brenda is still big boned and tall and . . . an adult. Of all the crazy damn things, Brenda is an *adult*. We embrace again, this time laughing. She remembers me, like Zeb said. She remembers in the same way I do, as if there has been no time in-between. We hold each other's childhoods in the core of us. We own them.

"Damn, Willa," she says, smiling huge. She bends at the waist and rolls up her pant leg to show me a well-scarred knee left over from our annual pacts. We both laugh, and we embrace again. "Blood sisters," she says. I tell her yes, we've always been family, always will be family. I introduce her to Christina.

I'm shaking with elation, and at the same time cinched with sadness. Our reunion is missing one person. It's hard to do, but I know waiting won't make it any better. I hear my breathing crack a little as I take a deep breath. I tell her and Raymond about Polo and the tracking, and I tell them about seeing Zeb.

"Is he okay?" she asks.

I shake my head. "Remember Chet," I tell her, and she says yes, and she remembers that Zeb left home just after Chet's death, and I explain to her that the story we all told back then was not the true story, that I'd known all along that Zeb had killed Chet. "It's what they had him on this time," I said. "He confessed." I can see by the way she nods knowingly that part of her knew all along, too. "He never went far away from your home," I tell her. "He stayed in town or on the mountain the whole time. It wasn't Polo or any of the men. They were not responsible for what happened to Zeb," I tell her. "I would've stopped them." I take a breath, finding the words. "But he died. Zeb died on the mountain. Not by his own hand, but by his own choice."

Brenda doesn't flinch. She's a lot like her father in that way. She sits upright, and tears fall, and she wipes them away without shame. After a while, she says, "It was the lion that got him, wasn't it?" She knows the lion, and she knows Zeb's entangled relationship with it.

I don't think about my answer. It just comes out. "Yeah. It was the lion." I leave it at that. Because there's more to truth than the actual facts of a story can ever tell.

She nods, knowingly. "I wanted to see him again," she says. "I wanted him to see who I am now." I comprehend her love for him, and for the first time ever, I understand that Zeb must have been happy, at least for a while, with her. He must have felt loved.

When Raymond hears the news, he holds Brenda and lets her cry. Then we all sit in silence for some time.

After a while, Raymond stands up, hands on knees, stiff back. "Well," he says. "I got some work to do."

Brenda stands too. "We all have work to do." She nudges Christina and me. "C'mon," she says.

We all walk together out to the dog kennel that he and Brenda were tending to when we walked in. He lifts a corner of the blanket, and from the slightest glimpse, I see her, and I know her. "Ciela." I look up at him, desperate. "Where's Hector?"

"We were just getting ready to get her back out there with him. Wanted to get it done before you came back. She's healed now."

It feels like a punch in the chest. "Healed?"

He tilts his head and glances sideways at Brenda. "Long story."

"*Tell*," I say, to him, using his own, forceful word.

He takes a deep breath and says, "She was stunned. Badly stunned," and Brenda adds, "By me." She takes over then, tells of leaving her cabin on the mountain, driving here, her confusion. Then she says, "I'm responsible."

"We're all responsible, Bren," Raymond says. "I thought Ciela reinjured her bad leg at first," he continues. "But I finally got a chance to look at that thing up close." He nods with certainty. "That limp she's had—it's an old injury. Probably a four-and-a-half trap, but either way, it was some kind of trap. No two ways about that. My guess is, that's the reason she wasn't able to skedaddle as fast across the highway as Hector. But this new wound, it's not going to cripple her. And as far as I can tell, this wolf got confused and ran headlong into the truck after

Brenda had stopped, not the other way around. She stunned herself good. Gave herself a concussion, a few scrapes."

"She's healed for sure?" I ask again.

"If you ever quit jawing on and asking questions, we can take her out where she belongs, and you can see for yourself."

He gestures to Christina and Brenda. "Take a corner. We're lifting this crate, as gently and quietly as we can, into that truck." He points to the semi sitting in front of his place.

The four of us move together as smoothly as possible. We lift Ciela's crate into the trailer of the truck.

Brenda's the only one who can drive this monster, so Christina, Raymond, and I sit in the trailer with Ciela while Brenda drives. Raymond sighs. "It gets to me, you know, seeing these animals, any animals, injured." He nods his head, staring at Ciela's crate.

I let his words sink in a little. Then I take a chance. "You ever shoot one of these wolves, Raymond?" I ask.

His eyes turn too quickly toward me. There's a momentary stare, and he stutters and says, "Yes." Then more directly, "Yes, I did that." I can see the words sinking into him, owning him in a way that becomes more comfortable as he says them out loud. "Complex thing," he says. And then he starts telling a story I need to hear so badly. He speaks with his eyes glazed, staring blankly. He says, "I was bringing in animals to rewild on my own, me and a group of people. You know all about that. We wanted to restore the plains and desert, you know, to how this land was before civilization even walked here. Before people of any nation caused this devastation. But I got caught, like you almost always get caught when you're doing something *that* stupid. It was when Brenda was here, living with me." He points with his head toward where Brenda sits, driving the rig. "The cops gave me a choice. Do time away from Brenda, or help control the wolves. Community service, they called it." He says, "Brenda was with me then. It was after she'd come back, when she was a teenager, and before she left again." He thinks on it. "I only did it once. It killed me to shoot a wolf; I mean, it left some part of me dead."

"You were on the management team?" I say to him, after a while.

He nods. "I was 'controlling' the wolves. Taking the lives of the ones they deemed unfit to live in the wild." His eyes are glazed and empty. "I didn't have a choice. If they put me away, I'd lose my daughter again."

He quits looking at me now, goes back to staring blankly. I take in what he says. I know operations like this go on all the time. It's the paradoxical part of any rehab plan, one I have never supported. After I've had enough time to filter what he's saying, I reach over and rest my hand on his. He looks at me then. Nothing more or less than that.

The truck rumbles on, and we can't see where we're going. Like Ciela, we're blocked in on all sides, no views to anything or cues to where we might be on the land. I understand now why they transport scared animals this way. There *is* something calming about it. We're crowded in by plastic containers stacked behind us in the trailer. I tap one. "So what's this?"

Raymond glances up. "Brenda took Zeb's route," he says. "But after we're done here, she's driving this rig back to Colorado and telling Mike he can shove it up his ass." He looks satisfied, even proud. "After that, she's coming back here to live. We'll get her a place. She wants to stay."

"I thought she couldn't come back after she left the reservation?"

"Yeah," Raymond laughs. "We're rewilding her."

"So what's in the crates?" Christina asks.

"Oh." Raymond hesitates. "Body parts."

Christina gives me a look. I give Raymond a look.

"Yeah, she was hauling the this-and-that's left over after glamorous folks have sucked and clipped themselves to bodily perfection." He slaps the side of a carton.

I punch his arm like a high school kid ribbing a friend. "You're shitting me."

"I would not shit you about human flesh."

"So she's going to tell Mike to shove someone else's ass up his own ass," Christina says.

"Many someone else's asses. Yup."

Somehow, the absurdity of it all makes us laugh harder than we should. We laugh, trying to keep the sound quiet on account of Ciela, and that just makes it harder to keep it in. We laugh till we're holding our guts and physically worn out and tired. We still have no idea where we are or what time of day it's getting to be. And in the aftermath of our levity, all three of us are silent, a little stunned, I think. In this odd place, life begins to feel comfortable again.

We can feel the truck slowing down now, heading off the highway onto a dirt road. A few minutes later, Brenda opens the doors to a dusky desert evening just beginning to come down.

Brenda hasn't taken us to the wolf reserve. These wolves, Raymond says, have found their way back to this land that is close to his home and a good distance from the WWA designated area in Días de Ojos. He had argued all along that they had never left here, and now, this is where Ciela and Hector's pack has returned. It makes sense to release them here, whether it's legal or not. We know the risks and the rewards.

Now, there's no laughter, no talk. We work together. We lower Ciela's crate from the truck and onto the ground. She scuffles inside it, and it rocks the balance, but the four of us hang on. From here, we have a short trek to the release spot Raymond has picked out. He saw the pack here last month, he says, and has monitored them off and on since then. He knows this is part of their territory. He knows they're thriving on this land.

By the time we get to the spot Raymond has picked out, the muscles in my legs burn, and my gloved hands are creased from the crate and cramped from holding one position. I'm grateful for it all. With these crates, once we loosen the latches, we can step back and pull on two heavy ropes to break the entire contraption apart. There's no way for a wolf to retreat back inside, and we're far enough away for our own safety and for the safety of the wolf.

It's grueling work, every muscle of your body tight with emotion and physical strain. It also feels like prayer, this quiet work we do, but it's a type of prayer that's neither dependent on an answer or a god. It's deeply holy. With the release cage set up, the latches loosened, the ropes in our hands, and our positions taken, we're ready. Raymond gives the word. We pull. The crate breaks apart, and Ciela runs. Her long legs stretch out as far as they can, a wide open gait, and then she is gone.

That trapped bird in my ribcage—it flies every time we do this. It flies again and again, and there's a soreness from the release and an emptiness in my chest, and I'm filled to the brim with it all.

· · ·

CIELA IS OUT OF sight now. It's past twilight, the crepuscular hour when great horned owls start up and coyotes yip and the pinon and sage turn to silhouettes and shadows. The horizon softens, then fades away completely. Soon, we'll only be able to see a few feet in front of our faces—no city lights here, no street lamps. Just stars and a crescent moon that's already high in the sky, made more visible by the darkness.

We gather the pieces of the crate and haul them, one by one, back to the truck. We can't help looking back to see if she is anywhere in sight. The biggest part of me wants to see her as she runs away. But I know it's best if I don't. I pray for her safety in this territory. There's always the chance that Hector will have already chosen a new mate, that Ciela will be rejected. If that happens, I know she has only a small chance of survival.

These are the things I'm thinking as we pack up. They layer with the events of the past week. This twilight, this time in-between, it seems like a gap between two worlds, as if we—all of us—are walking on that seam now, and sometimes it opens to us, and we see something beyond what we thought was possible, and we enter it, and we know. Because in the end, *this* is possible:

Across the land, one wolf howls. There is a gap of time when there is nothing. And then, another wolf answers. They go back and forth like this, the howls like brushstrokes hollowing out the night with sound.

No one moves. The four of us stand silently, together. Even our own breathing nearly stops.

The wolves, though, they move. You can hear them growing closer together, their howls closing that empty gap, Ciela's howl working its way farther and farther away from us, the distant howl waiting for her to arrive.

resources

THE MEXICAN GREY WOLF is the most endangered mammal in North America. For more information about their natural history and conservation, visit the following websites:

Colorado Wolf and Wildlife Center
www.wolfeducation.org

Defenders of Wildlife
www.defenders.org

Endangered Wolf Center
www.endangeredwolfcenter.org

Grand Canyon Wildlands Council
www.grandcanyonwildlands.org

Grand Canyon Wolf Recovery Project
www.gcwolfrecovery.org

Great Old Broads for Wilderness
www.greatoldbroads.org

Lobos of the Southwest
www.mexicanwolves.org

New Mexico Audubon Council
www.newmexicoaudubon.org

New Mexico Wilderness Alliance
www.nmwild.org

Sierra Club-Grand Canyon Chapter
arizona.sierraclub.org

Sierra Club-Rio Grande Chapter
www.nmsierraclub.org

Sky Island Alliance
www.skyislandalliance.org

Southwest Environmental Center
www.wildmesquite.org

The Center for Biological Diversity
www.biologicaldiversity.org

The Rewilding Institute
rewilding.org/rewildit

UNM Wilderness Alliance
unmwa.wordpress.com

Western Watersheds Project
www.westernwatersheds.org

White Mountain Conservation League
azwmcl.org/blog

WildEarth Guardians
www.wildearthguardians.org/site/PageServer

Wildlands Network
www.wildlandsnetwork.org

For more information on Parkinson's, please visit the following foundations' websites:

American Parkinson's Disease Association
www.apdaparkinson.org/userND/index.asp

The Michael J. Fox Foundation for Parkinson's Research
www.michaeljfox.org

National Parkinson's Foundation
www.parkinson.org/

The Parkinson's Disease Foundation
www.pdf.org

The author is not now and never has been associated with any of the aforementioned organizations.

acknowledgements

FIRST ON MY LIST of people to thank is Lisa Cech. I'll get back to this.

Huge thanks to Doreen and Joe Piellucci for your unwavering love and support. It is, as they say, simply beyond.

Special thanks to Liz Darhansoff, who keeps it simple, direct, honest, and compassionate. To me, that's the pinnacle of agenting.

To Kelly Dwyer, the Fairy Godmother of the book: Your insights and intelligence offered a clear turning point twice. Next year in Iowa, the drinks are on me. And huge thanks to Sarah Saffian, Peggy Lawless, Monica Mesa, the Professor of the Canine College, and Loml, who have all read sections of this book and offered essential insights throughout the process.

I also need to gratefully acknowledge the best friend I've never met, the writer-biologist Harry Greene for his vast knowledge and meaningful conversation.

To Terry Meyer Stone and the Canadian contingent: You know who you are, and you know I adore you and your completely weird and inexplicable ways.

Susan Feniger; Liz Lachman; Kathryn, Mary-Gaye, and Queen Mother Mary Kinsala; Beth, Susan, both Barbara Bogners; Patty Delarios; Katie Barak (come home, Katie!); Georgine Balassone; Ellen Newberry; Regina Stewart, and the Trevor

Cechs—your support has been a solid foundation for me throughout the years. Thank you all!

The residency programs at the Ucross Foundation, Jentel, and especially Colorado Art Ranch (and Grant Pound) generously offered me the quiet time I needed to work on these pages.

To the editors at Counterpoint: You make me believe that the writing world will retain its integrity far beyond all the bleak predictions flying around the book-o-sphere these days. Your integrity as publishers, your respect for language and for the art of writing, your regard for authors—I have to believe these will be the future of writing, not relics of the past. You're leading the way. Thank you.

My deepest gratefulness always circles back around to Lisa, without whom this book would not exist. Explanation is the thief of awe, and I never have to explain myself to you, Lisa. That makes you the beginning of awe, for me. Oh, and you make me laugh. What else is there? You've taught me to embrace it all.

In gratitude to all,
BK

BK LOREN has worked as a naturalist, professional brainstormer, assistant chef, ranch hand, furniture maker, UPS driver, and college professor. She currently teaches writing at Chatham University's low residency program, the Iowa Summer Writing Festival, and many other venues throughout the United States and Canada. She is a winner of the Mary Roberts-Rinehart National Fellowship and has also received The Dana Award for a novel-in-progress for *Theft*. Loren currently lives with her partner, two dogs, and two cats in Colorado.